I0676538

CAPT. MARLENA BRACKEBUSCH

The Ultimate Voyage

Island Sailing Publishing
Naples

Island Sailing of SW Florida, Inc.
PO Box 472
Naples, Fl. 34106

Please visit our website at www.sailnaples.com or
www.islandsailing publisher.com

Printed in the United States of America

ISBN: 0983533431
ISBN-13: 978-0-9835334-3-6

For my nephew, Tim. I am so proud of you.

Rum & Tonic.
May we soon sail the high seas together...again!

ALSO BY CAPT. MARLENA BRACKEBUSCH

Nightmare Voyage

Treacherous Voyage

Thanks to all who helped with this novel.

Special thanks to my dear friend, Gay Utter. Chapter 10 is yours.

Special thanks to my marine patrol friend for his technical assistance in Chapter 16

Extra special thanks to my Key West editor.

Chapter 1. The Atlantic Ocean

All eyes were glued to the big screen television mounted above the console of the gently rocking yacht. The only sound to break the silence was the hissing of air bubbles, escaping from the mini-sub 200 feet below us.

"They should be getting close." My husband, Eric, ran a hand through his mussed, sandy-brown hair. His ice-blue eyes squinted while deciphering the hazy images transmitted from the submarine.

"How long have they been down there?" Martin Sandering directed this question to Tom, who was not only the captain of this mega-yacht but my husband's elder brother.

"It's getting close to an hour. The sub should be able to stay down another thirty minutes or so."

"Don't you think they should have found something by now?"

"Not necessarily, Martin. Looking at the images from the bottom, it appears as though the visibility is poor." My husband looked away from the video monitor. He rubbed his tired eyes while giving me a tiny smile of encouragement.

Our attention returned to the video. Abstract images scampered around the glass panel.

"This search is like looking for a needle in a haystack," said my ex-partner Joey.

Martin suppressed a self-satisfied smile. "Yes it is. Keep in mind the sub is equipped with the latest version of my Lokator equipment. Finding the boat should be a very simple process."

Our new boss and owner of this mega-yacht was a very wealthy inventor who had a research company based in Naples, Florida. Among the multitude of reasons for organizing this trip, Martin wanted to test the viability of his new Lokator technology.

A sound gurgled out from the depths, echoing on the speakers surrounding the crew.

Gage's deep voice penetrated our thoughts. "I think we've got something. It looks like a big white hull." The former Navy SEAL and expert scuba diver piloted the mini-sub, hovering in the depths of the mighty Atlantic Ocean below us.

"I'll shift the camera to give you guys a better view of what I'm seeing. It will blow your minds."

The white reflection from the sub's spotlights was a stark contrast to the murky silt, swirling around the depths. The mini-sub maneuvered to a hover over a fuzzy, white object. Directly below the camera, tiny black dots merged into indistinct images. The edges of the black lettering slipped into focus.

Joey stroked the stubble on his haggard face. "Sweet Jesus."

"We've found it!" Martin Sanderling peered at the words transmitted from the deep abyss.

"Guys, I'm going to try to improve the focus of this camera. Stand by one."

The black smudges blurred, then clarified into letters. The pilots fine-tuned both the position of the submersible and the focus of its attached high-tech camera. This enabled everyone in the pilothouse to see exactly what was on the bottom of the sea. The picture sharpened.

"*Wind Rose*." Were my eyes playing tricks on me? Was this the wreck of the sailing yacht Joey and I were delivering two summers ago? My throat dried. Eric edged closer, squeezing my hand.

"I can't believe we're actually looking at the boat. If this were Vegas, I never would have placed a bet on finding her," Joey said, echoing my thoughts.

Despite the many months of hard work developing this new technology, there were doubts about finding this yacht. She lay on the bottom of the ocean, a hundred miles to the southwest of Cape Hatteras, entombed in an extremely turbulent stretch of the Atlantic.

"Would you guys like to see a wide-angle view?"

Martin moved to his left. "Yes, Gage, by all means. I'd like to see as much as possible."

Our captain slipped away from the helm for a moment, to peek at the video. "Linda, it's damn sad to see a boat end her life torn and broken on the bottom of the sea."

The camera panned out to give us a wide view of the once pretty sailboat, partially buried in the sand.

Capt. Marlena Brackebusch

While the submarine pilots attempted to improve our view of the yacht, let me try to explain this confusing situation. My name is Linda Williams. Life started out as an average American kid growing up in a neighborhood of Boston called Dorchester. I hated the snowy winters. During the summers of my youth, I explored endless tidal pools dotted along the beach, near the JKF Library.

The bridge of my nose peeled from sunburn. My curly, golden locks were forever tangled and encrusted with salt as I raced barefoot along the cool sand. No crab or tiny fish was safe from my curious inspection. This fascination with the sea led to a degree in marine mammal biology along with my captain's license.

My first job was aboard a research vessel. All of us kids were trying to save the whales. In reality, I froze my butt off. At twenty-three, the decision was made to leave the frozen north for the land of swaying palms and nice warm breezes.

The plan was to sail south, though the actual process of moving a boat with the wind was not in my skill set, yet.

"Maybe a handsome sailor will whisk me away on his yacht. I'll explore the world with my soul mate," I said to my sister one icy afternoon, many years ago.

She shook her head in disbelief. "Linda, why don't you get a real job? Settle down with a nice guy."

"Eva, you know that's not my style."

In reality, a man had lured me into the cruising lifestyle. Joey.

"Look at the sails." The shout from my ex interrupted my reverie. The video monitor showed the entire sailboat beneath us. The torn and ragged sails streamed out from the twisted rigging. It looked like the boat was desperately struggling to fight her way out of her watery grave.

"Those sails looked like you trimmed them, Linda. What a mess." His voice, along with his irritating laugh, made me wonder what I ever loved about this man. Sure, he was a sweetheart when we first met at his yacht club in Beantown.

Joey owned a successful trucking company in Boston. The time he spent away from home, shuttling freight to all points of North America, took its toll on his family. His wife threw him out. The divorce quickly followed. When he finally disentangled himself from the transportation business, he was on the prowl. Guess who was his prey?

We dated for a short time before buying a used Westsail 32 sailboat. After many hours of backbreaking labor, her hull was painted a stunning emerald green. Our new yacht's name, *Dark & Stormy,* was carefully painted along her canoe stern. Though our boat's name reflected our favorite drink, it was also a premonition of our relationship to come.

For several years, we happily sailed all over the eastern seaboard and the Caribbean. Despite the years of loyal commitment on my part, Joey never managed to put a ring on my finger. Was there too much emotional baggage?

"At least I bothered to put the sails up instead of sitting on my lazy butt like someone I know." My wicked stare darted across the motor yacht's pilothouse.

"Linda, if you ever listened when I tried to teach you how to sail maybe we wouldn't be having this conversation right now."

"Joey, I can't believe you are blaming me for losing the sailboat. I wasn't the one on watch, you were."

Disaster struck two summers ago. The delivery of a thirty-eight foot sailing yacht, from Boston to Ft. Lauderdale, started out with several awesome days. The early segment of our trip was filled with excellent breezes accompanied by smooth seas.

The following night everything changed. A jarring crash slashed a hole in the hull. The yacht was sinking. A huge wave broke over the cockpit, spitting me into the ocean. With lungs burning, the sea finally allowed me to surface. Waves spat in my face as the dark silhouette of *Wind Rose* drifted away.

The ocean calmed. Swim. Kick. Fight. Armed with only an inflatable life jacket, the ensuing twenty-two hours was a tremendous battle for my life.

I remembered shouting..."Where the hell are the rescue boats?"

When all hope was nearly lost, a faint green light appeared in the distance. This glimmer of hope was on the bow of a fishing vessel manned by Eric and Tom.

The duo were taking a break from their crab fishing boat on the Bering Sea. Lucky for me, the two brothers were tuna fishing with a friend off the Carolina coast. They plucked me from the sea. An instantaneous bond formed between Eric and me.

Now, this luxury mega-yacht was anchored sixty miles to the southeast of Beaufort, NC, due south of Cape Lookout. Situated right on the edge of the Gulf Stream, the world below us was fantastic. The Stream was one of the most prolific fishing areas in the world. Swarms of tuna and swordfish cruised the depths below us. They were stalked by one of the world's largest apex predators—sharks.

"Li'l Sis, don't let him get under your skin." Tom was perched on a leather chair at the helm. His eyes never left the sea when he addressed my ex. "Hey, Joey, keep in mind you are outnumbered on this boat. It would be a shame if a bad accident happened. There is always so much paperwork when you lose a crew member at sea."

Tom's eyes hid behind his dark sunglasses. It was difficult to tell whether or not the threat was serious. From the tone of his voice, I thought so.

"Once again the older brother has to defend poor little Linda. Why is that? Maybe her husband is simply not man enough."

"You don't know when to shut up, do you?" Our captain swiveled around in his chair. After removing the dark shades, his eyes glared at the former truck driver. The black Harley muscle shirt, clinging to Tom's chest, bulged as my brother-in-law drew in a deep breath.

"Boys, can we please concentrate on our business?" Martin's rebuke quieted the situation.

The big crab fisherman returned his gaze to the sea. Tom was a very handsome man, in a dark, rugged sort of way. Despite his quiet demeanor, he was quite a ladies' man. Dutch Harbor, Alaska was his usual hailing port. There he managed and co-captained the brothers' crab fishing boat—*Denali*. Here his gig was captain of this yacht.

"Is there a boat out there?" My eyes scanned the cobalt water, surrounding our floating platform. A dark silhouette slid across the horizon.

"Let's hope not. We don't need any interruptions when we lift the sub back on board." Tom's eyes diverted to the radar. "His course and speed shouldn't bring him much closer. It looks like a sport fish hunting tuna. No problem."

The Atlantic showed her gentler side today. A cat's paw danced across the mirror-like surface. Bright rays of sunlight bounced off the smooth sea, reflecting in the dark sunglasses on our captain's bearded face. He continued to keep watch over our vessel.

Sighing, I turned back to Eric. "I never thought I would see the bow of *Wind Rose* again."

My statement was interrupted by static accompanying Gage's voice from deep below. "Linda, there's a jagged hole on the port side near the bow. The gash is two foot long by one foot high. Multiple cracks extend in all directions both above and below the waterline. All along the cracks are dark, rusty streaks. Hang on a second while I focus the camera for you."

The video panned down along the white sloping edge to a dark void on the left side. The camera zoomed in on red scrapes. These discolorations ran along the tiny cracks framing the jagged edge of the fissure.

"There are fish hanging out in the hole in the bow. If this scene wasn't so sad, it would be a pretty place to check out the sea creatures." Gage's voice crackled through the speakers. "Look at this one." A little blue fish pecked at an unseen morsel of food nestled along the gash.

"Linda, it looks like whatever you hit punctured the fiberglass here. It must have been a sharp object to create an oblong crater like this. This hole doesn't look like it was caused by a collision with another boat. I'll have Ricky snap pictures, then we'll head up to the surface."

Martin Sanderling's finger jabbed at a red button on the submarine communications control panel in front of him. "Good job, guys. It looks like the new Lokator gear is working well. Why don't you two come on up, then we'll celebrate."

Our small group watched a few moments longer as the sub circled around the front of *Wind Rose*. The plow anchor, nestled in its bow roller, sat at a nasty oblique angle. The entire yacht rested on the ocean floor at an unnatural slant, as if the boat was heeled too far over. Green algae invaded every crack and crevice. The sea inundated the yacht. The image of the derelict sailboat faded into the dark gloom.

Capt. Marlena Brackebusch

"Seeing the boat again makes me think of the night we lost her. Do you remember how beautiful the moon was, Joey?"

My mind drifted back to the night we lost the sailing yacht. A sliver of moon lit up the night sky as we cruised toward Beaufort. Our mainsail and jib were eased to port, filled by a gentle north wind.

"All I remember is you yapping about the landfall in Beaufort. You probably jinxed us."

"Joey, you're such a jerk."

My daydream continued thinking about the warm breeze. It caressed my face while I sat curled up on the starboard cockpit cushion. The only sounds were the creaks of the rigging along with the hum of the autopilot.

The slight roll of the Atlantic almost lulled me to sleep. My ever vigilant eyes scanned the horizon for other boats or danger on this fifth night out of Boston.

"You know what is really weird? We never saw any fishing boats when rounding Hatteras. Usually, there are plenty of fishermen out there looking for swordfish and tuna."

"Li'l Sis, you're right. When we picked you up out of the water, the fishing zone around us was deserted. The rest of the fleet was way out to the east, beyond the one-hundred-fathom line. They must have wasted tons of fuel motoring out there. What a shame. There were plenty of fish in close."

Back aboard *Wind Rose,* my gaze took in the stars. Billowing clouds were building in the western sky.

The night air was heavy with dew. A salty, fishy smell hung around the cockpit. Streaks of lightning flashed against the black clouds.

"Joey, it's your watch." My voice broke the silence aboard. He struggled into a pair of old blue jeans with a ratty Red Sox T-shirt. I headed below for much needed sleep.

The cool pillow felt great against my tired cheek. Spare sails were crammed in the V-berth, creating a nook into which I snuggled. The musty smell from wet canvass didn't bother me too much. It was time for sleep.

My brain relaxed to the creaking jib sheet. Ting, ting, ting. One of the halyards rapped the mast in rhythm with the wind. Through the open doorway to the V-berth, my tired eyes watched Joey drinking coffee. He was staring at the black sea.

There were only three short hours until the dog watch, in the wee hours of the night. When I finally dozed off...*Smash!*

"Gage?" My call went down through the gallons of water separating the yacht from the sub below.

"Yes, Linda?"

"Can you guess the size of the object, we collided with, from the dimensions of the hole?"

"Not exactly. It would depend on the angle of the collision. Why?"

"I was thinking about the crash. When we smashed into the object, the boat was nearly stopped dead. Whatever we hit must have been huge."

Capt. Marlena Brackebusch

The sails slammed across the deck of *Wind* Rose. What the heck happened? Still half asleep, I staggered into the main cabin. My body was thrown against the bulkhead by the building seas. Pillows, blankets, and a dinghy floorboard were jammed into the hole up under the forward berth. Water poured in.

The desperate fight to keep the yacht afloat dragged through the next couple of hours. Sweat dripped off my brow. Bucket after heavy bucket were scooped up, lifted overhead, then tossed to the cock-pit. The cold water ran back down my arms. The water level rose.

Desperation trickled in. On deck, Joey was fran-tically jerking the handle of the manual bilge pump. The steady trickle of water wept past our makeshift repair. My cold and tired body shivered. Time had no meaning.

"Linda, dammit, pay attention. Grab the EPIRB. Get your ass out here in the cockpit. Make another call to the Coast Guard before we lose power." Joey's voice was a hundred miles away.

An icy wave sloshed through the open compan-ionway, slapping me squarely in the face. After lifting the emergency beacon from its bracket, I scrambled into the cockpit. Desperation galloped through my brain.

"Mayday, Mayday, Mayday." I barely recognized the voice speaking into the microphone. It was incred-ibly hard to keep my emotions together. I'd never made a Mayday call before. Hell, I'd never lost a boat before either.

My eyelids blinked away salt while trying to focus on those same numbers flashing on the GPS mounted next to the television monitor aboard the mega-yacht—thirty-four degrees twenty-six minutes north and seventy-six degrees twenty-three minutes west. I would never forget those digits.

"I didn't see anything. When we hit the object, it was after my last scan of the horizon. There were no boats anywhere near us." Joey's voice snapped me back to reality. He looked nothing like the man I knew before the accident. My ex was a strong, handsome man and one heck of a sailor. Now his appearance was only a shadow of his former self. Joey looked skinny and haggard.

The Robert Redford smile which once attracted all the ladies degenerated into a crooked sneer. Those formerly broad shoulders slumped beneath the white *Lady Diana* golf shirt he was wearing. Thick, sexy salt and pepper hair grew thin. The shock of the collision, along with the horrible shark bite which ravaged Joey's left leg, caused the amnesia he battled.

A drug dealer and his goons plucked Joey from the sea. They beat my ex mercilessly while imprisoning him aboard their dirty smuggling boat. Carlos, the captain of the converted shrimp boat, was a nasty South American drug lord. He was one bad dude. After my horrific experience with Carlos in Trinidad, the hate was locked in a secret place in my soul.

There was deep emotional baggage from the sinking. Though I tried to ignore it, simply being at sea again stimulated a near panic in my brain. Some days I felt extremely anxious. The sheer nature of my work made these feelings difficult to deal with. The ocean had been my life.

"Martin, darling, are you still playing with your toy submarine? It's so lonely sitting on the back deck without you. Would you please rub this sunscreen on my back? The sun is so hot it's scalding me." Martin's wife, Diana, paraded into the wheelhouse like the prima donna she was. Eric caught the look on my face along with the disdainful roll of my eyes.

"The wicked witch of the east," I whispered. Diana sashayed across the salon. Since our meeting several months ago, the first lady of this yacht treated the crew like subservient beings.

"*Shh.*" Eric gave me a warning look. His attention diverted back to the boss' wife. A pink bikini clung to her body. The swimsuit was not well hidden by the sheer silk coverup loosely tied around her slim physique. The salacious outfit seemed inappropriate for a middle-aged mother of two.

Martin's wife made a show of tossing back her shoulder-length wavy red hair. Her shoulder brushed along her mate's arm, like a cat marking its territory. You could almost hear her purr from across the room.

"My dear, we are nearly finished up here. Once the sub is brought aboard, we can all sit down for a nice cocktail before dinner."

Martin took his wife's arm, guiding her toward the door to the aft deck. The snide glance thrown over her shoulder telegraphed her displeasure. She was not pleased with "the crew" impinging on her private cocktail hour.

Eric nudged me. We followed the Sanderlings out the door to the spacious back deck of the yacht. The sun blazed over the calm sea. Long ocean swells rolled the big yacht ever so slightly.

"How are the surface conditions?" Gage's voice resonated through our headsets.

"The water surface is nice and calm. What's your depth?" Eric asked the former Navy SEAL. My husband was coordinating the retrieval of the sub.

"Twenty-five feet. We'll be up in a minute." A mass of bubbles burst from the calm surface of the ocean, announcing the arrival of the submarine from the depths.

Joey pushed the button which controlled the huge hydraulic transom of the mega-yacht. The heavy fiberglass panel swung upward, revealing a large storage area inside the ship. The mini-sub fit snugly inside the hull. What a great hiding place for this high-tech equipment. Any probing onlookers, innocent or otherwise, would see nothing but a typical mega-yacht.

"Eric, are you going to handle the lift control?" Joey asked. All eyes were on the sea.

"Yeah, I got it." My husband grabbed the push button remote control for the massive crane, sprouting out from the upper deck. A whirring sound was heard as the heavy arm extended over the ocean. Very precise control was needed on the joystick. It took a skilled touch to attach the crane's lifting hook to the bobbing submarine. Since the accident, Joey's hands shook, sometimes horribly. It was better to leave the precision maneuvering to Eric's steady hands.

Soon the lifting hook swung over the submarine to a position near the bow. A rounded steel u-bolt was located there. The top of the sub swung open. Gage appeared. A crew cut sprouted from his head. Dark aviator sunglasses camouflaged his eyes. His entire image reflected his military style.

The former Navy SEAL used a joystick to maneuver the sub beneath the lifting tackle. Joey reached out with a boat hook to grab the stabilizing line hanging near the stern of the submarine.

"Easy, Gage. Ease her forward a little," Eric whispered into his headset. The hook swung closer to the u-bolt. "Joey, pull the stern in."

"You've got it." The three men skillfully jostled the sub into position. Clank. The lifting hook clicked onto the bolt. My husband took up tension on the cable.

"Tom, go ahead and flood the ballast tanks." Not a sound was heard nor any motion felt as the mega-yacht sank a few inches deeper into the Atlantic. The ship was equipped with a secret water ballast system. This allowed it to submerge enough to slide the sub into its hull. Once the sub was secured inside the waterproof compartment, the excess liquid was pumped out. The yacht returned to its original waterline.

"Great job, men." Martin Sanderling stood behind us, supervising the choreography of the submarine retrieval. With a shake of my head, I contemplated how weird it was having my husband and my former lover working together on this new project. One reason they worked together so easily was the importance of the work. If the tests were successful, Martin Sanderling would sell his new technology to the United States Defense Department and the Drug Enforcement Agency for a ton of money. Much of this cash would trickle down to us.

A more important facet to this operation was the protection our Gulf of Mexico shores would receive from this top secret technology. The Lokator gear would halt the huge increase in drug traffic, brought ashore by mini-subs, similar to the one we had aboard the *Lady Diana*.

In the past few years, those lower-tech fiber-glass mini-subs, slipped by the DEA and Coast Guard because the hull material absorbed radar and sonar signals. This new technology would change the equation. Martin made it clear his mission was to stop the influx of narcotics which ripped so many families apart.

There may be an ulterior motive, allowing my husband and my former lover to work together so easily on this project. It was not normal for two men at odds to get along so well in such tight quarters. Could this have stemmed from Gage's visit to Naples several months ago? Though I tried to discuss this with Eric, he remained silent and stoic. There was not much doubt to my suspicions. These men intended to go after Carlos.

Chapter 2. Naples. Last Fall

Imagine my shock. Eric and I docked *Dark &
Stormy* in her slip adjacent to the Cove Inn in Naples.
We returned from a wonderful cruise to the Keys.
Guess who was standing on the dock? Only the man
for whom we'd searched for the past year and a half.

"Joey." His name slipped out in a whisper while I
stared at him in disbelief.

"Linda, where the hell have you been with my
boat?" Joey's greeting was gruff and challenging. His
eyes swiveled to Eric, who was securing the bow lines.

"Who the hell is this?"

"Eric Iverson." My husband mustered a smile.
The friendly look could not hide his astonishment.
While walking aft, he extended his hand to my former lover. How awkward was this? Joey ignored the
friendly gesture. His focus was on me.

"I asked you where the hell you have been." I
stared back at his glare. Familiar feelings of intimida-
tion and inadequacy surfaced.

"I was...I mean we were visiting Eva...in Key
West."

"I'm off fighting for my life while you entertain
this pretty boy on my boat. Linda, who the hell do you
think you are?"

"Joey. The last time I checked this was my boat, too." It was a good thing Eric slipped between us. I wasn't sure I could restrain from throttling this man.

"We just spent the last year and a half looking for you."

"Where in Key West?" Joey voice dripped with sarcasm. "Listen you thankless, b-e-e-e-ch, um."

"Careful." Eric halted the man's statement with a withering look.

"Get the hell off this boat. Now!"

"Linda, come with me." My husband grabbed my arm, pulling me off the boat.

"Where are we going?"

"We will get a room at the Cove Inn," Eric whispered as he dragged me away from my boat.

"No way. I'm not leaving. Why should I leave?" I stormed back down the finger pier. "Joey, why don't you get the heck off my boat?"

"Linda, let's not make a scene here at the hotel. We'll get a room so you can calm down in private. I'll come back to the boat to get some of our stuff off."

"But...Eric." It was obvious he was not going to relent, so I allowed him to lead me to the hotel. I would deal with Joey later.

Right at the head of the boat slip was the Cove Inn Hotel, a historic landmark here in Naples. All the rooms were decorated in a fun tropical style with splashes of cool, Caribbean colors. Nice lanais dotted the back side of the inn. The views of the bay were stunning. All around the perimeter of the building was lush tropical foliage and flowers. None of which made me feel any better after being thrown off my own boat.

After locating our room, I stood at the door to the lanai, fuming. Joey moved about the cockpit of *Dark & Stormy* like he owned it. Well, I guess he did.

"Linda, sit down. Take it easy."

"Eric, that's easy for you to say. How dare he?"

"Linda, fighting with Joey will get you nowhere. I'll go have a chat with him, to see if I can reason with him. You stay here and calm down."

"I don't get why you are allowing him to stay on my boat. None of his old stuff is even aboard."

"Honey, did you notice how Joey looked?"

"He is the same old bastard he always was."

"No, I mean physically. He looks sickly."

"You let him stay because you feel sorry for him?"

"Let me go have a chat with him. You stay here."

While standing on the finger pier, Eric engaged Joey in a chat. Judging by my ex's stiff posture, he did not appear receptive to the conversation. I would have loved to hear what was said. A moment later, my husband turned away from the pier soon returning to our room.

"He agreed to meet with you later. Linda, you need to talk to him calmly."

"I'll be damned if I'm going to do that. Who the hell does he think he is? We just spent the past year looking for his sorry butt. Now, he waltzes in here ordering me off my own boat."

Eric put his hand up. "Linda, honey. You could give him time to settle down. We can discuss the situation rationally. Let's try to come up with a reasonable solution. Aren't you a little curious to hear what happened to him?"

"I guess so." The rage trickled out. "You know, Eric, you shouldn't be taking his side in this. You could be more supportive of me."

"Linda, I'm not taking his side. He just looks so... pathetic. What good is fighting with him going to do?"

"Probably nothing."

"Also, I can't help but feel sorry for him. It must have been a huge shock, seeing his girlfriend on his boat with another man. I know I wouldn't be too happy."

"Damn you, Eric. Do you always have to be so reasonable?" The ineffectual swat at my husband's shoulder didn't make me feel better.

A couple of hours later, Joey and I faced each other. He sat on one side of the cockpit, huddled against a cockpit cushion. I was perched on the opposite seat.

After handing out cocktails, Eric settled down with a drink. Joey shifted uneasily in an attempt to sit up straighter.

"Thanks." Joey's black eyes pierced through mine like daggers. "Linda, I've missed you. I guess the feeling is not mutual."

"Joey." With my brain struggling, the right words wouldn't come out.

"Let me try." Eric squeezed my shoulder. "My brother and I rescued Linda from the ocean on a pitch black night. Finding her was a miracle in itself." He paused. Joey glared at him.

"She was in pretty bad shape. When we pulled her on board, her skin was cold. Linda was barely conscious. The next twenty-four hours were a battle with dehydration, hypothermia, and seasickness. It took her a day to come out of the shock."

"I wasn't seasick. I've never been seasick in my life, Eric."

"Well, whatever, you were heaving pretty badly."

"I'd swallow half the ocean." A deep flush crept across my face. Eric grinned. There was a dark scowl on Joey's mug.

"Eric, that wasn't very nice." Unconsciously, my hand rubbed the now-healed bruised ribs which twinged with the memories. I turned to Joey.

"We spent the last year or so trying to find you." I chewed on my lip. Why was he so belligerent? "I tried to swim back to the boat after the wave knocked me overboard. Didn't you hear me shouting to you?"

"How did you expect me to pick up any sounds over the howling wind?" Joey sipped his drink thoughtfully.

"In case you didn't figure it out, I had problems launching the life raft. The damn buckle on the raft's strap jammed. The piece of junk knife didn't help very much as I hacked away at the strap. Once free, it took a mighty effort to heave the canister overboard. Whoosh, the life raft inflated." His arms flew over his head. Eric and I flinched.

"When I looked up, you were gone."

"I yelled for you. The EPIRB was ripped out of my hands when a massive breaker swamped me,

23

driving me under. Even with my eyes open there was no telling which way was up. The wave continued to spin me until my lungs burned. Finally, when my head broke the surface, all I could do was watch the boat drift away."

"A big wave hit me also, snapping the painter to the life raft. I dove into the water as the boat went under. It was one hell of a long night."

"Keeping my head above water was a struggle. My arms and legs were already exhausted from bailing out the boat. Even though I was wearing an inflatable life jacket, I had to kick in the bigger swells. The water was so cold. My body was shivering terribly." I shuddered with the memories.

"There were bad thunderstorms. Hell, it felt like I was in a washing machine. It was about dawn, when the first shark arrived." A ghastly look flashed across his eyes.

"The bastard swam slow circles around me, like it was taunting me. My arms already felt like lead from treading water, so how the hell could I get away from this beast? The sun rose enough to see something orange, bobbing in front of me. With every last ounce of strength, I swam toward it, hoping it was the life raft. It was slow going, swimming against those waves."

My ex's eyes sank to the cockpit floor. "The first one hit me. Knocked the damn wind out of me. It slammed into my side. A huge, gray fin broke the surface of the water. I'll never forget that fin. It towered right in front of me. Then it submerged."

Joey took a long swig from his drink. He stroked the stubble on his chin. His dark eyes pierced through me. Those eyes looked devoid of emotion as he recounted the terrible ordeal.

"The life raft wasn't too far away, so I kept swimming. After three or four more big bumps, one shark attacked. Right before it's teeth sunk in, the monster looked me in the eye. I'll never forget those glassy, lifeless eyes. Murderer's eyes. It was either him or me.

"The eyes rolled right back into its head. Teeth clamped down on my thigh. Sawed right through the skin. Shit, the pain was bad. My only hope was to fight back. Punched it hard, on the snout. It finally let go. What a huge relief..." Joey's haunted eyes stared at the cockpit sole. "The real surprise was the surrounding water. It turned dark red. I was in some serious shit." His sad eyes turned to me.

"Linda, I can't talk about this anymore right now."

Eric nudged me. We left Joey to his thoughts. Back in our hotel room, Eric pulled me against him. "Linda, that was one hell of a story. What do you make of it?"

A variety of emotions swirled through my brain. Eric's hug didn't help ease the distress. Maybe some good old screaming or sobbing might work. Instead, I flopped down on the sofa. "It's been a long time since I've thought about the night of the accident."

"Linda, you always try to be so strong. My gut feeling is this whole incident affected you very deeply."

"Eric, sometimes I lie awake at night, shaking from the memories. In the darkness, I'm drifting alone in the ocean, isolated and terrified. Helpless. It was a huge effort, fighting to keep my head above the water. When the wave washed me overboard, I was already exhausted and freezing cold. In an instant, the boat was too far away to swim to.

"One bad memory was the feeling I wasn't alone, especially at night. It didn't take a degree in marine biology to know what was causing the swirls in the phosphorescence. The black water would light up. Something bumped me. When the moon rose, a fin darted by. The sea became very still. Hours dragged. I tried to tread water without attracting too much attention." My eyes rose to meet the compassionate look of my mate.

"Eric, all throughout the next day, I kept expecting to see a Coast Guard boat. There was no doubt the EPIRB was activated. Twilight led to the total darkness of the second night. You have no idea how demoralizing it was thinking about another long night adrift in the sea. My arm and legs were so numb from the cold."

He watched me, for a moment, before speaking. The demons needed to eke out.

"Linda, when I jumped into the water to rescue you, it seemed like you were in shock. I'm not sure you understood I was trying to help you."

"I couldn't figure out why the boat drove away. Why did it?"

"Tom and Mark wanted to do a quick spin around to see if your partner was nearby. If I could put a survival suit around you, they could search for a few minutes. You put up quite a struggle." Eric grinned at the memory. "You kept mumbling about sharks. I didn't believe you until one bumped us."

"It was a good thing the boat came right back to pick us up. My luck might have run out if I was in the water much longer." A cold chill slashed down my spine despite the warm evening.

"When I was holding your head above water, I had no idea how sick and frightened you were."

After a few moments of silence, Eric rose, pulling out his cell phone. "Linda," he said gently, "maybe Joey's return is a good thing. You two can talk about it. Maybe you can finally heal."

He reached down, tilting my chin upwards until our eyes met. "Jonathan Steele should be here. He deserves to hear the whole story."

Jonathan Steele, the narrator of Eric and Tom's popular crab fishing show, was instrumental in the futile search for Joey. He convinced his network bosses to spend a ton of money to finance our chase around the Caribbean which was all for naught. Yes, he should be involved.

"Eric, call him."

The next morning, Jonathan Steele arrived accompanied by our old buddy Jake Hammond. Jonathan used to be an ace TV reporter before his stint as narrator of the fishing show. At six-foot tall, skinny and wiry, he looked more like a marathon runner than the University math professor he once was.

He was a nice looking man, with a hint of Asian heritage hanging around his handsome, tanned face.

With a quick wit and a silver tongue, it was no wonder his career in television was such a success.

After a quick hug, I turned to Jake. He unfolded his six-foot-one bulky frame out of the small, red rental car. His huge arms surrounded me in a bear hug.

"Linda, it's great to see you." Our old friend held me at arm's length. This former Marine's face was scarred from the battles of a difficult childhood. His facade was of a man about to murder someone. He kept his kind, gentle eyes carefully hooded, but they managed to shine through whenever we saw each other.

We first met Jake a year ago. So much happened since our initial meeting in Beaufort. The former Marine flew us in his helicopter all over the Outer Banks of North Carolina, in a futile search for signs of wreckage after *Wind Rose* sank. Later, he helped us scour the Caribbean in our search for Joey.

"Jake, it's about time you came to visit. Doesn't it always seems as though we get together in weird circumstances? Why is that?"

"Lady, it's always good to see you. There's no telling why we can never meet at a calm moment. Maybe, just maybe we can get the answers to all of our questions. Are you holding up OK?"

"I'm fine. This whole thing is one big shock."

After checking the guys into the Cove Inn hotel, we formulated a game plan to approach Joey.

"Eric, why don't you talk to him? Invite Joey for a drink at the Chickee Bar. I'll be there to meet him." Jonathan leaned casually against the door frame. The reporter's eyes gazed past the lanai which overlooked the yachts and the rustic bar by the swimming pool. "If we can get Joey to relax, maybe he'll tell us the rest of the story."

My husband left for *Dark & Stormy*. Jonathan and I settled in by the Chickee Bar. Sonya, an awesome bartender at our favorite watering hole, chatted with us.

A light breeze rustled the palm fronds overhead. The sun journeyed to the west after another warm Florida day. To the east, a line of black storm clouds brewed. Could they be a precursor to this imminent conversation?

A moment later, Eric and Joey approached. We grabbed seats at one of the tables along the water. While the fisherman went to the bar for beers, I introduced Jonathan Steele.

"Joey, this is the guy who financed the search for you this past year." My ex watched the TV man suspiciously over the icy cold Budweiser placed in front of him.

"Why would you go ahead and do that? It seems like a waste of good money, looking for me."

Jonathan reclined, trying to look casual. After a moment, he leaned forward with both elbows on the plastic table. The reporter spoke directly to Joey.

"We looked for you because of the amazing story. Who wouldn't want to hear about a yacht mysteriously sinking? Linda drifts around the Atlantic, only to be plucked from the ocean by famous Bering Sea fishermen. Top it off with your rescue by a drug trafficking boat. All of this seems like great television to me."

"So, you're a TV reporter?" Joey's dark eyebrows narrowed.

"Used to be. Now I'm the associate producer and narrator of a fishing show."

"Well, I'm not talking to any damn reporter."

Jake walked up, towering over us. "Can I join you guys?"

"I was just leaving." Joey rose, but was stopped by Jake's massive hand on his shoulder.

"Friend, don't leave on my account. I'll pull up my own chair." The big Marine deftly slid another chair next to Joey's while signally to Sonya for more drinks.

"Let me buy you a beer. It's a real honor to finally meet you. I'm Jake."

My ex peered at this grizzly bear of a man who sat next to him. Joey eased back into the chair.

I chimed in. "Jake is a former Marine. He was shot in the leg in Trinidad while searching for you."

Joey eyeballed this big man before speaking. "I'm sorry you took a bullet for me, but I'm not talking to any reporter. I don't want what's left of my life splattered all over television."

Jake placed his huge paw on Joey's forearm. "Friend, I completely understand where you are coming from. It took me a while to warm up to this skinny ass reporter dude, but I did it for Linda. Don't you think you owe her an explanation?"

My former lover glared at the rings on my left hand. His right index finger wagged in front of my face. "I think I'm owed an explanation more than she is. You didn't go ahead and marry this pretty boy did you?"

Joey tossed Eric a frigid stare. "What kind of crap are those rings on her finger? A pirate ring? You've got to be kidding me. Her cheap husband couldn't even afford to buy her proper rings. Geez."

A nearly silent breath escaped from Eric. I was about to explode at Joey when Jake's calm voice penetrated my rage. "She did have a big, shiny rock on her finger until Carlos kidnapped her down in Trinidad. The ring was stolen from her." The Marine tipped back his bottle of Bud light while watching Joey's reaction out of the corner of his eye.

"Carlos!" my ex barked. "What the hell were you doing messing around with Carlos? He's bad news."

"No kidding, Joey. We were in Trinidad, looking for your sorry butt. Carlos told me you...died from the shark bites and the infection."

"I probably would have, if the Coast Guard hadn't rescued me." The man leaned back in his chair, obviously exhausted.

"The Coast Guard rescued you?" Eric asked. "When the hell was that?" A look of fury passed between Eric and Jake.

"You don't have to yell at me, my hearing's not bad, only my memory. It must have been early July. A large Coast Guard cutter pulled alongside Carlos' shrimp boat. They sent a bunch of guys aboard armed to the teeth. The lieutenant asked me who I was and what I was doing there. The realization hit me for the first time. My memory was messed up. I had no idea who I was." Joey dragged a long, slow swig from his beer. His haunted eyes stared off into the distance.

"They took me off the drug boat. Later, the Coast Guard transferred me to the Navy hospital in Bremerton, Washington. It scared the hell out of me, not knowing who I was. The doctors said the amnesia was caused by the trauma of the shark bites and the blood loss. After a couple of surgeries to fix my leg and a little rest, my memory slowly came back. Though I was in a daze for a few weeks, every once in a while tiny bits and pieces of the accident and my former life drifted into my mixed up brain."

"Why didn't you call me? I was so worried about you."

"It really looks like you were worried about me, Linda," Joey said sarcastically, again glancing at Eric.

"Joey, you son-of-a-bitch. You weren't the only one injured by this thing. It's just like you to only worry about yourself. Who gives a damn about Linda?"

"Geez, woman, take it easy. I couldn't call you because the Coast Guard wouldn't allow it. They wanted to keep the whole thing quiet because of the drug war. There was talk about Carlos being a big shot in a drug cartel in Venezuela."

"He's not just a small time drug runner on a shrimp boat?" Jonathan asked.

"No, but the Coast Guard made me promise not to talk about this, so I'm not saying anything more. As soon as they released me from the hospital, I came back. I came back for my boat and my woman. Silly me, expecting you to be here...alone."

Joey leaned close to me, whispering so only I could hear. "What a disappointment you turned out to be."

Before the shock of his statement wore off, my ex turned back to the rest of the group. "I gotta get out of here and get some rest. We can talk more tomorrow." Joey struggled to stand. After fumbling with his cane, he hobbled off toward *Dark & Stormy*.

"What a bastard." I didn't allow the thought to slip out.

Jake's voice again penetrated my anger. "If Joey can't tell us about his rescue from Carlos, I sure as hell know someone who can and he better have a good explanation." The ex-Marine sprung from the table, pivoting for the hotel.

Chapter 3. Naples-Beaufort, N.C.

After paying the bar tab, our group went to Jonathan's room in the Cove Inn. We had to place a very important phone call. Jake pulled out his cell phone, while the rest of us huddled on the couch. Eric paced.

The ex-Marine's large fingers pounded on the small keys of his phone. After a quick glance through the numbers stored there, the big man pressed the send button. A familiar voice soon filled our ears.

"Hello Jake." Mitch's voice came through, loud and clear.

"Mitch buddy, I'm in Naples with Jonathan Steele, Eric, and Linda. You're on speaker phone."

"Hi, guys. I wish I was down there with you. I'm at a meeting in Boston. The fall chill has already worked its way up here. I'm freezing my butt off."

Jake sounded like he was attempting to keep his voice casual. "Mitch buddy, guess who we were just talking to?"

"I have no idea. Who?" Mitch's voice flooded with caution. He must have picked up on the tension in former Marine's voice.

"Joey. As in Linda's ex Joey. Remember the man who supposedly died from shark bites? We found out this same Joey was rescued by the Coast Guard. The

United States of America Coast Guard. Imagine my surprise when I found out Joey was rescued, by the Coast Guard, before Linda was kidnapped by Carlos." The ex-Marine paused for a second. He drew in a deep breath.

"Could this be the very same Joey you knew nothing about when I called you from Trinidad last summer? Do you remember the call I made right after Linda's kidnapping? Or did I call the wrong Mitch? Not the same Mitch who is an officer for the United States Coast Guard in the Drug Interdiction Unit."

This bear of a man continued his soliloquy with his voice a deep growl. "Mitch, tell me you didn't know about Joey's rescue."

From the phone, there was silence.

Eric lunged toward Jake, grabbing for the cell phone.

"Mitch, Eric here. The speaker phone is off. You didn't answer Jake's question."

The Coast Guard man's response was too muffled to hear.

The crab fisherman slowly closed the phone. He handed it back to Jake.

"Son of a bitch."

The college-aged stewardess aboard the *Lady Diana* efficiently brought cocktails and snacks to our group seated in comfortable lounge chairs. The sprawling aft deck looked more like a swanky hotel lounge than the deck of a yacht. The floor consisted of scrubbed, natural-colored teak. The lounge chairs were polished mahogany with yellow striped cushions. The crew chatted about the discovery of *Wind Rose* earlier this afternoon.

"Today was a very productive day. I'm quite pleased with the Lokator. Despite the challenging conditions, you had little trouble locating the sunken yacht," our boss said.

Martin and Diana Sanderling soaked up the late afternoon sun. Diana's chair was nestled against her husband's. Her pale face was turned skyward, carefully shaded by the dainty, pink canopy, extending out from the back of her lounger.

A slim glass of vodka tonic, with a tiny slice of lime, sweated and dripped. Tiny drops of condensation pooled on the teak to the left of the lounge chair. Long, delicate fingers, dangling from her right hand, rested on the left forearm of her husband. Our boss swirled the amber neat bourbon around his tumbler. He appeared deep in thought while pensive eyes scanned his crew. "If we keep on this pace, it should be no time at all before we round up all the drug smugglers."

"Yes, Martin, including one particular drug smuggler," Eric said.

My husband and I enjoyed the cool shade of the tropical blue awning with Tom sitting to our left. Gage's six-foot-three heavily muscled, yet lean frame stretched out on a recliner, right at the edge of the late afternoon shadow. A nearly empty aluminum bottle of Bud sat on the deck to his right.

"What a great ride in the sub today. It was really something finding the sailboat." The former Navy SEAL looked to his left. His sidekick, Rick, was seated nearby.

"It sure beats deep diving. We were nice and snug in the mini-sub."

This stocky man was also a former Navy SEAL, though his physique was completely opposite Gage's. Rick was five-foot-nine. His body looked like a solid, rectangular block with a head sticking out of the top and two legs poking out the bottom. In between was solid muscle. His personality was quite different too, being a good Italian boy from Jersey.

His fire came from his mother's Irish heritage, giving him a short fuse. Sometimes it was difficult to keep up with his fast talking chatter. On deck that night he was quiet, absorbing the conversation around him.

"With the mini-sub, we should be able to sneak up on any drug runner."

Just like the Navy SEAL snuck up on me. Thinking back to the night of the rescue from Carlos' drug boat, Rick never said a word. When I followed Gage from the dirty stateroom, this other Navy man, shrouded in black, occluded the hallway. A carbine protruded from his right hand. Intense eyes flicked back and forth. Deadly serious eyes. Black streaks bled down his face.

Fear sizzled through me. His hand snapped to my shoulder, twisting me in the direction of his retreating partner. A stiff jab between my shoulder blades nudged me along.

"Yeah, Rick, with the Lokator, even the black of night won't keep us from tracking the mini-subs at sea."

The black of night merged with the sea and sky when Gage dragged me from the drug boat. I struggled with every last once of strength.

"Get me out of this water, now." Rick lashed out. His fingers gripped my wrist with a vise-like hold. Gage spun me around. His forearm locked around my neck.

"You guys did a great job finding the sailboat today. The smuggling mini-subs are next." Martin Sanderling nodded at the two Navy SEALs.

Gage tipped his beer bottle in our boss' direction. A knowing smile crossed the tall man's face. "The new equipment you invented is great. We had nice clear water down to 175 feet. Directly below, a sub-ocean current had all the silt stirred up. It took some circling around with the Lokator to home in on a strong signal return, but without it, we never would have seen the hull of the sailboat."

The sub's pilot turned his attention to me. "Linda, after close examination of the crack in the side of the boat and the rusty scratches, I would think you hit a partially submerged object. Shipping containers are lost off vessels all the time. Give them a month or so to rust and you have a great battering ram to poke a hole in a sailboat. You would never see what you hit because the bulk of the container would be submerged, like an iceberg.

"I'd like to get scuba gear on to take a closer look. Since it would be a technical dive, I'm not sure you could come down with me. If it's OK with Martin, we can take the sub for a look."

Before I could answer Gage, the wicked witch chimed in. "Enough of this business talk. Martin, I can't spend another night on this rocking boat. With all this motion, I simply cannot get enough rest. Can we go ashore? There must be a decent restaurant in Beaufort. After dinner, we can spend the night at a nice hotel. If we can find one in such a little town."

"Absolutely, my kitten, anything you please. Jake, do you mind firing up the helicopter?"

"No problem, boss." The former Marine hoisted his bulky frame off the lounge chair. His half-empty bottle of Perrier was deposited on the cocktail waitress' tray. The big man climbed the ladder to the upper deck of the yacht nimbly. His motion was reminiscent of a chimp climbing a tree. The speed with which he scurried up the steps was impressive for such a large man.

On the top deck was the spacious helicopter pad sporting the chopper with "SI" (Sanderling Industries) printed on its side.

When Martin and Diana rose from their chairs to bid us goodbye, the boss turned to our captain. "Tom, after you guys finish the last couple of tests tonight, could you bring the boat into Beaufort tomorrow morning? That is, after Gage takes Linda down to see the sailboat." Martin winked in my direction.

Was he being gracious or could he read my mind? I didn't want to go 200 feet underwater in a mini-sub, though it would be interesting to see the wreck of the *Wind Rose* for myself. It could help put my demons to rest.

"Yes, sir, we should be in around noon," Tom said, half-rising out of his seat.

"Don't get up. We'll see you all tomorrow." Martin shook our captain's hand before following Diana into the main cabin. The whine of the chopper's motor warming up broke the evening silence.

"Rick, do you want to give me a hand running the diagnostics on the ship's Lokator gear before we pack it in for the night?" Tom turned for the wheelhouse. "We should run armament tests, too."

"Sure." Rick followed our captain leaving Eric, Gage, Joey, and myself alone on the back deck.

"Linda, how about a swim before dinner?" Gage knew it would be a huge step getting me into this water again, exactly where we lost *Wind Rose*.

The tall Navy SEAL casually glanced in my direction, watching my reaction through his dark aviator sunglasses.

"Are you freaking' nuts?" Joey asked. "I would never get into this water again."

Eric's eyes seared into my skin, though he remained silent. Gage rose, towering over me with his hand extended. "Come on, Linda, it's a warm evening. A swim would feel great."

Mustering up as much courage as possible, I accepted the former Navy SEAL's hand. We stepped down the fiberglass steps to the transom. After his sunglasses were carefully set on a shelf, his anthracite eyes burned into mine. A cocky smile eased some of my tension. He gripped my hands firmly.

"Linda, I know you don't want to get into the water again, but trust me. I won't let anything happen to you."

The tall man pulled off his shirt. His foot kicked the boarding ladder down into the crystal-clear blue water. After tossing in the life ring, the ex-Navy SEAL dove in. A second later, he bobbed in the calm water only a few feet from the back of the yacht.

My mind drifted back to the dark ocean water near Trinidad when Gage rescued me from Carlos' evil talons. The Navy SEAL dragged me into the black water which had been infested with sharks only a few hours earlier.

As I stood on the swim platform of the mega-yacht, fear and dread crept up. A hand grazed my elbow. Eric brushed past me, diving into the placid water. A clump of yellow Sargasso weed meandered by, disappearing behind the men. Despite my hesitation, I leapt off the transom like a little kid at a lake.

I was submerged for only a faction of a second before bobbing to the surface. Panic seeped into my brain. It was an incredibly weird sensation, drifting in the same water which imprisoned me only a year and half earlier.

Thinking about it, how weird was it to be involved in two water rescues about a year apart? The first was the sinking of *Wind* Rose. The second was the liberation from the drug boat in Trinidad. It was amazing I went anywhere near the water, much less swam in it.

My brain dragged me back to my last night adrift, after *Wind Rose* sank. The darkness engulfed me. Absolute, pitch blackness made it impossible to differentiate the sea from the sky. The knowledge of being completely alone, a hundred miles out to sea, adrift, was terrifying. The bone-chilling cold stiffened my limbs and numbed my brain to a point where I simply didn't care anymore. My hope was for the end to be quick and painless. Since the disaster, my mental recovery had been a slow road.

Eric tugged me back to the boarding ladder. "Let's shower off and get dinner."

Thirty minutes later, we joined our friends on the back deck. A nice table was set on a pretty coral tablecloth topped with a vase holding a single bird of paradise. We invited the rest of the crew to eat with us. The dinner of grilled lamb medallions, with a fresh garden salad, was delicious. We savored an excellent wine as the sun sank into the blue sea. Conversation flowed until darkness enveloped us.

Later, I was alone on the aft deck, gazing out at the sliver of moon, peaking over the horizon. The only artificial lights, interfering with the velvety carpet of stars overhead, were our navigation lights. A dim glow radiating out of the main cabin.

A cool breeze prickled my skin. I lost myself in the salt air. Relaxation overtook me for the first time in a long while. Despite all the challenges of the past two years, I still loved being at sea.

Tom and Eric were in the wheelhouse, finishing up the final tests on the sophisticated electronics aboard this secret ship. Though this yacht looked like a typical mega-yacht, it not only sported the latest in high-tech electronics and sensing gear, but was armed with the newest anti-piracy systems. Even though our main objective was surveillance, we needed to be prepared for an attack by the ruthless drug dealers.

A rough hand grazed my elbow. I looked over to see Joey standing to my right. His gaze was also on the placid sea. My ex rested against the rail. After a moment, he turned to face me.

"What a beautiful night, Linda. So much has gone on since we last sailed these waters together. Could you answer one question?"

"Sure, Joey. What?"

"Why did you go off and marry Eric, especially when you didn't know what happened to me? It seems as though you should have waited longer."

A long, deep sigh escaped from me. How do I answer this one?

"Joey, when Eric rescued me, I was devastated, lost, and frightened. I had no idea what to do or how to find you. If it wasn't for the kindness of those fishermen, I would have been penniless and on the street. You have no idea how terrifying it was. Without a credit card or any ID, I couldn't even fly back to Florida."

"That's no reason to go off and marry the guy."

"How do I explain this? Eric..."

My answer was cut short. Joey grabbed me. His arm snaked around me.

"What the heck are you doing? Let go of me!" I was jerked against my former lover. My head was yanked against his coarse, scraggy beard. The smell of old whiskey was nauseating. It took my brain a moment to register exactly what this man was attempting.

"I don't want to hear any more of this Eric crap. After all the years we were together, you must still have feelings for me. I'm twice the man he is. Linda, I still love you, dammit."

The man's cold, rough hand slithered down my neck. Disgust and fury raged.

"Joey, let go of me!" His arm tightened around me. I was about to elbow him in the gut when a big shadow traversed the dim light to our right.

"What the hell is this? Let her go!" Jake materialized out of the darkness behind Joey. He towered over us, sizing up the situation pretty quickly. The former Marine grabbed my ex's wrist, deftly wrestling his arm from around me.

Jake's huge paw of a hand closed around Joey's throat, lifting him clear off the deck. The helpless man's feet dangled mere inches off the ground. His eyes bulged in their sockets.

"You son of a bitch. If you ever touch her again, I'll murder you." Jake face contorted with fury, hovering inches from Joey's.

Gently, my hand was placed on the former Marine's massive arm. "Jake, let him go."

A moment after the Marine dropped him, Joey doubled over, gasping for breath. He retched over the rail. Jake's eyes blazed.

"Now apologize to the lady." The bulky man seized Joey's arm, spinning him around to face us.

"Jesus, you and I can't even have a conversation without this gorilla interfering."

The furious Marine looked like he was about to grab the gasping man's throat again. I intervened.

"Joey, you are as big a jerk as you always were. It took finding Eric to realize what a mistake you were. I'm actually glad the boat sank. And no, I have no more feelings for you, other than repulsion. Come on Jake, I owe you a drink. Let's go." I led the ex-Marine away before he tore Joey apart.

Chapter 4. Naples. A few months ago

After Joey's mysterious re-appearance in Naples, there were a few tense days of bickering over possession of *Dark & Stormy*. Eric convinced me to allow Joey to live aboard the boat until we could sort out a reasonable solution. My ex continued to be a pugnacious cad, while I refused to give up ownership of my beloved yacht. The unresolvable standoff continued.

Jonathan Steele tried everything, in his wily book of tricks, to persuade Joey to agree to a television special based on the sinking of *Wind Rose*. There was little progress. It appeared as though the lost sailor was happy being a belligerent sod. What the heck did I ever see in that man?

Jake spent his days prowling the sugar-white sand beaches of Naples. Once the sun set, the Marine cruised the bars, chatting with all the sun-drenched ladies. His affable charm more than made up for his rough exterior. On several occasions, the former Marine entertained multiple pretty ladies at one of the local watering holes.

Early Friday evening, Eric, Jake, and I were enjoying cocktails at the Chickee Bar. One of our favorite bartenders, Jan, entertained us with stories while the sun set over the historic Dock restaurant. Earlier that evening, Joey was dressed in clean, pressed jeans with a nice tropical shirt. He leaned over the bar, chatting away with Jan. On the prowl again, Joey? Interesting.

A light breeze wafted the scent of jasmine and other tropical flowers around the patio area. Eric leaned on the bar, grasping his plastic glass of rum. I was tilted against him. We laughed at the last of Jan's tale. Jake perched next to us, exchanging flirtatious glances with a couple of red headed ladies, across the bar. His massive bulk took up a two full spaces along the wooden rail. A ceiling fan slowly rotated above the bottles carefully lined up along the rustic bar.

"Is there anything good to drink at this establishment?" a familiar voice asked, over my shoulder. My husband and I swiveled around to come face to face with Gage, our ex-Navy SEAL friend. The man who saved my life.

To his left was Rick, his longtime pal and cohort. To their right stood Mitch Connolly, the U.S. Coast Guard officer who used to be our friend. Jake swiveled around on his bar stool. The big man lurched toward Mitch. "What the hell are you doing here?"

The former Marine's lips were pursed in a tight line. Not many people were strong enough to be able to intercept this former Marine when his fury erupted. Gage was one of the few who could. He slipped between the two men. In an instant, his hand was flat on Jake's bulging chest, stopping him in his tracks.

"Chill out, Jake. Listen to what we have to say." Gage's coal black eyes burned with intensity. When

Eric made a move toward Mitch, Rick and I grabbed his arms.

"Easy, cowboy." The conversation in the Chickee Bar died off. Tension and hostility settled over the Friday crowd. All eyes were on the newcomers.

"Hey, Linda, it's great to see you." Gage smiled at me while keeping a hand on Jake's chest. "Why don't we all sit down and have a drink?"

"Gage, what the hell were you thinking, bringing him here?" Eric nodded at the Coast Guard officer. "Did you forget Mitch knew about Joey's rescue, before Linda was kidnapped? Despite the fact we owe you a huge debt of gratitude, it would be a good idea for all of you to leave." An unintelligible growl escaped from Jake.

"Eric, it's nice to see you too. I know you guys aren't too pleased with Mitch right now, but we have interesting news about a mutual friend. News I know you want to hear. Why don't we all sit down? Ricky is just dying to buy everyone a drink."

"Here, Eric, why don't you have a seat?" The shorter Navy SEAL might not be the biggest man in the world, but his physique reminded one of a stocky bull dog. He firmly nudged my guy into a seat at one of the tables. After gallantly pulling a chair out, he motioned for me to sit next to my husband. The whole scene was surreal.

Gage manhandled Jake into the place next to Eric. Once they were settled, the tall man grabbed another chair without removing his hand from the agitated Marine's shoulder.

"Mitch, why don't you sit here?" The Coast Guard man folded his six-foot-two lean frame into a chair next to Gage. His blue USCG cap was placed on the plastic table.

Rick returned a moment later with cocktails. An uneasy silence persisted. My husband stared at the Coast Guard man with blatant hostility.

"Eric, here's the deal." Gage leaned over the table, speaking in hushed tones.

"As you know, Mitch was transferred to the Drug Interdiction Unit of the U.S. Coast Guard." The tall Navy SEAL leaned back, surveying our small group. I'm sure he saw nothing but fury and rancor from both my guy and Jake.

"Eric, listen to me, man. Mitch is one of the good guys."

My husband took a deep breath before speaking. "Gage, you've got ten seconds to spill out whatever you have to say before we leave."

"Recently, Rick and I met a real interesting guy. A man with the IQ of Einstein and a pile of money to play with. It seems this guy is also a real patriotic American. He doesn't take too kindly to all the drug trafficking coming onto the Florida shores these days."

"Gage, what the hell are you talking about? What does this have to do with our former friend?" My husband's cold stare roamed over Mitch, who was trying to look as innocent and friendly as possible.

"Eric, hear me out. There are some things I cannot tell you, because they are top secret. What I can tell you is this guy lives right here in Naples. Let's say the work he is doing...overlaps with Mitch's Coast Guard responsibilities. As a matter of fact, our Coastie friend is here in Naples to liaison with this man. He needs to figure out how this guy's project will benefit the servicemen who protect our shores along with the Drug Enforcement Agency."

"What the hell does this have to do with Eric and Linda?" Jake was finally calm enough to speak.

"Actually, it has to do with all of us. Ricky and I gave this guy a proposal today. He's real interested in all of our knowledge and individual skills. There should be an offer forthcoming within the next twenty-four hours."

"What kind of offer?" I asked Gage.

The former Navy SEAL spoke in a whisper. "An offer which could bring us all a boat load of money... and the chance to track down and deal with Carlos."

"Carlos." Eric gazed into the distance.

"Yes, Carlos. I thought that might get your attention."

"Where do we fit into this plan?"

"Eric, I can't tell you the details right now. This guy is putting it all together. By the way, where is Joey?" Gage asked no one in particular.

"He's probably aboard *Dark & Stormy,* over there." The former Navy SEAL followed the direction of my finger which was pointing to my pretty emerald-green sailing yacht. The sloop was located a few slips away.

"I'm going over to talk to him. Don't kill Mitch while I'm gone."

With a grin, Gage stalked over toward the sailboat. It always amazed me to watch him move. He was such a big, strong guy who moved with the grace and agility of a cheetah.

Though well north of six feet tall, he slinked along. His deep, black eyes burned with intensity, taking in every detail of his surroundings. Like the great cats of Africa, he could spring upon his prey in a flash. He proved this aboard the drug smuggling boat anchored off an island near Trinidad last year. Using the darkness as cover, his cat-like prowess allowed him to rescue me from Carlos' grasp.

In the dead of night, he crept up, silently. I lay bound in the dirty prison cell of a stateroom. As he edged closer, I tensed, ready for a battle. The fight was over in three seconds. The former Navy SEAL pounced on me in a flash. He pinned me down, stifling my cry with the huge palm of his hand.

"Relax, my name is Gage. I'm a Navy SEAL here to rescue you." His rough voice hissed into my ear.

The big man liberated me to the cold, black ocean. My attempts at resistance were futile. Like the wild African hunters, he dragged his prey away with little effort.

Once aboard the rescue boat, the former Navy SEAL's gentler side became apparent. He tended to the wounds inflicted by the brutal drug dealer. It was quite a surprise to find out how sensitive the guy was, a caring man who could become a heartless killer in an instant.

After the SEAL's departure from the Chickee, both Jake and Eric peered at Mitch. I'd never seen such a glare of hatred out of my husband. The Coastie returned the stare. He fidgeted for a second, then spoke for the first time tonight. "Eric, will you give me a chance to explain?"

"There is nothing you can say which will make me change my opinion of you. You can answer one question. How could you not tell us about Joey's rescue when you knew we would be heading back to Trinidad?"

"Eric, I was hoping, well, maybe after the wedding, you guys would drop it. If I knew you were going back to Trinidad, I certainly would have tried to stop you. By the time I found out you were there, Carlos had already kidnapped Linda. At that point, there was no reason to tell you about Joey. What good would it have done?"

"You son a bitch. YOU should have called us the minute you heard about Joey's rescue." Eric rose half way out of the chair. Rick leapt up, grabbing a tight hold of my husband's arm.

"Geez, man, give me a break. I couldn't tell you because it was top secret. If I spilled the story to you, it could have cost me my job. The brass have thrown officers in jail for divulging much less important information."

"That's a load of crap. You could have found a way," Jake shouted while rapidly opening and closing his fists.

Rick looked frazzled because he was losing control of this situation. "Hey, you guys, let's try to calm down and talk about this."

"Jake, you're a Marine. You know how the chain of command operates, need to know and all that," the Coast Guard officer said, ignoring Rick.

"Look, Mitch." Eric grabbed my hand, pulling me up from the chair. "If you expect us to accept your mea culpa here and be friends again, don't hold your breath. Get the hell out of here because we're through with you."

"Listen, cowboy, you can hate me. I can deal with that. Keep in mind, we may be working together very closely over the next few months. You are going to have figure a way to get beyond your anger."

"Not very likely." We hustled away from the Chickee. In our hotel room, we tried to relax, but sleep was very elusive that night.

The next morning, the ringing of Eric's cell phone woke me. A quick glance at my watch showed eight already. Where was Eric? I found him on the balcony, reading the newspaper with feet propped up on the railing. The morning sun gleamed through the sliders.

"Eric, honey, your phone just rang."

"Who is it?"

"I didn't check."

He listened to the voice mail while I search out the coffee pot.

"You're always such a morning person."

"Who was on the phone?"

"Gage. He wants to meet us in a half an hour in front of the hotel."

"Half an hour? I'd better get in the shower."

A short while later, we walked out the front door of the Cove Inn to be confronted by a big, black stretch limo. Gage leaned casually against the back door. A cocky smile lit up his face. "Good morning. Your chariot awaits."

"Gage, what the heck?" Eric asked.

The former Navy SEAL casually turned to open the back door to the limo as if this were an everyday occurrence. He motioned us inside the luxurious car. My husband and I settled down on the soft leather backseat. The Navy SEAL sat across from us.

"Not a bad set of wheels, huh?" The Navy man leaned back like he owned the car. The uniformed driver fired it up.

"Government?" Eric asked.

"No, it belongs to a friend of mine. We have a meeting with him shortly."

"The friend with a ton of money and the IQ of Einstein?"

"You know, Eric, it might be too early in the morning to discuss business."

Gage nodded at the limo driver. My husband's eyes followed mine out the car. We were stopped at the stop sign near the corner of Broad Avenue South and Gordon Drive.

Our driver made a left. The spectacular, mani-cured roadway leading to Naples most exclusive neigh-borhood passed by our windows. We gazed at the tow-ering royal palms, lining both sides of the street.

Another left turn on Galleon Drive was followed by a quick right onto Schooner Landing. The limo stopped in front of an imposing wrought iron gate. Behind it stood a huge Mediterranean-styled mansion. The gate opened efficiently, allowing us to enter this tropical enclave. A veritable jungle surrounded the entrance to the grand staircase, leading to the front door. The entrance was framed by two huge banana plants. Immature clusters of green fruit dangled below the stalks.

A stocky guy in a dark suit, with a earpiece nearly hidden in his ear, opened the car door. His tailored jacket didn't hide the bulge beneath his lapel. He gestured toward the massive front door. "Mr. Sanderling is waiting for you in the study."

"Thanks, bro." Gage grinned at the man in the suit. We ascended the white marble staircase to the house. "Rent-a-cops, he'd a been down in two seconds. I need to work on the security around here, also."

After swinging open the heavy oak entrance portal, our friend casually ushered us across a huge entry hall into a posh great room. Exotic stone spanned the floor. We crossed the space by the sliding glass doors. A glance outside revealed a lovely pool area immersed in a jungle of lush greenery. Gage rapped on a tall wooden door.

"Come on in," said a muffled voice. The former SEAL opened the passageway to a cozy study, richly lined with polished mahogany. Volumes of books dominated both walls, leading into the nook.

An imposing man, of medium build, glanced up from his post behind a formidable desk. His attire consisted of the typical Florida golf outfit, including a collared teal shirt. A jagged, three-inch scar blemished his right temple. Mid-fifties would be a reasonable guess for his age. Seated nearby were Rick and Mitch.

"Good morning, Gage. I see you brought your friends." The man rose as we approached. Eric extended his hand.

"Martin Sanderling. Welcome to my home." After generously guiding Eric and me to comfortable chairs, our host perched on the edge of his desk. There was something about his easy going demeanor which commanded respect.

Martin examined Eric and me before speaking. While he scrutinized us, my eyes fell upon a statue of a bottlenose dolphin sculpted in black stone, much like ebony. The sculpture occupied a prominent position near the front of the polished mahogany desk.

"I assume you know Rick and Mitch." Martin Sanderling watched my husband's cold glare at our former friend. The Coast Guard officer nodded with a stiff smile. I didn't bother to acknowledge him.

"My understanding is you were told nothing about why I invited you here this morning."

"That's correct." Eric shifted his gaze from Mitch to Martin Sanderling. We waited patiently for the man to speak again. Our host's intense look made me think he was sizing us up.

"I've been working on a project for some time now. If successful, it will be very important for our national security. Also, my work is vital to the health and welfare of both my corporation and my family. Normally it would take years acquainting myself with someone before I invited him into my inner circle.

"When I met Gage months ago, there was something special there. Maybe it had to do with the way he carried himself, or quite possibly his former profession. After our initial meeting, I knew he could be trusted." Martin Sanderling nodded in our friend's general direction. The ex-Navy SEAL's face was a blank mask.

"You two," Martin nodded at us, "I don't know too much about. Eric, you have quite a reputation on TV. My two teen-aged daughters love your fishing show. I would venture to say you are their favorite captain. They can't wait to meet you." Martin paused, allowing a smile of pride to play around his lips. Eric looked embarrassed by the compliment.

"Seems damn crazy to go fishing off the Alaskan coast in the dead of winter. I've only caught a little of the show, but it always seems like a big storm is pounding the boats. You obviously know how to handle your ship, a skill that may come in very handy for me."

The man narrowed his eyes in my direction. The faint smile persisted. "Linda, treading water for as long as you did tells me you have great survival instincts. Also, I've heard bits and pieces about your nasty encounter with a friend of ours. The way you handled yourself was impressive." I attempted to return his smile, not really sure what this man was getting at.

"There are a couple of things I will not tolerate. There will be no infighting among the ranks of my team. Eric, it's obvious you have a problem with Mitch. If you join me, you need to work it out." Martin Sanderling glared at my husband. "Also, I expect complete loyalty and vigilance in protecting this very important project."

"What exactly is this project?" Eric asked stiffly. I guessed he was uncomfortable with the domineering attitude of our host. My husband was used to being in charge.

"There is not much I can tell you much until you have signed confidentiality agreements and further agreed to all of my conditions of employment." Our host again stared hard at Eric.

"I can tell you this. I've invented some very interesting technology, thanks to a pair of clever bottlenose dolphins. We are only in the testing stages with these electronic components, but if they work as well as I think they will, the U.S. Government will pay me tons of money to get a hold of them.

"Even better, with the help of the U.S. Coast Guard, we should all but eliminate drug trafficking in the Gulf of Mexico. We will work to eradicate all the drug dealers supplying our wonderful country. That is an accomplishment I would greatly enjoy."

Chapter 5. Somewhere in the Everglades National Park

The yellow seaplane skidded across the glassy, aquamarine water of the Gulf of Mexico. Salt spray billowed, jettisoned by the float plane's pontoons.

Moments before, my neck was craned at nearly a right angle with my forehead pressed against the window along the fuselage. Where was this island we were headed for? There was nothing but thick, tropical foliage below the circling seaplane. We were about to land in an area of dense mangroves.

Eric eyed the landscape below us. "Linda, look at these islands. They are tiny clumps of trees surrounded by sand. The cays all look alike. What a great hiding place."

We bumped to a stop on the sugar white sand beach. A man dressed in a tropical "Tommy Bahama" type shirt jogged over to open the passenger door. Martin Sanderling sprung out of the plane, followed by Gage, Rick, and Joey. Eric and I were the last to slide out. Whew! As flying was not one of my favorite pastimes, it was good to be on the solid land again. My sandals easily slipped off my feet, allowing my toes to squish in the hot sand.

"Welcome to Paradise." Martin Sanderling grinned at his own pun. "Paradise" was the code name the United States Park Service gave to this remote enclave craftily hidden in the Ten Thousand Islands, south of both Marco Island and Everglades City. There were not many maps showing the location of this facility. The few that did, had this area marked as a United States federal research facility. Access, by the general public, was strictly forbidden.

The location, on the charts, was intentionally altered to further protect the secrecy of this cay. Because of a jurisdictional agreement between the State of Florida and the U.S. Department of Homeland Security, the island was never visited by any state or local authorities. This enclave was secured by a private security force provided by the U.S. Department of Defense.

Eric pulled me aside for a private chat. "This island is the perfect hiding spot. It would be tough to try to find this tiny cay amongst all the mangroves in this area. It's a maze of waterways."

"Even flying overhead, you couldn't see anything. This research facility is all but invisible. Come on, Eric, let's catch up with the group." We broke into a jog across the beach to rejoin our cohorts.

Our bevy meandered along the soft, white sand beach to a collection of buildings spread around a small clearing.

Joey wiped the sweat from his brow. "It sure is a hot day today. This humidity is a killer." The faint breeze barely allowed the beads of sweat to evaporate from our skin.

After another short hike, several dwellings materialized from the native plant life. One large edifice, made of sheet metal painted green to blend in with the mangroves, dominated the clearing. While wandering along, I observed a heavily armed man, patrolling the edge of the dense brush. Gage followed the guard with his eyes.

"These are the living quarters." Martin pointed to a group of thatched huts which looked like camping lodges. "The big building up ahead is where we do most of the research. Over to the right is the dolphin pen. Come, I'll introduce you."

We wandered toward the water. A bright blue lagoon awaited us. Crude wire fence enclosed a pool of pale aquamarine water. At the bottom of the shallows, bright white sand sloped off toward the deeper blue of the Gulf. Our group paused at the water's edge.

Suddenly, a five-foot-long dolphin torpedoed toward the beach. He came to an abrupt stop in mere inches of water, three feet from us. With a flick of his head, a big blast of water erupted from his mouth, spraying over us. Rivulets dripped off Martin's canary-yellow golf shirt.

The wily mammal bobbed his head up and down. Sharp whistles squeaked from the slick gray mouth which was arched in a smile. It appeared as if the dolphin was laughing at us.

"Meet Jet." Our grinning boss stooped over to rub the dolphin's head. "He's Flo's son. This bottlenose dolphin is one of the most intelligent beings I've ever run into on this planet. He's a troublemaker as you can see. Being a young adolescent, he loves playing practical jokes on you."

Martin whistled sharply while clapping his hands. A second dolphin gracefully swam over, stopping in the deeper water eight feet off the glistening beach. Her head rose above the surface. A few staccato clicks greeted us.

Our host waved, while smiling at this second dolphin. "Hello, Flo." For such a serious man, he sure looked like a kid when interacting with this aquatic duo.

"Later on, we can put on swim suits so you can be properly introduced to these wonderful mammals." Martin turned away from the beach. "Now, I would like to show you the research lab."

Our group followed the boss back up the beach. We came to a stop outside a nondescript whitewashed door to the metal building. It looked like a diminutive warehouse. A few small windows dotted the front side. Roll-down hurricane shutters covered the exposed glass.

Once inside the cool, air conditioned building, we strolled into an expansive room. Brightly lit computer screens blinked away. There were several tables housing a variety of tools along with partially disassembled machines. Drab gray paint covered the walls. No artwork or pictures adorned the workspace. Bright florescent lights glared down from above.

"This place sure looks sterile," I whispered to my husband. "They must be extremely serious about their work."

A man and a woman, clad in starched white lab coats, leaned over the guts of a machine. The female tweaked something with a tiny screwdriver. Once she was satisfied with the adjustment, she glanced in our direction.

"Sloan, I would like you to meet the new members of our team."

After introductions, my eyes were not the only set taking in the female member of this research pair. Joey gawked at this woman who had the body of Rachel Welch. Long, lustrous brown hair was carefully twisted in a neat bun. The bundle was pinned to the back of her head. Her golden bronze tan glowed. The librarian spectacles, perched at the end of her nose, didn't hide her beautiful black eyes any more than the lab coat hid her sleek body.

Martin Sanderling looked down at the unimpressive machine with a gleam in his eyes. "This is my baby." He placed his hand on the unit. The machine was six inches long by five inches high. Attached to the disassembled apparatus was a small readout, resembling a radar screen on a yacht. At the other end of a long cable was a cylindrical black plastic tube. The entire instrument looked like a depth sounder with transducer from a sailboat.

"Sloan, how is our Lokator gear working?"

"It appears to be functioning properly, Mr. Sanderling. We really won't know how well until we've completed the open water tests."

Eric's eyes diverted from Sloan to our boss. "What exactly is this?"

"Let's head into the conference room where I will explain." Martin led us into another area at the back of the building. Our chief motioned for us to sit down at the long, industrial table surrounded by chairs. A large white board with diagrams drawn on it, plastered the wall in front of us. Next to the white board hung nautical charts of the area.

"The Lokator is based upon echolocation. The same system used by dolphins and whales to locate things in the open sea." A serious look was etched upon our boss' face. He stared at each of us in turn.

"It appears to be very simple process. In reality, echolocation is a very complicated, sophisticated system. Let me explain.

"First, you must understand what an echo is." Martin paused. His glaring eyes narrowed when my ex sighed loudly. "Joey, am I boring you?"

"No, I just didn't expect to return to grade school on this trip."

"What a jerk." Eric smirked at my whispered comment.

"Joey, you are free to leave anytime." Our host could not hide his irritation. He glared at my ex once again.

"No offense, but let's get to the action. After we find out what happened to *Wind Rose,* Carlos needs to be dealt with."

"All in good time." Martin Sanderling ignored my former partner.

"Echoes are simply vibrations in air or water which stimulate the auditory nerves of the ear, allowing you to hear them. These vibrations can be thought of as oscillations of air or water molecules. This allows a transfer of energy to the surrounding ones." Martin pointed to a diagram on the white board. "This energy is passed along to other molecules. The movement of these particles allows the sound to travel through the air or water."

The door to the lab opened. Sloan poked her head in. "May I join you?" The female researcher entered, sitting to Martin Sanderling's right.

"Sloan, you are always welcome. Now where was I? Oh, yes. When the sound wave reaches the surface of an object, it bounces off. The return pulse travels in the opposite direction. The sound is received by an instrument, or in the dolphin's case, their ears." The serious lady researched chuckled at this statement.

"Maybe I should correct myself as dolphins don't really have ears." Martin smiled at his own faux pas. "They do have very complicated auditory systems. We will discuss these at another time.

"This sending and receiving of sound waves is basically how radar and sonar work. For the optimum echo, the waves must bounce off a surface perpendicular to the source of the waves. Ideally, this surface should be a dense, hard material...like steel." Martin's eyes scanned our group.

"The problem we are trying to overcome, is getting these molecules to bounce off a fiberglass object. The dilemma is two-fold. The first problem is fiberglass absorbs the typical sonar and radar signals. The second difficulty is the shape of most boats. The rounded hull makes a poor reflective surface."

Our new boss paused one more time. A smile darted across his face.

"The breakthrough finally came in an odd way. One day, I was piloting the family fishing boat, off Naples, when a small pod of dolphins came over to play with us. The water was very murky on this particular day, yet the dolphins had no trouble swimming alongside the boat even though they couldn't see the hull clearly.

"I know you all have witnessed this and probably didn't think much of it. It's obvious they are using their echolocation. How is it they can bounce sound waves off a fiberglass boat? Most yachts have a rounded area at the bow. Maybe a simple demonstration would be best."

Martin rose out of his chair. "Why don't you all change into swim suits. Meet me at the dolphin pen. I'll show you how good this echolocation is."

Eric and I wandered along the grass roof huts looking for number five, marked on the key given to us earlier. We entered the comfortable, well-appointed room. The center of the left hand wall was dominated by a queen-sized rattan bed with a fancy oval head-board of flowers woven in the rattan.

There was a nice seating area to the right with two bamboo chairs on either side of a glass topped table. A ceiling fan, with blades shaped like palm fronds, rotated overhead. We found our luggage next to the varnished teak dresser.

I searched through my bag for a swimsuit. "What do you make of Martin Sanderling? He seems like a very complicated man."

"Yes, he is a complicated and very intelligent man. The next few days should be interesting. What do you make of Sloan?"

"She certainly is stunningly beautiful. Judging by the manner of her dress, she is either self-conscious of her good looks or too busy working to care very much."

"They make an unusual duo."

"Yes, Eric. A strange duo in a strange place. It's right out of the *Twilight Zone.*"

After changing, we walked to the beach where the group had already assembled. Joey stood at the water's edge wearing a T-shirt and shorts. No swim trunks were visible.

"Don't you want to swim with the dolphins, Joey?" I could not help but goad my former lover.

"I'm not getting in the water with those beasts," he whispered. His face twisted into a nasty sneer.

"Chicken." Three quick strides took me into the water.

"Hey, Linda. Watch out for the sharks," Joey said.

I stopped swimming. A flash of uncertainty was quickly replaced by aggravation. "Joey, you're such an idiot. It's an enclosed pen. Martin wouldn't allow any sharks in here."

"Yeah, but I made you blink, didn't I?"

"Your quick wit was something I always loved about you."

"At least there was something. Gee, Linda, the way you act with Mr. Wonderful, an outsider would think I was the bogey man."

"You said it. I didn't."

To extricate myself from my irritating ex, I swam a few short strokes to the center of the lagoon.

Martin waved to me from the edge of the sand. "Be careful with the dolphins. Don't try touch them."

As soon as he warned me, Jet rushed over at full speed. The little guy stopped on a dime, only inches from me. The young dolphin cocked his head to look at me with one eye.

"He won't hurt you." Sloan called out, while rushing in my direction. They must have thought this was my first time in the water with marine mammals. Lucky for me, Joey was always there to save the day.

"Linda's a so called marine mammal biologist." He scoffed at my former profession. "What a joke. She thinks she's a damn dolphin whisperer or something."

After a few graceful strokes, Sloan was beside me. Jet circled us, watching me carefully. I made no attempt at physical contact, knowing it was better to let him come to me. Finally, he glided to a stop, lifting one eye out of the water. The little male followed my every move while staying out of reach.

"Martin didn't tell me you are a marine biologist." Sloan brushed back a lose strand of hair self-consciously as we bobbed side-by-side in the calm water.

"I'm not sure I told him. It's obvious my ex doesn't think much of it."

"Biology is my undergrad degree also."

"What is your graduate degree?"

"I have my PhD in engineering from MIT." Sloan smiled awkwardly.

Jet flew at us, furiously beating his tail. He leapt, clearing our heads by a mere couple of inches. The resultant flop into the water drenched us. In a flash, he was back in front of us, clicking and whistling for attention.

"He wants us to play with him." Sloan laughed like a kid. She swam off on her back toward the beach. Jet followed, cruising around and jumping over her. Out of the corner of my eye, I noticed Gage break off his conversation with Martin. He approached Sloan and Jet cautiously.

"Can I join you?" The former Navy SEAL eased into the water near the scientist. This tall, lanky newcomer immediately received the adolescent male's attention. The mammal cruised over to the Navy SEAL, prodding him with his bottle nose. Jet didn't want any competition for the ladies' attention.

"Don't push him away, unless he gets too rough. Let him check you out." Sloan instructed the tall man. Soon the three of us were swimming around the pool on our backs with Jet circling and jumping over us.

Martin stepped into the knee-deep water. "Now, we will have a demonstration of his great echolocation abilities." He tossed a cloth with a strap on it to Sloan. The researcher called the little dolphin over. The cover was carefully placed over the juvenile's eyes. He swam around easily, having great fun with this game. Martin tossed a round plastic ball to Gage.

"Put it in the water in front of you. Don't make a splash, just set it down." The former Navy SEAL did as he was told.

"Jet, Gage has a ball." The young dolphin spun in a tight circle. With a flick of his tail, he accelerated toward the Navy man. Without being able to see, the young dolphin easily snatched the ball away.

"That's amazing." The little guy cruised back to Sloan, who removed the covering from his eyes. She rewarded him with a rub on his jaw.

"My cetacean friend demonstrated a very simple lesson in echolocation. Though he couldn't see the ball, the sounds waves sent out quickly located the object he knows as a ball. By pulsing the signals, he could home in on the object as he swam over to grab it. All in a matter of a few seconds with very little effort. His echolocation is exactly what we are trying to duplicate."

After a few more moments enjoying the dolphins company, we waded out of the water. Eric and I stopped at our hut for a shower, before taking a late afternoon stroll along the beach.

My husband bent down to pick up a shell for closer inspection. A brown pelican dove into a school of bait fish, surfacing with a pouch full of brine. The unwieldy bird pointed his beak skyward as the water drained from it. With a couple of shakes of his head, an afternoon snack of tiny fish slid down his gullet.

Our wanderings brought us to a private sitting area isolated amongst the twisted mangrove roots at the water's edge.

"Hi, Sloan." The scientist reclined on a lounge chair, sipping a Corona. Her librarian spectacles perched on her perky nose. A thick textbook was balanced on her lap.

"Hello." The researcher's eyes rose from the hardcover. She smiled at our approach. "Why don't you two join me? You're welcome to help yourselves to a beer."

"I hope we're not disturbing you." Eric reached into the cooler, pulling out two ice-cold brews. The red fireball of a sun descended into the Gulf of Mexico. Two tiki torches blazed away on either side of the lounge chairs. The smell of citronella did a good job, keeping the mosquitoes at bay.

"You're not bothering me at all. I would love a break from all this technical stuff."

"Do you live here full time?" Eric asked after we settled down on a couple of lounge chairs. Sloan straightened up, leaning in our direction.

"Yes, this is my research lab. It's either this or a stuffy workshop in Cambridge, Massachusetts. I much prefer this."

"Tell us about your research."

Before she could respond, Gage ambled up. "Hi, guys." He threw an admiring glance at Sloan.

Her cheeks blushed red. "Corona?" She tipped her nearly empty bottle in the ex-Navy SEAL's direction.

"Let me get it." Gage pulled two beers from the ice, flipping off the bottle caps. He gave the first one to the researcher, keeping the second for himself. His tall body folded onto a lounger next to this very attractive lady. She looked embarrassed by his attention.

"I'm studying the mechanisms of echolocation." She paused a moment to glance at Gage, who sipped his beer, while giving her his full attention. She blushed again.

"Dolphins send out a series of clicks, but at a much higher frequency than the ones we hear. These pulses are emitted from an opening right below their blowhole. This area, called the oily melon, amplifies the pulses sent out by the dolphin, giving their echolocation great range."

As a marine mammal biologist, I was extremely interested in her research. It was obvious my husband and Gage were interested in other aspects of this beautiful scientist.

"The return echoes are received, by the dolphin, near the lower jaw. An intricate set of nerves transfer the pulses to the middle ear. Due to a combination of instinct and learning, the dolphin's brain can interpret the electrical impulses transmitted from the inner ear to the brain to be able to figure out what the object is."

"It seems like duplicating the frequency of the sound pulse along with amplification should be no problem. The difficulty would be in the interpretation of the return pulse, because so much of it is absorbed by the fiberglass and dispersed by the rounded surfaces of a boat." My response lit up the scientist's pretty face.

"Exactly." Sloan sat up so quickly both Gage and Eric flinched. The excitement plastered on our faces caused my husband to shake his head.

"Gage, do you have any idea what the hell they are talking about?"

"Nope." Gage winked at me. This former Navy SEAL was a very intelligent man. My husband was no slouch either. They were just teasing us. It was obvious Sloan didn't get it. Scarlet stained her cheeks.

"Here it is such a beautiful evening and I'm boring you with physics. Sorry." The scientist rose to leave but was stopped by Gage's lightning fast reflexes. His hand was on her forearm in an instant.

"Lady, don't ever apologize to me for being smart. I love smart women. Eric and I sort of understood what you said. We were just kidding you."

"Well, whatever. We should be heading off to dinner." The researcher scurried away in the direction of the lab building.

"She'll be a tough nut to crack, Gage. Don't you get the feeling all her beauty has left her feeling a little...awkward?"

"Eric, I can't believe you were checking her out, when you are here with your wife." He stared at me for a moment, as if trying to figure out whether or not I was teasing him. Gage interrupted Eric's contemplation.

"It would be tough not to notice a body like that."

Chapter 6. Paradise

The next morning, Eric and I were checking over the twenty-five foot, center-console motorboat. A trio of 350hp outboards clung to the transom. The boat was moored at the end of a short dock, running out from the beach.

While walking out here, we stopped by to see Flo and Jet. When the male dolphin noticed our feet sloshing through the shallow water, he flew over.

"Hi, Jet. How are you this morning?" The young dolphin grounded on the soft sand inches from us. A greeting of staccato clicks and whistles followed. After giving the little guy a quick stroke on the jaw, we strolled down the dock. A short jump landed us aboard the speed boat.

A few moments later, tiny beads of sweat rolled off my husband's brow while he measured the oil in the port engine. I leaned against the gunwale. The big engine cowling was balanced carefully on my lap. A familiar figure walked down the beach. He turned to head down the dock in our direction.

"Tom." My face lit up with a smile at the newcomer.

"Hello, brother." Eric stopped what he was doing, jumping easily on the pier. The brothers exchanged a handshake-hug. "What the heck are you doing here?"

"Hey, bro. About a week ago, I got a phone call from a guy, offering me a job." Eric's older brother stepped aboard, embracing both me and the engine cowling at the same time. I was careful not to drop the expensive motor cover. Tom's dark, black beard scratched my face as he gave me a brotherly kiss. A Harley T-shirt, dark cut-off shorts, and black suede boots looked very out-of-place on this tropical island.

"It's great to see you, Li'l Sis." The older brother turned his attention back to my husband. "I thought the phone call was a joke until Gage called, confirming it was on the level. I spent the past few days in West Palm, going over this guy's mega-yacht. It's very impressive."

Tom wiped the back of his hand across his sweaty brow. "Sanderling and his wife flew in to get acquainted. She's a piece of work. Have you met her?"

"No, not yet." Eric replaced the engine cowling. With a laugh, he turned to face his older sibling. "Brother, you need new clothes if you're going to spend any time in Florida. You look like a castaway dropped off a plane from Alaska."

"Watch it, little bro. It was the best I had on short notice. Anyway, we went over the yacht from bow to stern. He wants me to bring it over here so we can run tests on the new equipment he invented." Tom helped Eric remove the second engine cowling.

"We are going to head out in a few minutes with the dolphins to test this gear. It's some pretty interesting technology." My husband pulled the dipstick out of the second engine. With a wipe of a rag, the oil level was checked.

"Did you hear where Martin Sanderling wants to head next, after we finish the tests here?"

"To Cape Lookout, to try to find the *Wind Rose*." The answer came from Gage who ambled stealthily down the dock. The former Navy SEAL loomed over us.

"You can thank your favorite Navy SEAL for the idea. I'm the one who suggested it. Martin wanted a real world scenario. Something to search for with a geographical position we knew approximately, but not exactly. He wanted to see how well this new equipment works."

"Cape Lookout." The memories of the fateful night off the Outer Banks flooded back. "I guess it would explain why Joey is here."

"Joey is here. As in your ex-Joey?" Tom asked incredulously. "No shit."

"None other. He's been such a jerk since we arrived back in Naples. It was a shock to see him come down here with us."

"Martin hired him for several reasons. One, he is the only one, other than you Linda, who knows where the *Wind Rose* is," Gage said. "Also, he has intimate knowledge of Carlos. Mitch thinks Carlos is one of the big links in the international drug war. The Coast Guard suspects he is launching mini-subs off his shrimp boat, sending them ashore all over the Gulf of Mexico. These subs are loading with drugs: heroine, crystal meth, all the real bad stuff."

"Is Martin hoping to use Joey's knowledge of Carlos' activities to try to stop the drug flow into the United States?" I asked Gage. His answer was interrupted by Sloan's approach. The researcher was dressed in a sleek, teal one-piece bathing suit, mostly covered by a wispy white wrap, carefully tied in a knot on her chest.

"Who the heck is this babe?" Tom asked under his breath. Gage turned his attention to the approaching lady. The former Navy SEAL straightened his frame. A smile played around his lips.

The big crab fisherman climbed to the dock, in an attempt to intercept this newcomer first. The dolphin lady definitely needed to be rescued from these fawning men.

"Hi, Sloan." In an instant, I stood beside her. "Let me introduce Tom, Eric's brother."

"Hi." The pretty researcher glanced up at the bearded man before averting her eyes. "Are you another Bering Sea fisherman?"

"Yes, I'm captain of our fishing vessel." Tom's statement brought a smirk to his younger brother's face. Both Tom and Eric skippered their fishing vessel, depending on what type of crab or fish they were hunting for.

"Nice to meet you, captain," Sloan said formally. With an involuntary flick, a few strands of hair were tossed over her shoulder. This caught all the guys' attention.

"Linda, I was wondering if you could give me a hand?"

"Sure, Sloan, what do you need?"

"The fence around the dolphin lagoon needs to be checked for holes. A sensor went off a few minutes ago, indicating something big tried to get in. It was probably a large bull shark. If a shark gets in, it could hurt one of the dolphins. Since they were born in captivity, their natural fear of predators is not as strong as it should be." Sloan brushed a loose strand of hair off her face. Once again, this was not missed by any of the men.

"Jet is in particular danger because he is young and everything is a play toy to him. I need to snorkel around the perimeter to make sure there are no gaps."

"I'd be happy to help you," Gage gallantly offered. "I'm not bad at snorkeling and could offer you extra muscle for any repairs, or to fend off any nasty sharks."

The scientist looked helplessly to me with a slight roll of her eyes.

"Come on, Sloan. Gage we'll be sure to call if we need you." My quick pat on the Navy SEAL's shoulder kept him at bay. After grabbing the dolphin researcher's arm, we strolled back down the dock. A slight pang of fear was quickly pushed aside.

"Thanks, Linda. It's not like I don't like the attention. It's just, well, I've worked so hard on my education so men would see me for my brains not my looks." Sloan stopped, facing me at the beginning of the dock. We looked back at the guys, who were following us with their eyes.

"Sloan, I get it, but watch out for Tom. He's quite a ladies man."

Capt. Marlena Brackebusch

"He intrigues me a little. 'Captain'." She laughed softly. "It's so funny how the guys get all tongue tied. The SEAL guy puffed up when I walked down the dock. The next thing will be a duel to determine who claims the maiden." We shared a laugh before heading over to the dolphin area.

Soon, we were swimming along the perimeter of the enclosure. The cool water felt great as we glided along ten feet off the sandy bottom, slowly kicking our swim fins. All kinds of brightly colored fish darted out of our path. The pretty blues and yellows sparkled in the morning sun. After a few minutes of swimming, we came upon a large hole in the wire fence, leading out to the Gulf of Mexico. Jet swam in and out of the gap, making a game of our discovery.

Sloan glanced uneasily around the enclosure. "I hope no bull sharks got in."

"There are no sharks in view, only Flo and Jet. Do you need help fixing the hole?"

"No, I don't think so. I'm going to bend the wire back, then lace the loose edges around the unbroken part of the fence. Come on you two, get in here." The repair was complicated by the curious dolphins who insisted on inspecting the scientist's work. After completing the repair, the electronic sensor was reattached.

"The dolphins seem fine. If there was a shark inside, Flo's instincts would make her nervous. Let's head back to the beach."

After toweling off, we met up with Martin, who was heading down the dock. He cradled the display unit and transducer components of the Lokator equipment in his hands. We turned as a group for the motorboat.

"Sloan, is everything all right with the dolphins?"

"Yes, Mr. Sanderling. I repaired a hole in the fence. We didn't see any sharks in the enclosure."

"*Hmm,* maybe we'll take a quick spin around in the boat before heading into the Gulf with the dolphins. After all I've invested in them, I'd hate to lose them to sharks."

Aboard the launch, the three of us joined the guys. Eric maneuvered the skiff away from the dock, steering us toward the dolphin pen. Sloan leaned over to unhook the gate to the enclosure. As it swung open, Jet and Flo cruised over. They seemed delighted to play with the powerboat.

After entering the lagoon, Sloan reattached the rope to close the gate.

"Why don't they escape? They could swim out of the pen when you open it up. The dolphins would be long gone by the time we'd catch up. It would be like *Free Willy* or something," Tom asked the researcher.

She glanced at me with a roll of her eyes. "They don't leave because this is their home. These dolphins were raised in captivity. As an adult dolphin, Flo is relatively happy here. Jet won't leave, especially at his age, because his mom is here. Eventually, we may have to provide company for the little guy to keep him from wandering off."

As the lady scientist finished her statement, we arrived back at the beginning of the pen. No more holes were found in the enclosure. No large predators lurked in the deeper recesses of the lagoon.

Gage reached over, opening the gate before Sloan could get to the bow. Martin Sanderling blew a high-pitched whistle, calling the two dolphins over.

"They'll follow us. One of my crew members put an oblong fiberglass object, similar but smaller than a mini-sub somewhere on a course due west of the research facility. The dolphins know they have to find something new. Let's see if they find it first. It would be interesting to see if my Lokator gear will discover it before the dolphins do."

Eric throttled up the skiff. We skimmed along the aquamarine water with Flo and Jet leaping alongside the planing boat. All of us enjoyed the exhilarating speed and the natural show put on by the lightning fast dolphins. When we reached the approximate area of the fake mini-sub, our captain slowed the boat. Sloan called the two dolphins over, showing them a model of a submarine.

"Submarine." Sloan repeated the word a few times. Jet tried to grab the toy from the scientist.

"He just want to play," Tom said.

"Actually, marine mammals understand much more than we give them credit for. By repeating the word 'submarine' a few times, the dolphins now associate the word with the object. You'll see."

Martin deployed the black tube from the Lokator equipment over the side of the skiff. All eyes were on the monitor as Flo and Jet nudged the gear, reacting to the high frequency waves emanating from it.

Sloan leaned over the side. "Flo, Jet. Go find a submarine."

The dolphin pair systematically searched, back and forth, in front of us.

"Having the dolphins actually increases the range of the Lokator gear, since we managed to duplicate the frequency they send out exactly. Any reflected signals from their echolocation can be read by the machine." Sloan paused, squinting at the readout.

"Our biggest challenge is designing an algorithm to be able to decipher the return signals from both the dolphins and the Lokator. We worked up a program to interpret the signals based upon a pre-programmed set off possibilities. Also, the computer can learn new objects entered into the database through the receiver."

"Like the dolphins, the Lokator can learn what new objects are, like artificial intelligence." I looked toward the unimpressive machine with new respect.

"Exactly." Sloan seemed pleased at least one of us understood.

"Eric, it's a good thing you and I can drive the boat. Otherwise, these chicks wouldn't need us one bit." Tom eyed Sloan. The smile on his lips radiated to the creases surrounding his eyes.

"Tom, you'd better be extra nice to us chicks. Remember, I know how to drive a boat, too. I can handle this." My elbow playfully nudged the elder brother out of the way. I reached for the wheel in Eric's grasp. Before Tom could respond, the Lokator beeped.

"We have something." Martin stared at the screen. About twenty yards ahead of us, the dolphins circled furiously, madly clicking and whistling. Jet was so excited he leapt five feet into the air, landing with a splash. Martin switched to the video mode of the machine. Lying fifteen feet below us was a white cylindrical object, shaped like a sub, with the blue "SI" logo on it.

"We've found it. The Lokator works. Now, we progress to the big boat tests."

Chapter 7. A Boatyard near West Palm Beach

The flight from Naples, aboard Martin's private jet, was quick and smooth. The limo cruised along the West Palm Beach waterfront. The uniformed driver made a couple of turns before stopping in front of a tall chain-link fence topped with barbed wire.

Martin Sanderling's eyes fixated on a building on the other side of the fence. "It's an old, defunct boatyard. I bought it to be able to build a platform to house both the Lokator gear and the first of my mini-subs. The combination of the two should go a long way in the war on drugs."

The electric gate was opened by a man whose posture looked very stiff as if he was ex-military. The man wore no uniform, only blue denim coveralls. His dark, black hair was topped by a navy ball cap with the now familiar "SI" logo on it.

After opening the gate, the guard motioned our car inside. We stopped outside the huge, white building. It had the look of a dilapidated warehouse. A pier extended out from the boathouse into a narrow waterway. We were about to slip inside a metal door, when Tom grabbed my arm. "Wait until you see this."

Inside the brightly lit space was a huge white yacht, bobbing gently in its slip. Several workers scrambled around. Boxes of gear were passed aboard. Another crew cleaned and polished the brilliant fiberglass along with the equally shiny stainless steel.

Martin Sanderling's face lit up with pride while looking at his beautiful new yacht. "Come aboard. I'll show you around."

Our group stepped aboard the huge swim platform. Our host led us to the lower deck. Tom slipped off his shoes. We followed his example before heading into the interior lounging area of the yacht.

"This is the main salon." Martin showed off the exquisitely furnished sitting room featuring two huge sofas clad in cozy white leather. The soft beige carpet caressed our feet as walked across it. A marble bar stood against one wall. Polished glasses hung from the ceiling. The whole room resembled an elegant hotel.

Martin and Tom led the way through the dining area, another sitting area, and a media room. Around a corner, we were confronted by a metal door with a keypad next to it.

Gage stepped forward, placing his hand on the door. "This is the armament room. You can only enter this room with Tom, Rick, Jake or myself. We'll check it out later. Tom, why don't you show them the engine room?"

The former Navy SEAL had a curious, yet strange look on his face as he steered us away from the locked egress. It would be interesting to see exactly what was located behind the white steel door.

After descending the steps, we filed into the spotless mechanical room. Two monstrous engines dominated the space. Everything was neat and tidy. All the electrical wiring ran in organized conduits with every strand labeled and cable tied securely in place. Even the lights illuminating the space were trimmed in polished stainless steel.

"These are twin MTU 3650HP, 16V4000 engines. This baby should really fly." Tom grinned as he patted one of the massive engines. We looked around the engine room for a moment more before heading on deck.

Martin motioned to a huge steel arm with a block and tackle attached. "This crane can lift the mini-sub out of the water."

"We are going to carry a mini-sub aboard?" Eric asked.

"Yes, we need to fight fire with fire. You'll see." The tour continued to the wheelhouse.

An impressive array of navigation instruments, along with video monitors, a big screen television, and joystick controls for the engines made this area look more like a spacecraft than a yacht. Big picture windows allowed great visibility in front of and alongside the decks.

"The video cameras, along the aft deck, are able to rotate 180 degrees. These allow us great visibility behind the ship." Tom pointed out each individual piece of equipment on the expansive bridge.

Martin Sanderling proudly listened to the conversation, before leading us back off the yacht. "I've booked everyone into a hotel for this evening. Tomorrow morning, we will take the *Lady Diana* out of the boathouse. We will dock her outside, briefly, before heading to Key West. There are last minute preparations my mechanics need to do before departure. If the weather is good, we can make the passage to Keys in the afternoon. Of course, the decision is Tom's."

"The weather looks good, Martin. I don't foresee any other issues."

"Good. Why don't you all get some rest?"

The following morning we were up early, preparing the mega-yacht for the quick run to Key West. While perched on the swim platform, I examined the stern dock line. Tom instructed me to remove it on his command.

A scuffling sound caught my attention. Out of the corner of my eye, I watched a woman walk up, dressed to the nines in high heels. Her chic pink outfit looked more appropriate for a country club than a boat. The lady straightened her matching hat, sporting a gaudy fuchsia flower wrapped in coral-colored bows. She made a point of looking down her nose at me.

"Sweetie, do you mind getting my bags out of the car? Make it quick and be extra careful not to drop them."

My eyes rose to meet hers. I was sure my face was plastered with disbelief. Martin Sanderling materialized out of the aft lounge area. He swooped down to the swim platform, gallantly extending his hand to the lady. She threw him a disdainful look before accepting his help aboard.

"Diana, my kitten. I didn't think you would arrive in time."

"If your darn pilot would learn how to fly, I would have been here much sooner." Diana huffed. After a pause, her attention returned to me. "What? You're not gone yet? Don't you speak English? Chop. Chop. Get my bags." She gripped her husband's arm, strolling off toward the lounge like visiting royalty. "Martin, I'm so in need of a cocktail. My lips are absolutely parched."

"Yes, my kitten. Come inside. I'll get you a martini."

I was about to give her a few choice words of my own, when Tom jumped down from the flybridge. He grabbed my arm, turning me away from the Sanderlings, who stepped into the main salon.

"Diana, Martin's wife. I told you she was a piece of work." Tom's eyes crinkled as he attempted to stifle a laugh at the look on my face. "Easy, Linda. I wouldn't cross her. Our boss dotes on her like she's the queen bee." Tom hustled over to the limo. He snatched the matching pink leather bags, trimmed in faux fur, out of the trunk.

After stepping aboard, he grinned at me one more time before heading back to the bridge. "Li'l Sis, relax. Get the stern line. Chop, Chop."

Soon after the finishing touches were put on the *Lady Diana,* she cut through the calm water, inside the Gulf Stream. A frothy wake was left behind as the yacht cruised at a speed of twenty-eight knots. Tom was right, this craft really did fly. The electric-blue water shimmered as we made our way outside the reef south of Miami. The weather was fine and the sea was flat.

"Eric, I don't know this area too well. Why don't we head south outside the reef?"

"Good idea, Tom. There should be much less small boat traffic. We'll get a slight set from the Gulf Stream, though it shouldn't bother us too much at this speed."

I reclined in the left hand watch seat with Tom at the helm. My husband stood behind me, enjoying this exhilarating ride. At Alligator Reef, our captain tweaked the autopilot, heading us on a more south-westerly course.

A couple of hours passed before the red and white striped buoy, at the entrance to the Key West ship channel, appeared.

The yacht cruised easily down the waterway with Eric pointing out the route since this was Tom's first trip to the capital of the Conch Republic. Near Mallory Square, he guided the big boat alongside a huge slip.

Our captain was stationed on the bridge wing. He nudged the boat into the dock, with the joystick for the bow thruster. I was positioned on the stern, manning the aft dock line.

"Linda, go ahead and give the dock hand the stern line. Have him cleat it. Take the slack aboard." Tom's command came into my headset, loud and clear.

I tossed the inch and one half warp to the waiting shore crew who slipped the eye over a bollard. With the bitter end wrapped around the electric winch, the stern squeaked against the huge, black fleece-covered fenders. Soon the mega-yacht rested alongside the rough cement of the wharf. Eric appeared a moment later.

"I'll grab the shore power cords." His shoulder muscles flexed as he tugged the twin thick, yellow electrical cables out of their home on the transom.

After cleaning up, we saw the owners off the boat. Rick and Joey stayed aboard to secure the yacht. The rest of us strolled off for a visit with my wacky sister Eva.

She was a tarot card reader who lived in Key West along with her husband Merlin. A few years ago, she abandoned her high pressure accounting job at a Fortune 500 company in New York City for the simpler life of a yachtie. Thanks to her husband's stock market proficiency, they enjoyed comfortable living with their two poodles aboard a restored forty-two foot motor yacht right in the center of Old Town.

A short stroll down Caroline Street brought us to the pier near Schooner Wharf Bar. We paused a moment to watch a big silver fish swim by.

"What's that?" Tom asked.

"Just a shark," Eric said.

The older brother didn't take the bait. "Sloan?"

The scientist crinkled her nose at Tom as if she was trying to decide whether or not to go along with this game.

Gage glared at the elder brother. "It's a tarpon, for goodness sakes."

We continued down the dock, finally arriving at the trawler. Eric and I climbed aboard followed by the rest of our group. My husband knocked on the teak door to the motor yacht.

"Linda and Eric, it's wonderful to see you." Eva motioned us into their main salon. Hugs were exchanged with the Key West couple amid the barking of their two pups. When everything settled down, our group was introduced.

"Eva and Merlin, you already know Tom. These are our other friends Gage and Sloan." Introductions finished, Merlin served drinks. Eva glanced over our colleagues as the conversation flowed.

"You know, Linda, I haven't read your tarot cards in a long time." Uneasiness swept over me. I didn't want our friends to think my sister was a complete wacko.

"Eva, I don't think this is a good time."

Eric had a grin on his face. He must have picked up on my uneasiness. Before he could speak, Sloan joined the conversation.

"You read tarot cards? My grandmother used to do that. When I was little, my family would visit her in Bermuda. Most of the locals would come over to her house on Saturday nights. She was always very accurate with her readings."

"Great, let me get my cards." Before I could protest further, Eva ducked out of the cabin. She returned with her tarot cards wrapped in a purple scarf.

"Oh no, not again," I said, under my breath, to Eric.

"It wasn't so bad the first time was it?" My husband referred to my sister's tarot card reading, two summers ago. Her interpretation predicted our marriage, months before we were seriously involved.

The cards were shuffled. Eva looked to Sloan. "Shall I read yours first?"

Gage grinned his cocky grin. "She's going to fall for a hot Navy SEAL." Tom grunted something unintelligible. Sloan rolled her eyes.

Eva ignored the two men. "Shuffle the cards. Remove the top four from the deck. Place them in front of you in a diamond pattern."

We leaned over to look at the brightly colored cards displayed on the varnished teak table.

"*Hmm*." Eva examined the cards. The Tower Card was at the top of Sloan's pyramid.

"Oh no." The lady researcher glanced from Gage to Tom.

"The Tower." Eva gazed at Sloan. My sister grasped the scientist's hands.

"You must have a major conflict in your life. The Tower card, when accepted and welcomed, allows wisdom and enlightenment to flow freely through your body. You have been blocking this energy. Are you hiding behind something?"

"No."

"Remember the Tower card is both a destructive and a creative force."

"With the Star to your left," Eva pointed to the Star card at the left hand position of the pyramid, "hope will appear when all seems lost. After the light of the Tower destroys your false path, the gentle gleam of the Star will guide you."

"Eric, why don't you shuffle the cards." Sloan abruptly gathered up the cards. She thrust the disheveled deck at my husband. It appeared as though she suddenly became very uncomfortable with the Tarot reading.

"Sloan, don't fight the Tower." Eva again grasped Sloan's hands. The mood lightened a moment later, when my sister turned to Eric. "Your turn, cowboy."

My husband shuffled the cards, arranging the top four in a similar diamond pattern.

Eva studied the four cards; Death, The Devil, Judgment, and Strength. I never saw her so upset by the placement of four cards.

"Well, maybe we should have another cocktail. We can do this later." My sister forced a smile while gathering up the cards scattered on the table. Eric grabbed her hand. Their eyes locked.

"Eva, what's wrong?"

"Nothing, nothing. Linda was right. This is silly."

"Eva, what do the tarot cards say?" My husband demanded, suddenly becoming very serious.

"Of course, it's only an interpretation. These four cards suggest something devastating is going to happen. Someone, who is close to you, will betray you. A great danger will inundate you. All of your skills will be tried and tested. A tremendous amount of strength and fortitude of character is necessary to not allow the future to destroy you."

Chapter 8. The Bering Sea

After Joey's inauspicious return to Naples, the stress of constantly fighting with him was taking its toll on me. Why didn't he go away, leaving *Dark & Stormy* and me alone?

The past month, our entire group worked very hard to get the Lokator gear functioning properly. Many long days were spent ironing out the bugs while allowing the computer algorithm to learn new objects.

After spending a couple of weeks testing the new mega-yacht and the mini-sub at the Paradise location, Martin Sanderling suggested we all take time off for the holidays. As more work was needed installing the last of the anti-piracy equipment on the *Lady Diana,* we were not really needed on the project for now.

Tom flew to Alaska to check on the new captain the brothers hired to run their crab-fishing boat. Everyone else went to their respective homes for a little down time and to catch up on other business. Eric thought it would be nice to spend the holidays at the ranch in Dallas.

It was early January. A cold wind nipped at the front door as we relaxed in the living room. A cozy fire blazed away in the hearth. My husband and I reclined side-by-side on the big, comfy couch. He leaned against the sofa arm, reading a horse magazine. My head rested against his shoulder.

The warm, flannel shirt my cowboy wore felt soft against my cheek. A faint hint of the his spicy cologne mingled with the scent of the logs in the fireplace. The roaring flame nearly lulled me to sleep. For the first time, in a very long time, I relaxed enough to allow my mind to wander.

"Linda, I'm going to grab a coffee from the kitchen. Would you like one?" Eric set down the horse magazine.

"Let me get it." I puttered around the well-appointed kitchen, pouring two cups of java. Did I hear a phone ring?

While Linda was out of the room, Eric's phone beeped. He checked the Caller ID on the screen. "Blocked" flashed boldly. With a shrug, he put the phone to his ear.

"Eric, Carlos. Did you and Linda have a nice holiday? My sources tell me you are in Dallas. Such a pretty city. Maybe I need to make a trip out there. I bet it's very cold there now. Keep your lady close to you. It would be quite a shame if she became ill. I haven't forgotten our encounter in Trinidad. Payback will be when you least expect it." The phone call disconnected before Eric had a chance to respond.

"Who was on the phone?"

"It was a wrong number."

My husband forced a smile as I sit down next to him. Strange. After a few moments of relaxation, his phone rang again. He looked at the Caller ID before answering. His face looked taut until he recognized the phone number.

"Hi, Tom. How are things in Alaska?"

"They were fine until the good-for-nothing captain I hired decided his girlfriend was more important than our fishing vessel. She dumped him. He flew back to Seattle to try to get her back. With only one week until opilio crab season begins, we have no one to run the boat."

"Damn. What do you want to do about it?"

"We have no choice. I'll have to call Martin. You need to get up here right away to skipper the boat."

"All right. I'll get the first flight out. Have the guys load the bait and food. Make sure they stack the opilio crab pots properly." My husband closed his phone slowly. His eyes locked on mine.

He sighed heavily. "Linda, I have to go to Alaska to run *Denali* for opie season. Our captain quit."

"OK," I said guardedly, thinking back on the huge fight which ended our relationship one year ago. Eric was too overprotective at the time, not allowing me to accompany him on the snow crab fishing season. What really infuriated me, was his decision making process. He simply made a declaration, without considering my opinion.

Now, one year later, Eric stared hard at me. A few seconds ticked by. The hesitation in his eyes told me everything. Here we go again. "You need to stay here and take care of the ranch."

"Eric, we're not going through this again. I'm coming with you."

"No way. It's too dangerous."

"Do you really expect me to sit here, like a good little wifey doing nothing, while you risk your life fishing on the Bering Sea in January? I don't think so."

"I thought you understood, after our talk last spring. If the ice gets bad, the boat could sink. Every year, the fishery loses a few guys to the violent storms."

"We'll have to be in survival suits together because I'm coming. This year the decision is not negotiable. A year ago, when we were only friends, you made your choice. You walked away. Now, I'm you wife. I'm not going to sit by and possibly become your widow, without a fighting chance of helping you."

"Shit." Eric stared hard at me. "Why do you have to be so difficult?"

"It's one of the reasons you love me so much. Let's go pack."

"Linda, I'm not taking you to Alaska."

"Eric, one of the reasons we broke up last year was your inability to listen to me. Do you remember making your decision without consulting me?"

"Yes, I do and for a good reason. I don't want to lose you."

"You are not going to lose me. I'll be right by your side."

"Dammit, Linda. You are not going."

I took refuge, in the bedroom. My suitcases were packed in no time.

Eric was in his office, furiously banging away on the computer. A look over his shoulder confirmed the matching airline tickets. His look of anger sent me back to the bedroom.

The next morning, Ricardo drove us to DFW airport. After connecting in Seattle, our next stop was Anchorage, Alaska. After a brief layover, we boarded the turbo-prop plane. Turbulence bounced us around the frozen sky. Eric held my hand until we skidded to a stop on the icy runway in Dutch Harbor. Tom jogged up to the plane after we came to a halt in front of the frozen terminal.

"Welcome to the North Pole." The elder brother hugged me. He steadied my arm when I slipped on the frozen ground.

My teeth chattered in the frozen air. "It must be twenty below up here."

"Actually, it's only a couple of degrees below zero. It's a nice warm day by Alaska standards." Tom turned to his brother. "I guess we don't need to worry about her going on deck this time."

"I don't want to talk about it." With a bag in each hand, Eric strode for the terminal.

Tom grinned at me. "He's not too happy to have you here, I guess."

"No he's not, but I wasn't staying behind this time."

"Li'l Sis, opie season is serious business. Make sure you do what he says."

"I will, Tom. Let's get out of here before we freeze." My brother-in-law grabbed our other two bags. Tom navigated the icy roads on the way to the boat.

When we arrived at the pier, *Denali* looked like a big, frozen ice sculpture. Icicles clung to the crane and rigging high above the surface of the water. It was after dark. No crew members scurried around the deck. The fishing vessel appeared to be locked in a frozen tomb.

Eric climbed aboard first. He turned around, extending his hand to me. "Be careful getting on board. You don't want to go swimming between the boat and the dock." The fisherman yanked me aboard. "Get inside."

"Thanks, honey."

"Since returning to the frozen north, my bro's become the abominable snowman," the elder brother whispered after climbing on board behind me.

Eric turned on him. "Tom, stay out of this."

"Aye, Aye, Captain." The elder brother winked at me. We followed my husband into the superstructure of the vessel. The interior was cozy warm. Brett was the first crew member to greet me. We became good friends when I was aboard the boat during the fall king crab season over a year and a half ago. That trip was before my breakup with Eric last winter.

"Linda. Hey how are you? It's great to see you." He half-rose out of his seat, at the galley table. He sat back down when he saw his boss' icy stare.

"I'll be in the wheelhouse." Before leaving, he turned back to Brett, the deck boss.

"What's our Coast Guard clearance status?"

"They're doing the final inspections tomorrow at ten A.M. We'll be ready to leave whenever you want to afterward."

My husband stared hard at me. "Make sure you practice putting on your survival suit ahead of time. I don't want any delays."

The frost hung in the warm cabin air for a few seconds after my husband stormed out.

"Don't ask," Tom said to the crew. "Let's just do our job until he sorts this whole thing out in his head."

"Jeez," Brett said while refilling his coffee. "Last year he was miserable without her. This year he's miserable with her."

My husband's icy demeanor lasted throughout the night. He hardly said a few words to me. The next morning, he was in the wheelhouse going over paperwork when I walked in. "Eric."

He turned to look at me with a frown on his face. My husband silently accepted the steaming coffee I extended as a peace offering.

"Are you still mad at me?"

"No, I'm mad at myself. You should not be here."

"Listen, I'll be fine. Tom helped me with a survival suit practice drill. I managed to get the suit on in fifty seconds."

"Good." Our captain turned back to his paperwork. His cold attitude toward me continued throughout the morning.

"Stay in the wheelhouse while we pull away from the pier." The big, steel fishing ship slipped out of the bay to do battle with the Bering Sea. Once beyond Priest Rock, the navy-blue steel behemoth dove into the freezing swells, crashing head first into the seas. White water blasted across our bow.

The forecast was for twenty to twenty-five knot winds with fifteen-foot seas, increasing to forty knots over the next twenty-four hours. Freezing spray could become a deadly problem since we were carrying a full load of crab pots. The added weight made the vessel particularly top heavy and vulnerable to the waves. This added stress further burdened my already tense husband.

Later the next evening, Tom and I kept watch in the wheelhouse, while Eric took a break. He must be enjoying the hearty meal of pot roast with lots of potatoes and veggies. I struggled to prepare the meal in the bouncing galley. It was amazing more of the dinner didn't end up on the floor.

"Are you hanging in there, Li'l Sis?" Tom's eyes glanced to me after scanning the radar. Several other crab boats steamed within twenty miles of us on a similar trek to the opilio crab grounds.

"Yeah, Tom, I'm fine. I just wish Eric would lighten up a little. This is a side of him I've never seen before."

"Give him some time. Once we splash these pots and start filling the tanks, he'll be in a better mood."

There was a scuffling sound behind us. Eric appeared, fully dressed in foul weather gear. A life vest was strapped around his chest.

"Tom, slow the boat down. The guys and I are going to beat ice off this ship."

I was tempted to ask if I could help, but the look on my husband's face silenced me. After he went on deck, I made my way to the galley. Due to his neat crew, there was not much to clean up. I was starting to feel useless on this trip.

Back in the wheelhouse, my eyes were glued to the guys slipping and sliding around the deck. Metal on metal clanged as they beat the solid mass of ice from the rails. Whack, whack, whack.

The frozen water relented. Most of the super-structure of the massive boat reappeared. After a couple of hours, our captain reentered the wheelhouse. He displaced Tom at the helm. The boat was quickly powered back up to cruising speed.

"Hey, bro." Tom slapped his younger brother on the shoulder. "When we were kids, you would never be quiet. What gives? I'd love to know the secret, so I can shut you up at any time in the future."

Eric's icy stare was the only response to Tom's attempted quip. The elder brother shook his head before leaving.

After another twenty-four hours of steaming, there was another marathon ice bashing session. The waves picked up to eighteen feet. *Denali* bounced around like a plastic toy in a very rough bath tub.

We finally reached the opie grounds. The crew stood fully dressed, ready to do battle with mother nature. Eric slowed the boat a couple of knots. He summoned the crew on the loud hailer.

"Get the pots in the water."

The guys streamed out of the ready room. They went about their business of baiting and splashing the huge steel traps. Every move made was a tremendous effort. Each frozen pot had to be beaten free from the solid block of ice, holding the stack together. The trap doors were pounded on, until they broke free of the mighty ice crystals welding them to the surrounding metal frame. Endless frozen bags of herring were hung inside the traps.

All this work was done in temperatures of ten degrees below zero. With the tempest blowing close to thirty knots, the wind chill was much lower. Towering seas added a whole new dimension to the term "sea legs."

"This is going to be one hell of the season." One of the crew's comments could be heard over the deck intercom.

Tom slid across the deck to grapple with the next trap in line. "Hustle up, guys. When finished, we can get off this frozen purgatory. Maybe Linda will have a treat cooked up for us."

The elder brother glanced toward the pilothouse. The only visible part of his face were the icicles hanging from his beard and mustache. I bet he had a smile hidden under there.

After many hours of freezing repetition, all the pots were finally soaking. My husband still manned the helm. His eyes squinted from exhaustion. Determining the ideal trap placement was mentally draining. Armed with the latest NOAA surveys, it still was a guess where the biomass of crabs was located.

The boat had a six hours steam back to retrieve the first pot. Fortunately, the wind and seas had moderated. The deck crew was below, napping.

"Eric, would you like me to keep watch while you rest?"

Much to my surprise his voice was calm, with some of the old warmth in it. "Sure. Keep us on a course of due east. Wake Tom is you have any problems."

The autopilot steered us back in the direction of our first string of pots. All I needed to do was to ensure there were no other vessels crossing our path. The sun rose. It looked to be a clear, crisp day with a brilliant-blue sky. Something off the starboard bow caught my eye.

Whales. Killer whales to be exact. They frolicked alongside of us, much to my delight. Slick black and white torpedoes sliced through the icy waves. In unison, they responded to an unseen signal, disappearing into the white foam. Maybe today would be a good day.

After four hours of watch, Tom slipped up behind the helm chair. "Hey, Li'l Sis. I didn't expect our multimillion dollar crab boat to be in the hands of a woman." I turned my head in time to catch the twinkle in his eyes. He could never resist the temptation to tease me. "Did you throw Eric overboard?"

"No, he needed rest. It really surprised me when he agreed to leave me on watch."

"Great. The boys and I are going to beat more ice off the boat before we get to the first pot. Make sure you keep a close eye on everyone. Don't forget this button is the man overboard alarm, in case someone slips."

My nerves ratcheted up a couple of notches as the guys slid around the floes of frozen water on deck. Though I was not a complete novice at handling this boat, a special touch was needed if one of the crew should go overboard. Relief flooded my brain when Eric came back to take over command.

"What's going on?" His voice still resonated with gruffness.

"The guys are beating ice off. I was a little nervous with them on deck."

"*Hmm.*" We stared eagerly at the rail when the first pot erupted from the freezing brine. It was a long trek up the sixty fathom rise through the water column. As it broke the water's surface, a crew member leaned over. The crane hook was snapped to the bridle. The trap was yanked into view. Mud dripped off. Hundreds of squirming crabs clambered for freedom from the dripping cage.

"Oh yeah!" A broad grin spread across the fisherman's face. His clenched fist pumped in the air.

The next twenty-four hours were a race, with mother nature, to haul as many crabs as possible before the next storm arrived. A major blow was forecasted. The winds were expected to reach hurricane force. This monster churned across the North Pacific, heading directly for us. Sixty to seventy knot winds with thirty-foot seas were likely. It looked to be the biggest storm I had encountered while at sea.

The guys raced around with no rest. Eric and Tom monitored the forecast. They huddled over the weather faxes while discussing their plans. In addition to high winds, freezing spray and ice were also on the menu.

"I wish we had an offload scheduled. It wouldn't be a bad idea to spend some time in St. Paul Harbor while this blow goes by," my husband said to his brother exactly one day before the gale was due to arrive.

"With the forecast wind direction, the harbor could be a frozen washing machine. We'd be better off anchoring up behind the island for a few hours."

"That's exactly what we are going to do. I'll set a course. Secure the deck."

The guys suspended their pot hauling for now. *Denali* raced to gain the shelter of the rocky island before the storm descended upon us. Huge waves broke over the bow. Northeast winds howled. The blizzard charged up behind us.

A huge wall of water eclipsed the horizon.

"Hang on." Eric yelled into the intercom. Our bow dangled over the edge of a monster. Bang! An enormous wall of green water cascaded over us. The wave devoured the entire forward half of the ship. She shuddered terribly. Thousands of pounds forced our bow under.

The whine of the engines faded. Our captain hauled back on the throttles. The ship continued down. Would the air trapped in our forward holds allow the naturally buoyancy of the bow to haul us back to the surface?

Time stopped. The growling beast roared over the pilothouse. Our windshield was submerged beneath the churning green foam. It felt as though we were headed straight down. I gripped the sides of the watch chair. White fingers clenched the arm rests. My knees locked against the navigation console. Alarms pierced the roaring din of the monster.

There must have been a slight correction to the pitch of the boat. A glance at Eric's hardened face gave me no reassurance. His brow was furrowed. He must have felt something. The throttles were jammed forward. With engines screaming, we exploded out the backside of the wave. More gray monsters loomed in front of us.

Tom burst into the wheelhouse. "Shit, that was a bad one."

"Everyone OK?" Eric asked through gritted teeth.

"Yeah, we're good. Brett is checking the engine room." The elder brother lumbered over next to my chair. He slipped his arm around my tense shoulders.

"You OK, Li'l Sis?" No sound would come out of my throat. I simply nodded my head.

Denali dodged more towering walls of water over the next several hours. Finally a dark smudge on the horizon became the barren twin peaks of the rocky isle. We crept by the tiny village dotted with red-roofed houses. Chimneys puffed away.

A pair of horned puffins huddled together as we passed the wind-swept Seal Rock. In lee of the island, our anchor chain rattled out of the hawser. The massive anchor dug into the muddy bottom. The big crab boat strained against the anchor rode. Darkness descended.

Blasts of icy air screamed over the ridge of rock. The mountain provided little protection against the now hurricane-force winds. Huge swells crept around the edge of our refuge. *Denali* rolled hard from side to side. If there was ever a time for seasickness, this would be it.

"Whew!" Our captain's head drooped when we were finally secured. "Linda, why don't you go below? Try to get some rest."

I finally found my voice. "There is so much adrenaline surging through me sleep would be impossible."

"Why don't you both get some rest?" Tom sauntered into the wheelhouse. "I'll keep watch. Get her out of here, bro."

My husband and I staggered through the rolling companionway to the captain's quarters. A shower would feel great, but was nearly impossible in these conditions.

Instead, we took refuge on the full-sized bunk, snuggling under a blanket. Even though I was wedged between my husband and the bulkhead behind me, the roll was terribly uncomfortable.

Eric snored lightly. Despite the warm, safe feeling of this haven, the synapses of my brain wouldn't quit firing.

Trying not to wake my exhausted husband, I climbed out of the bunk. The galley was deserted. The floor felt chilly through my slippered feet. With all the recent work pulling pots, securing the deck, and anchoring, there would soon be very hungry men aboard this fishing boat.

I spent the next hour bouncing around the galley like the shining orb in a pinball machine. The wonderful smell of rosemary chicken, with all the fixings, wafted around the damp, chilly fishing vessel.

"What the heck smells so good?" Looking up from the sink full of soapy dishes, my eyes met the sleepy smile of our captain. He ran his hand through his mussed hair before collapsing at the galley table. Even though Eric managed to get a few hours of solid sleep, it took a long time to catch up with the many hours spent on stressful watches.

"Just a little dinner."

"Maybe having you on board this trip wasn't such a bad idea."

Our conversation was interrupted by more sleepy crew members. Their jabbering about crabs and the weather was silenced by steaming plates of food. Strong, hot coffee was downed in gulps. Before bothering to eat, I climbed the stairs to the wheelhouse to relieve Tom on watch.

"You'd better get a share of the food before it's all gone."

"Thanks, Li'l Sis."

Tom turned for the stairs to the galley, leaving me alone in the twilight-lit watch area. The sounds of the storm and the creaking vessel were amplified from this vantage point twenty-five feet above the deck. The anchor rode moaned as the vessel snapped backward driven by a huge gust of wind.

Though the wheelhouse was heated, icy blasts whistled by the windscreen gaskets, prickling the skin on my exposed face and neck. Even the leather of the watch chair felt cold and rough through the jeans hugging my hips. Whiffs of diesel exhaust drifted by.

The anchorage was plunged in darkness. My senses were heightened by the exaggerated sounds and motions. The glowing green radar screen was the only light in the cockpit other than the amber glow of the depth sounder. A steady four fathoms blinked in this tentative anchorage at Lukanin Bay. The wind screamed out of the west.

Several other white lights bobbed around us. This gave me the comforting feeling of companionship amidst this battle with mother nature. The problem was, those other steel vessel could become a deadly hazard if their anchors dragged or their warps parted. This would create dangerous battering rams.

The tempest's shriek was occasionally interrupted by the crackle on the VHF radio. Other fishing captains chatted with one another, making sure every ship kept their position during this vigil.

About a half an hour later, Brett entered the wheelhouse to take over the watch. I was happy to head below for a quick snack before attempting sleep. This time, when my head hit the pillow, I barely heard Eric's voice before dropping off.

"I'll be right back. I'm going to check on Brett."

A rumbling noise roused me from sleep. The vibrations of the engines were felt though the steel of the cabin. Squealing against the strain, the anchor rode wound around the capstan. After pulling on my clothes, I scrambled to the wheelhouse to see what the problem was. Eric was at the helm. His brother hovered nearby.

"What's wrong?"

"Nothing, Li'l Sis. The wind's come down. We're heading back out for round two of the crab battle. Why don't you get a little more rest?"

"I'm fine. What time is it?" There was only blackness in front of the windscreen.

"Four-thirty."

On our way back to the crab grounds, the waves continued to crash over our bow, though the wind moderated. The frigid sea created more ice aboard our vessel.

"Tom, I'm going to get the crew together to bash ice."

"Can I help?" I tentatively asked our captain.

Eric stared for a full minute before answering. "Oh, what the heck. If you want to freeze your butt off, I'm not going to stop you. Do not go near the rails. Put on a life jacket and stay right next to me."

After donning every warm piece of clothing I had aboard, my slim figure now looked like an overstuffed, yellow dough ball. Eric laughed as he handed me a hammer. An icy blast greeted us as we struggle out the heavy steel door.

I braced myself. My first swing, at the solid wall of ice on the superstructure, barely made a dent.

"Hey, guys, it looks like Linda managed to knock off a couple of snowflakes. Give her a hand," Tom said over the loud hailer from the pilothouse. The entire crew turned around. They clapped their gloved hands in unison. My husband made a poor attempt at stifling a laugh.

My fist was raised in a most un-ladylike gesture. This salute to our relief captain caused a round of jeers to erupt from the crew. No amount of their teasing would send me back inside before I was ready to give up.

After an hour of banging solid ice, the crew managed to clear a good portion of the superstructure. My toes were numb when we finally retreated to the warmth of the cabin. The ache in my shoulder would surely hurt much more later on. For now, we returned to the business of pulling crabs pots.

During the next several weeks, *Denali* filled with crab. The holds were emptied, several times, at the processor. Our quota inched toward its maximum. It was a relief to finally steam back into Dutch Harbor for the last offload of the season. After a day of hard work putting the boat to bed, we flew back to Dallas.

Chapter 9. Dallas

"What did you think of opilio crab fishing?" Eric asked when we were safely ensconced back on the sofa at the ranch.

"It was interesting. The weather was much worse than it looks on TV."

"You know," Eric said lightly touching the back of my neck. "You never did answer my question."

"What question was that?"

"The one I asked when we were aboard Mark's fishing boat. I asked you something right after we pulled you out of the water."

"Gee, what did you ask?"

"Don't you remember? After waking up from the daze you were in, Tom was trying to put the intravenous line in your arm. You fought him until you realized who we were, the guys from the fishing show. Remember?"

"Yes."

"You never told us who your favorite captain from the show is?"

My cheeks blushed at least two different shades of scarlet. "Isn't it obvious?"

Eric laughed as his cell phone rang. "Hi, Jeb. How's it going."

The caller was a fellow rancher and horse breeder. Two of his mares were pregnant with the offspring of Blackjack, Eric's champion horse who died after breaking his leg in the Kentucky Derby last year. Because of the severity of the break, my husband's winning stallion had to be euthanized.

It nearly broke his heart along with the hearts of everyone who worked at the ranch. Now, a long eleven months later, we eagerly awaited news of the new foals' births. My husband engaged the speaker phone.

"Eric, I'm great, but one of my mares went into labor. I thought you and Linda might want to come over for the delivery."

"Jeb, we're on our way." We bundled up in warm clothes. The night was unusually cold for March. My husband drove his pickup truck like a madman toward the ranch on the other side of Dallas. We skidded down the icy ramp from the highway.

"Eric, slow down. Take it easy."

"I got it. Don't worry, lady." Traffic was light. We made good time, careening down the dark roads to the nearby homestead.

We rushed into the barn. Jeb and a ranch hand were in a big stall. A pretty black mare stomped around. Even though the barn was heated, the horse's breath came out in foggy puffs. She struggled with the early contractions of her labor.

The floor of the barn was padded with bales of fresh hay. The crisp March air was laced with a sweet, grassy aroma. A subdued light danced around the barn, provided by the overhead lights. A couple of gas lanterns flickered.

The mare lay down. Clearly uncomfortable, she quickly regained her feet with a snort. Her swollen abdomen expanded and contracted. Jeb eased in behind the horse.

"Easy, girl." He soothed her with his gentle voice while stoking her hind quarter.

"Eric and Linda, look at this. Do you see the tiny hoof? That's the front hoof almost all the way down the birth canal." We leaned over to see a little foot, surrounded by a bluish, white membrane.

"The nose and other hoof should be right behind this one," Eric whispered while squeezing my hand. Suddenly, the mare's water broke. It was a good thing Jeb wore rubber coveralls and boots because a tremendous rush of fluid followed. The mare whinnied loudly, then lay down again.

After a few more strong contractions, a tiny nose appeared followed by a second hoof. The wet, compacted hair above the foal's nose looked black with small, white spots. Eric gripped my hand, hardly able to contain his excitement.

Jeb stroked and encouraged his nearly exhausted mare. "It shouldn't be long now." She rose again, whinnying loudly. The mare stomped her hooves a couple of times before pacing around the stall, with an uneasy gait. The expectant mother stopped right in the middle of the wooden enclosure. She shuddered a couple of times. Half the foal slid out.

"Eric, give me a hand." Jeb grabbed a hold of the small horse. The ranch hand steadied the struggling mother. The rest of the foal slid out. Eric and Jeb eased it to the hay. It lay very still.

"Linda, grab those towels. Give us a hand drying the foal." The little animal stirred under our care. Jeb inserted a rubber bulb to the baby horse's mouth in an attempt to suction fluid out of his throat.

"Keep rubbing. It should stimulate him to breath," Eric said. The three of us dried the black coat of the newborn. The baby black horse shook its head, opened its eyes, and stared right at Eric. The two of them made eye contact.

The mare came over, nudging me out of the way. She licked her newborn baby's face. It struggled to get its tiny hooves beneath it. The spindly legs shook from the great exertion. With a mighty effort, the new foal sprang to its feet. He staggered to his mom, who had backed off a short distance away. Loud suckling sounds echoed around the barn.

"It's a boy!" Jeb laughed after looking under the newborn foal. "I should have brought cigars."

Eric and I scrutinized the baby horse. Standing before us was the spitting image of Blackjack. He was black as coal with the same white blaze down his forehead. The only difference was a white stocking on the lower part of his left rear leg.

This white patch of fur was in the exact same place, on the same leg, Blackjack broke while running the Derby. I wondered if Eric realized this. A moment later, the small back horse pulled his head from under his mom. After an ungainly pivot, he trotted toward us on wobbly legs. The little guy arrogantly stuck out his head to nuzzle Eric's hand. With a quick flip, the baby boy tossed his head up, pushing my husband's hand away. An adorable whinny squeaked out of him.

"He has Blackjack's attitude also," Eric laughed. The little horse strutted back to his mom's side.

"Eric, I guess he picked you." Jeb referred to our agreement, giving my husband his choice of foals. "Any idea what you are going to name him?"

"I was thinking of 'Ace'. It plays off Blackjack's name. His racing name can be 'Ace of Spades.'"

"Aren't you getting ahead of the game by planning his racing name?"

"Maybe. This little guy has a big reputation to live up to."

We spent a few more minutes enjoying the sight of the newborn foal with his mom. It was not long before the exhausted baby lay down in the soft bed of hay. His small white nose tucked under his leg. We decided to head back to our ranch for a shower and much needed sleep.

The next morning, Eric called a meeting for his ranch employees at lunchtime. Maria, his housekeeper and excellent chef, prepared beef brisket sandwiches.

They lay steaming on the table when Daniel, our horse trainer, strode into the kitchen.

He used to be a tentative, shy teenager who would never march into a room the way he just did. The young ranch hand grew up so much in the past couple of years. I affectionately though of him as the son I never had. Daniel was a sweetheart through all my trials and tribulations. After Blackjack's death, our relationship grew close.

The Derby disaster nearly crushed the young man's spirit. Prior to that, our horse trainer would knock tentatively on the door while waiting to be invited in. Today, he marched in after a loud rap on the window.

After shaking Eric's hand with a firm grip, Daniel leaned over me with a rough hug. "Linda, it's so dog-gone good to see you, if you don't mind me saying so, ma'am."

"It's great to see you too, Daniel."

The young man leaned toward me. "Linda, is everything all right? Mr. Eric, I mean Eric seemed mighty upset on the phone."

"Everything's fine. He has great news for you."

Ricardo, our lanky ranch manager, strode in next. Maria and Ricardo live in the small house adjacent to the main ranch house. The duo had been taking care of the house and ranch for several years. Their support was crucial during the dark days following Eric's nasty divorce. The pair also provided great comfort during our split last year.

Right behind our ranch manager was Manuel, the jockey who rode Blackjack in the Kentucky Derby. I had not seen him since the horrific day of our horse's death.

"Manuel. It's so nice to see you." He seemed perplexed to be invited to this meeting. Eric handed out beers. Maria distributed the brisket sandwiches.

"Thank you all for coming. Manuel, it may be premature having you here, but I thought you should be included in this good news." Daniel's bright green eyes stared at Eric.

"Last night there was a new foal born at Jeb's ranch."

"I knew it." Daniel's face blossomed into a grin. He nearly leapt out of his chair before settling back down.

"He's a healthy baby boy. The spitting image of Blackjack." Eric proudly surveyed the group. "I've decided to name him Ace. After he is weaned, I expect Daniel to start training him."

"Yes, sir. I can't wait to see him. All my chores are done here. Can I go see him this afternoon?" It was great to see Daniel so excited. So much of his spirit was quashed by Blackjack's death.

"Why don't you finish your lunch first, son? We can take a ride over together."

With their food finished, the guys went to Jeb's ranch. I enjoyed the quiet time relaxing in the living room. My eyes gazed at the painting of *Dark & Stormy*. The canvas was a wedding present from Eric. It was mounted in a place of honor over the fireplace.

The boat was pictured sailing through the bright blue waters of the Caribbean. Looking at it made me realize how crazy life had become.

The remainder of the week, we relaxed around the ranch. Eric and I attended to many of the tasks necessary to keep a cattle ranch of this size running. With the help of Daniel and Ricardo, we packed up many sacks of vitamins, containing medicine to rid the cows of worms. These heavy sacks were lugged out to the feed troughs.

This gave us a good opportunity to look over the new calves running around in the south pasture. The entire fence along the boundary of the ranch needed to be checked. Our task was accomplished on horseback with Eric on Outlaw and me atop Sonny. We even managed to enjoy a few quiet trail rides.

On our last day at the ranch, the pond was the setting for our picnic lunch. We relaxed on the dock. It was a chilly afternoon, so there was no swimming today. Eric stared out at the glassy, calm water. He chucked a few pebbles into the pond before turning to me.

"Linda, I wanted to talk to you about something."

"What's that, Eric?"

"It seems like you are having a really hard time with Joey's return."

"He's being such a jerk."

My husband gazed out at the pond. A long sigh struggled out of him. "Can you blame him? Joey must have been...shocked...when he came back to find us together."

"Why do you always take his side on everything?"

"Linda, I'm not taking his side. I wonder if you are feeling guilty."

"Guilty? You've got to be kidding. The only thing I feel is repulsion. I can't believe I put up with his crap for so long. When we get back to Naples, I want him off *Dark & Stormy*."

"Linda, I thought you both owned the boat."

"I don't care. I want him to leave."

"Maybe you should forget the boat. We can always get another one."

Chapter 10. Back in Beaufort

The morning dawned bright and clear. I took my coffee to the upper deck of the yacht still anchored over the spot where the *Wind Rose* sank. The sky was a brilliant blue. I stood at the same rail where Joey accosted me several evenings ago. A shiver ran down my spine. Now and again, I glanced over my shoulder. He could be stalking me right now.

Someone did walk up behind me but not Joey. It was Gage. He stretched his tall frame like a cat getting up from a nap. His back slowly arched, then relaxed. Big hands surrounded the rail next to me. He cocked his head in my direction, shaking the locks of his hair out as if to douse the last bits of sleep from his brain.

"Morning." He smiled lazily at me, but there was always a deep intensity in his eyes. He appeared casual, but I doubt this man ever completely relaxed.

"Hi, Gage. Sleep well last night?"

"About as well as I ever do." He smiled again, stretching his arms over his head. While leaning on his elbows, the tall Navy SEAL stared with his piercing gaze. A relaxed, cocky smile played around his lips. "Are we taking a ride in the mini-sub this morning?"

How was I going to get out of this one? "Well, Gage, I don't know."

"Come on, Linda. I thought you would want to see the boat close up. We can put trimix gear on, but that's a pretty technical dive. If you prefer to get wet, I could walk you through the technical stuff. We'd have to make a couple of decompression stops on the way up. Rick would be our safety diver and monitor those."

"What's trimix? I've dove with nitrox, but never heard of trimix."

"It's a mixture of nitrogen, oxygen and helium. In the Navy, we used it all the time for very deep, technical dives. We could do 200 feet on nitrox, but we'd have almost no bottom time. Our decompression stops would be much longer, also."

"Do we have trimix equipment on board?"

"Heck yeah. One nice thing about working for a wealthy, yet very intelligent man, is his willingness to outfit the yacht for any possible situation. Deep diving is not out of the realm of possibility, when we start chasing those mini-subs. One tactic the druggies have used in the past is to sink the sub when the heat is on. Rick and I may have to go down to recover one. We have individual tanks of oxygen, nitrogen, and helium aboard, so we can mix our own tanks to whatever individual dive requirements are necessary."

"Gage, I appreciate what you are trying to do, but my emotions are treading on pretty thin ice. The thought of seeing *Wind Rose* puts my mind at ease, but I wonder if it would break my spirit. The memories are like links in a chain. Seeing her again might break the weakest link."

"Linda, maybe breaking the link is exactly what you need. It could set you free."

"You may be right. Seeing her again could help me to get on with my life. What if my emotions go crashing into some unknown place? I just don't know, Gage. One side of me wants to go take a look, the other is telling me to leave things well enough alone."

"OK, Linda, you're the boss. You have forty-five minutes to make up your mind before I shove off in the sub. I've done all the talking I'm gonna do. Your emotions are not my responsibility. There is too much work to do."

Gage went below. My stare returned to the sea. Maybe the answer lay in the tiny ripples breaking the surface of the ocean. What was I going to do? Toss a coin? Walk away? Leave it alone? If I did, the whole disaster could haunt me the rest of my life.

Downing the strong, hot coffee, my eyes locked on the ocean. I took a deep breath...trying to breath in all of the good in Gage's offer...and breath out the fear. A soothing calm infused me.

The decision was made. Gage would take me down to see the sunken vessel. He promised nothing bad would happen. Once the reality of *Wind Rose* was faced in person, the demons would be put to rest.

Back inside the yacht, the search was on for the Navy SEAL. While dropping the cup in the galley, I peeked out the porthole to see a glimmer of peace on the horizon.

Where was that man? The last place searched was the submarine compartment. He was stooped over, checking out the scuba tanks. He looked up at me with a knowing smile.

"I'm ready, Gage. Let's go."

"I knew you would be. So are we going to dive or take the mini-sub?"

"I'd like to do the dive."

Rick joined us. The two men inspected the extra equipment necessary for the technical dive.

Gage glanced up from the buoyancy device. "Linda, you need to promise me something."

"What's that?"

"If you get frightened, tell me. I can't have you freaking out 200 feet below the surface. We can have normal conversations with the full face masks we will be using."

"OK, Gage."

"One other thing, Linda." The Navy SEAL stood up, placing both of his hands on my shoulders. "You realize, there is a good chance we'll see sharks down there. Can you handle that possibility? It's especially important to remain calm when we make our decompression stops. Rick and I will be there to help you."

"I think I'll be all right."

"Linda, you can't think, you must know. You've got to trust me."

"I do trust you, Gage."

"Good. We will be take along a protective device, in case we attract an aggressive shark." The tall man held up a small machine. It looked like an electric razor.

"What's that?"

"It's a little gizmo Martin's company invented. It sends out electromagnetic pulses that irritate the shark's electrical sensors. It should drive them away. If not, when the predator comes near us, I can discharge a small electrical shock right on the animal's snout. The pulse will stun it. No shark will hang around after that. The shock won't harm the animal."

"Oh, I see. The gizmo works like a stun gun."

"Exactly."

Eric walked into the sub compartment. "Linda, you decided to go diving with Gage?"

"Yes, Eric. I need to see the boat for myself."

"Good for you. Gage, I'd like to come along."

"Eric, I realize you've dove in the Bering Sea under very difficult conditions. But, I'm going to have my hands full taking another diver, with little technical experience, down so deep. I can't allow you to go."

My husband glared at the tall man. He didn't look pleased.

"Listen, Eric. My full attention needs to be on Linda. You want her safe, don't you?"

"OK, Gage. I'll stay topside," Eric said tight lipped. "Would you like me to accompany Rick to the decompression stop?"

"Why don't you suit up, but stay at the surface, in case we need you?"

After a few more equipment checks, Gage turned to me. "We are ready to carry this gear topside. It's time to get the heck in the water."

For the next twenty minutes, we lugged gear to the swim platform. It was a struggle to drag on the dry suits. Rick hefted a tank with rebreather onto my back. The full face mask fit snugly. Gage reached over to pry a few strands of my hair from under the mask's seal.

The tall Navy SEAL stared into my mask. "Linda, can you hear me?"

"Yes, Gage." A slight feeling of panic seeped into my brain.

"You look scared already."

"I'm all right, only a little nervous."

"Relax, everything will be fine."

"If the sharks don't get you." Joey lurked in the shade behind us. "Linda, you're nuts getting into this water."

"Thanks, Joey. I can always count on your support."

The Navy SEAL brought my attention back to him. "Forget him. I'm going to do a giant stride entry. Wait until I'm clear, then follow me in. Once you hit the water, breath normally."

Gage stepped off the swim platform. When the sea of bubbles subsided, he swam clear of the entry area.

"OK, Linda. Jump in."

After a moment's hesitation, I stepped into the blue water. The weight of the gear submerged me. When the buoyancy compensator overcame the weight, I popped back to the surface. Immediately, my mask was stuck into the water to look for any large predators. There were none.

"Linda, look up." The former Navy SEAL yanked me away from the swim platform. My mind drifted back to the night off Trinidad, when this same man dragged me away from Carlos' shrimp boat, in the dead of night. Those terrifying thoughts were buried for now.

A moment later, Rick jumped in. The two men rechecked all the gear, before we began our descent.

"OK, we're all set. Linda, hold on to the safety line. As you release air out of your buoyancy compensator, try to regulate your descent to match mine. If you have a problem, let me know."

Gage reached over to grab the line. Bubbles burst around me as the Navy SEAL descended into the sea. With a push of a button on my vest, small blasts of air vented out. I sank into the depths. My pulse raced as we made our way past fifty feet. Prior to this, I dove to 125 feet when my nitrox class did a certification trip.

The tall man looked up, now and again. We descend down, down, down. The SEAL halted his descent at a dark area of the rope with a big knot in it. We hung at this depth for a few seconds.

"You all right, Linda?"

"Yes, Gage, I'm fine."

"We're at 100 feet. This will be one of our safety stops on the way up. It is the most important safety stop. If we go charging to the surface, without enough time at this depth, we will get decompression sickness. Do you see this knot?"

"Yes."

"Feel for this knot on the way up. When you reach it, stop, even if you are having a problem. Rick can deal with any problems you could possibly have. We do not go above this spot, for any reason, until the safety diver clears us. Is that understood?"

"Yes."

"Rick, you good with this?"

"I got your back buddy. I'll be here waiting for you. Have fun at the bottom."

We left the other Navy SEAL at the safety stop. The sea darkened as we dropped farther into the gloom. The visibility decreased to fifty feet. A shadow streaked by the corner of my eye. Panic trickled into my brain.

"Gage, what was that?"

The former Navy SEAL stopped to look around. "I didn't see it. What did it look like?"

"It was just a shadow." My depth gauge showed 150 feet.

"Let's keep going. We're almost there." Gage continued down. While following him, uneasiness infused me. As we plummeted deeper, a chill crept in, despite my dry suit. The sea grew darker and darker even though the water was reasonably clear. At 175 feet, Gage turned on his dive light. "Linda, keep yours off for now, to save the battery."

We continued down. A shadow appeared out of the silt. Gage stopped. The depth gauge read 195 feet. Incredible.

"There she is." The former Navy SEAL shined his light on the hull of the sailboat barely visible through the silt. "Linda, we'll leave the safety line here. Follow me over to the bow. We don't have much bottom time, so head right there. We'll take a look at the hole. Stay close to me and be careful not to get snagged on anything."

We kicked our fins, propelling ourselves over the wreck of *Wind Rose*. As we swam above the bow, I shined my light on the black lettering. An eerie sight. *Wind Rose*. My stomach felt like someone kicked me in the gut.

"Oh my, Gage. When you guys showed me video of this from the submarine, it seemed so far away. Now, seeing it for myself, it's so much more real."

"It's awfully sad to see such a pretty yacht end up like this. Seeing her should make you feel better."

"How come?"

"Swim with me to the hole. You'll see the evidence of contact with a container. There is no way you could have seen what you hit at night. The collision was unavoidable. It was crappy luck." We kicked over the top of the boat. Another short descent dropped us down the port side. The gaping hole defiled the sleek lines of her topsides. The gouge looked like a terrible wound.

"See the cracks. It looks like she sustained a sharp blow. Look at all the rusty scrapes along the edge. Fiberglass doesn't rust. Whatever you hit must have left these red marks. My best bet is a container."

My hand brushed along the injured area of the hull. Wouldn't it be wonderful to heal this wound and make her whole again with the power of my touch? The heavy glove still allowed me to feel the sharp cuts along the jagged edge.

"Linda, we better start our ascent. Are you ready?"

"Yes...Gage?"

"Yeah, Linda."

"Thanks for bringing me down here. I'm glad I saw her for myself."

"You can thank me at the surface. A cocktail at a nice restaurant in Beaufort would settle the debt."

"You're on."

"We need to get back to the safety line. We'll head up nice and slow. The first stop will be at 125 feet, only for a couple of minutes." With a few kicks of our fins, we arrived back at the heavy rope. Gage began his ascent first, with me right behind him.

When the target depth was reached, we stopped, hanging in the underwater current. Rick's shadow loomed twenty-five feet directly overhead.

"You're doing a great job." Gage's voice encouraged me. "You didn't seem scared at all."

"I was concentrating too hard to be scared."

He looked at his watch. "Let's go up to Rick."

When we stopped again at 100 feet, we were greeted by the other Navy SEAL. "Did you guys have fun, while I hung around, bored to tears?"

"It was amazing, Rick. Seeing the boat. Oh no!" Over the man's right shoulder, not thirty feet away, loomed a shark. A big shark. Something clamped down on my right wrist. My hand jerked in an effort to pull away.

"Linda, chill out, it's me." Gage had a tight hold of my arm. He must have heard the increase in my breathing.

"Slow your breathing down, he's not bothering us. Now is not the time to panic."

"It's a short fin mako, like the one caught on Mark's fishing boat."

"There's a second one." Rick pointed out the second large apex predator.

"Gage, can we get the hell out of here?"

"Relax, take a deep breath, Linda. Let's all stay close together. We have two more minutes at this depth."

The only sound heard was my ragged breathing. We watched the predators cruise around us. One of the sharks seemed to really focus on us, arching his back. Finally, Rick nudged me.

"We can go up to seventy-five feet." The three of us ascended through the water column together. Rick gripped my vest until the sharks lost interest in us. Their shadows disappeared into the gloom. After two more safety stops, we popped to the surface. Eric was there, fully suited in dive gear, hanging on to the swim platform.

"How did it go?"

"Fine, Eric, but I'm ready to get out of the water."

Gage and Rick helped me slip off the tanks, tying them to a line hanging off the transom. After climbing aboard, I rinsed off with the cockpit shower before helping the two Navy SEALs carry the equipment back to the submarine room. The four of us sorted out the dive gear when the intercom buzzed.

"Hello."

"Linda, Tom. Are you all topside?"

"Yes, we're cleaning up the gear."

"Could you come to the wheelhouse? Send Eric to the bow. I'd like to get underway."

"Sure, Tom. We're on our way."

Ten minutes later, the yacht cut through the water at twenty-five knots on the way to Beaufort.

Our captain expertly maneuvered the *Lady Diana* down the narrow channel by Radio Island. The current was ebbing hard, making our approach into Beaufort challenging. The swift current swirled, creating small eddies. The large yacht was thrown off course a few degrees. Several small fishing boats lined the channel on either side of us.

"Eric, look at the wild ponies on the beach." We glanced off to our right. Several horses, also called banker ponies, cantered down the white sand beach of Carrot Island.

"I didn't know they had feral horses here." My cowboy studied the wild ponies through the binoculars.

"Their ancestors came from Spain. They probably swam ashore from wrecked Spanish Galleons."

"It doesn't look like there's much grass for them to eat on the island."

"That's why they are so small. They eat marsh grass and scrub. Their food doesn't have much nutritional value."

"*Hmm*." We watched the ponies move around, grazing and socializing, until we turned the corner of the channel.

We cruised into Taylor Creek. The Beaufort Docks were directly in front of us. Many types of sailing craft bobbed at these floating berths, interspersed with motor boats. Everything from runabouts to massive sport fishing yachts moored here. Their crews relaxed after their Gulf Stream battles, with elusive tuna.

Behind the boats, lay the main streets of Beaufort. As we moved closer, I could see the Dockhouse restaurant. Oh, there is the General Store with its great homemade fudge. Many of the buildings had gray wood-shingled exteriors surrounded by white picket fences reminiscent of the town's early seafaring days.

My ribs twinged with the memory of entering this channel aboard the fishing vessel that rescued me. How many times did Joey and I come into this port aboard our own boat? This was a very popular place to stop while delivering boats either north to New England or south to the Caribbean.

"Beaufort Docks, this is the *Lady Diana*. We'd like a starboard side tie. Once our lines are secured, we need to take on fuel." Tom spoke into the radio while tapping me on the shoulder. "Linda, wake up. Do you mind getting the stern line today?" Despite his sharp rebuke, Tom's gentle eyes always telegraphed his affection. He knew how difficult it was, coming back to this port.

"I'm on it." I handed the line to the dock hand, who whipped the thick rope around the cleat, securing us to the floating dock. For the next hour, we fueled the boat and washed the salt off the mega-yacht.

Tom was wiping the stainless rail on the transom, when he halted his work. The fishing captain's gaze rose to the gangway, leading to our slip. Walking toward us were Martin Sanderling and Sloan. The researcher's cute dress must have caught his attention.

"Permission to come aboard, captain." Sloan crinkled her nose at Tom, who stepped to the transom. He extended his hand to assist the pretty scientist aboard. Martin Sanderling casually strolled on board behind her. Our boss glanced at Tom, who looked rather smitten in his customary tough guy fashion. With a shake of his head, Martin went below.

"Thanks." The pretty scientist smiled at our captain. He gallantly slipped the bag from her shoulder.

"Hi, Sloan." Gage's tall frame leaned over the railing of the upper deck. His face broke into his cocky grin until he noticed Tom.

"Hi, Gage." She threw him a little wave before addressing our captain.

"Tom, can we go over the data you recorded from the Lokator device?"

"Sure, Sloan. I'll drop this bag in your cabin. Why don't we meet in the wheelhouse?"

"Hey, lady scientist, I would be happy to go over all my personal observations of the Lokator in action. Over a drink ashore?"

"Thanks, Gage. Let me take a rain check. I really want to look at the raw data first." Sloan rolled her eyes in my direction. "Linda, sometimes I can't figure out how you deal with all this testosterone around here."

"I just ignore it." We shared a laugh before the researcher followed Tom inside.

A moment later, Eric came out of the salon doors. "Lady, how would you like to accompany a handsome sailor ashore for a drink? A stroll down the boardwalk would be nice." My eyes searched his. The last time we docked in Beaufort, I went running from the fishing boat, so the fishermen wouldn't see me cry. Eric followed me to a bench right in front of this dock. His support during such a difficult time was invaluable.

"A drink with you, sailor, would be great."

Arm in arm, we strolled to the Dockhouse restaurant. The lower level had a rustic bar frequented by yachtsmen, fishermen, and sailors, alike. Tourists visited this bar to eavesdrop on the many yarns spun here over the years.

"Two Dark & Stormies," Eric ordered as we settle onto a couple of stools. The bar was packed with many sailors beginning the northward trek up the Intracoastal Waterway.

We sipped our drinks while listening to a couple of fishermen talk about a recent catch. "The swordfish 'round here are sissy fish, compared to what we catch off the Grand Banks up New England way," said an older, grizzled man wearing a wool watch cap and a scraggy beard. He could be right out of a fish sticks commercial.

"Aye, and all the fishermen around here are a bunch of babies, compared to the New Bedfahd lot. Everyone knows the toughest fishermen in the world come from, New Bedfahd."

Before Eric could stop me, I tapped the old man on the shoulder. "Excuse me, sir."

The old man swiveled around in his chair, gazing at me with red, bloodshot eyes. He allowed those squinting eyes to look me up and down. "Aye, and what can I do for you, sweethaht."

"Well, sir, I always thought Bering Sea fishermen were the toughest of all fishermen. Don't get me wrong, New England fishermen brave bad weather, but nothing compared to the storms off Alaska."

The old man took a long draw on his whiskey glass while sizing me up.

"Linda, knock it off. Don't antagonize the old guy," Eric whispered.

My sweet smile caused the old man to squint his eyes again. He scratched his stubble of a beard while examining my husband.

"What's da matter with your hubby. Let me guess, he's an accountant from New Yawk or sumtin' like that." The old man smiled through his missing front teeth.

"He don't like you talkin' to a real fisherman? Now, back to our conversation. I don't reckon I've met no Bering Sea fishermen. But iffin' one ever crosses my path, he'd likely be a sissy boy, too, just like these boys round herah. 'Specially the ones on TV. They just make it look scary, like special effects, ha! Like to see them boys in a real nor'easter."

Someone brushed by us. Tom. Sloan stood next to him, with her arm linked though his. "Hey old man, can I buy you a drink?" The elder brother ordered cocktails for Sloan and himself. As the salty, elderly man held up his drink to toast Tom, they clinked glasses. "One old sea dog to another."

"You a fisherman? Or are you another accountant, like this fella here, from New Yawk? A wannabe fisherman who takes his little rowboat on a little lake to catch a little trout." The old man broke into wheezy laughter.

Tom winked at us. "Oh, I think my little brother is a better fisherman than that. Even if he likes to fish for crabs."

"Crabs!" The old man doubled over laughing and wheezing. "Crabs. You're joshin' an old man."

"No, really. I like to fish for crabs, too. Only much bigger ones than my bro catches."

Eric made a *tssh* sound, while shaking his head and laughing.

"Crab boys. Where do you catch them? Off da dock with a little net?"

"No, we have a boat. A pretty big boat."

"Now boys, maybe one of these days you'll grow up to be a real fisherman like me. Maybe go off the Grand Banks for the big swordfish. That's a real fisherman's fish."

Eric seemed to be getting bored with this conversion, so he turned his back on the old man. His full attention was on his drink and me.

"Hey, mista accountant, don't you go turning your back when I'm a talking to ya." The old man reached over to grab Eric's shoulder. Tom intercepted the old man's hand with a lightning fast grip on his wrist.

"I wouldn't grab him if I were you old man." The elderly fisherman winced in pain.

Eric pivoted around on his bar stool. "Let him go, Tom. He doesn't mean any harm."

"Hey, old man, we don't want no trouble in here." The bartender scurried toward us. He leaned over the bar, swatting the elderly guy with his bar towel.

"Hey, Aldo. Knock it off. Did you have too much to drink?" Our captain released the old man's wrist with a pat on the senior's shoulder.

"There's no problem barkeep, just a little misunderstanding."

My husband extended his hand to the old man. "Eric Iverson."

The old man shook his hand while studying Tom. "Don't I know you boys from somewhere?"

"They're crab captains on television. I recognized them when they came in." With a laugh, the bartender refilled our drinks. "On the house, guys. We don't get many celebrities in here. Also, there aren't many opportunities for old Aldo here to put his foot in his big mouth."

The crowd near us laughed at this friendly dig. The old man stared at the brothers with his beady eyes showing new found respect. "Now, boys, I hope you don't hold all my joshin' ag'inst me. I knew right away you boys was real fishermen. I was just teasin' you."

"No problem, Aldo," Tom said benevolently, patting the old man on his back. During this conversation, Sloan watched our captain with renewed interest.

"Hey, old man." Eric lowered his voice, leaning toward Aldo. "Do you hang around this bar every day?"

"Yes, captain crab man. I'm herah about most days. Except maybe Sunday, when the missus 'spects me home. Sunday is the Lord's day ya know."

"I know." Eric leaned closer to the old man. "Have you ever seen an old black, rusty shrimp boat around here with a Hispanic crew?"

The old man rubbed his beard. He contemplated the question before looking back at my husband. "No, can't say I 'ave. I did hear tell 'bout an old shrimp boat landing out at Cape Lookout. Them boys off it come in herah 'board a black tender. I can't understand a word of dat Spanish. They throw a lot of money around."

"Do you know if they are out there now?"

"Don't know, young fella. But I'd be watchin' out for those boys. The word is they are bad news."

"Thanks, old man." After dropping a couple of twenties on the counter, Eric grabbed my hand. "Let's go for a walk."

He slapped his brother on the shoulder as we made our way out of the crowded bar.

Alone on the boardwalk, Eric turned to me. " I t sounds like Carlos' boat makes regular stops around here, probably to drop off drugs."

"How did you figure out he would come here?"

"It makes sense. Carlos had to be in the area in order to rescue Joey. What better place than along a coastline know for piracy. If I'm not mistaken, Black-beard the pirate used to ply these waters."

"Yes, I read about him when visiting here years ago. He and his crew captured a French merchant ship in the Caribbean, off St. Vincent. They kept the ship, renaming it *Queen Anne's Revenge*. The pirates took refuge between here and Ocracoke." I paused a moment while trying to recall the details. "I bet they hid at Cape Lookout."

"Linda, remember when we flew with Mitch and Jake in the helicopter to look for Joey. We flew right over Cape Lookout. The bay was surrounded by big sand dunes. I didn't see anyone living out there. The bay seemed big enough to harbor a fleet of vessels."

"You're right. The only inhabitants are the light-house keepers. I don't think they have a boat."

"You've been out there before. How deep is the entrance?"

"Certainly deep enough for a shrimp boat. Eric, do you think Carlos is out there now?" The thought of the nasty drug dealer being so close made me shudder.

"I don't know, but we're going to find out. Why don't we see if we can rent a boat? We'll take a ride out to Cape Lookout." My husband led the way down the boardwalk toward the charter boats.

"Eric, why don't we take the tender off the *Lady Diana?* With these north winds, the seas will be calm. The small boat should be fine."

"Linda, we can't take the tender because, for now, I don't want anyone to know where we are going."

"You're not telling Gage or Tom? What if we have a problem?" A chill bolted up my spine, thinking about my last encounter with Carlos.

"We'll be fine. Look at this boat." He pointed to a twenty-something-foot daysailer for rent.

"Let's take this boat for a sail. We'll cruise out to Cape Lookout for a peek."

Chapter 11. Cape Lookout

The crew was up early the next morning, having a light breakfast in the galley of the *Lady Diana*. Seated at the oblong teak table were Tom, Eric, and I. The elder brother's nose was buried in a local news rag. His brow furrowed as he examined all of the area's fishing gossip.

I couldn't help but smile thinking back to our days in Beaufort aboard Mark's fishing boat...shortly after these men dragged me from the cold clutches of the Atlantic.

Both brothers were so sweet and supportive, in a gruff fisherman sort of way.

Our fabulous chef, Henri, kept trying to make us omelets or crepes for breakfast. Instead, we opted for a couple of bowls of cereal along with excellent, fresh-ground coffee. Eric packed a small cooler full of sandwiches and drinks from the huge refrigerator.

The door to the galley opened. Sloan wandered in. "Morning." She carried her cup of coffee around the table to a seat next to Tom. Her hand lightly brushed his shoulder as she sat down.

Our ship's captain made a point of studying the swirls in his coffee. He gave Sloan a private glance out of the corner of his eye. The tough fisherman's eyes crinkled as a smile played around his lips beneath his rough, black beard. My eyes averted to Eric. He didn't miss the look the scientist returned to Tom. The younger brother stifled a grin.

"What are you two doing today?" The elder brother's voice turned gruff, after seeing the knowing smile on my face. The four of us had the day off.

"Linda and I rented a small boat. We're going for a sail."

"I haven't been sailing in a long time." Sloan looked to us. "I shouldn't go inviting myself."

My husband's stare let me know he was not pleased with the possibility of extra crew for our trip to Cape Lookout. "I'm not sure the boat is big enough for four people."

"That's OK, bro. Sloan and I will head for the beach. Where are you sailing to?"

The elder brother peered at his junior. He must have picked up on the tension in the younger brother's voice. Eric shifted uneasily in his chair. He made an effort to lighten his demeanor. "Oh, I don't know. We'll take a cruise along the beach. Maybe we'll see you two there."

Leaving the cereal untouched, he grabbed the cooler along with my hand. "You ready, Linda?"

We dashed for the steps, leading off the boat. Our getaway needed to be swift, before anymore questions were asked. The only problem was, we were not quick enough. Our captain stopped us at the bottom of the gangway. "Bro, wait up. What gives? What the heck are you up to?"

"Nothing, Tom. We're going for a sail."

"Like, hell. Your chat with the old man last night wasn't exactly a secret. Let me guess your destination. Cape Lookout? Is your brother psychic or what?"

"Tom, we're only going for a sail. Don't get involved."

"Don't you think you should have let me in on these plans?"

"No, brother. Stay out of it?"

"Does Gage know about this?"

"No. I would appreciate it if you kept quiet for now. We're only going for a look."

"You're not going for a look without us. You'll have to make room. Sloan should be out in a minute."

As soon as the scientist joined us on the dock, the four of us strolled to the boardwalk. We made our way down the Beaufort waterfront, past the General Store, to the charter boats farther down Taylor Creek. A few gulls circled the charter fishing boats, looking for an easy meal. The mates were sorting through small bait fish for their customer's hooks.

A north wind ruffled the waters farther out in the waterway. The current swirled by.

We stopped in front of the red sailboat. Though the small sloop's exterior was nicked and dinged showing years of neglect, her pretty lines promised good sailing ability.

A teenage boy, sporting sun-bleached hair arranged in dreadlocks, strode over to greet us. The young man seemed so full of himself, as he sized up his customers. From his attitude, it was obvious the kid was used to dealing with the touristas who had little boating experience.

"Any of you know how to drive a boat?" The kid, about Daniel's age, stepped aboard. His left hand rested casually on the boom. The young man extended his right hand to help us aboard. Tom let out a snicker.

Eric climbed aboard. "I think we can handle this."

"So, you're going to be the captain?"

My husband looked to me. "I guess so."

"That's fine, darling." My sweet smile of acquiescence hardened his eyes

After stowing our gear, the kid demonstrated the use of the outboard. Life jackets and other safety equipment were located.

"This rope pulls up the big sail here." The kid pointed to the dirty, worn main halyard.

"And this red rope pulls up the sail in front. If you're leaning too much, let this rope out and the sail will flap. You guys are due back at five, so try not to be late. It will take longer coming back in because the tide will be going out."

After jumping off the boat, the kid turned to watch us. Was he expecting us to run into something?

Eric tossed off the stern line. "We'll keep that in mind."

"He wasn't fishing for tips, was he?" Tom asked when we were out of earshot. "What a smart ass."

After departing the dock, our skipper turned the boat into the wind. A joint effort was made to hoist the mainsail because the frayed bolt rope had to be fed into the mast groove. Perched on the fatigued cabin top, with hands positioned on either side of the slot in the mast, I coaxed the decaying sail cloth into the worn groove. The elder brother heaved, hoisting the sail. With a tug on the tiller, the little sloop pivoted off the wind.

A wonderful silence surrounded the boat after the noisy motor was shut off. A ten knot breeze blew from the north. We reached off, heading for the open ocean. The sloop handled well. The few boats at anchor in the lagoon were easily dodged. With the fresh breeze astern, we happily clipped along.

After cruising out the channel by Radio Island, fighting a slight incoming tide, we made a quick jibe. Beaufort Inlet was right around the corner.

Sloan pulled off her cover-up, revealing a pretty yellow, one-piece bathing suit. "Could you put this sunscreen on my back, captain?" She handed Tom a bottle of lotion.

"Sure, wench. I'm always happy to help out a lady. Keep in mind, I'm not the captain on this venture. Today we are in the capable hands of Captain Eric." Tom's big hands gently massaged the sunscreen into Sloan's golden brown skin. She leaned back as the wind blew her long, auburn hair.

This lady seemed such a different person from the tense, shy researcher we met in Paradise only a few short weeks ago. Maybe she decided which man would receive her affection. Gage would be disappointed.

There was a fair amount of chop in the outer harbor, with all the passing pleasure boat traffic. Boats of every imaginable type crossed the shipping channel from small aluminum fishing skiffs to large fuel tankers. Water spritzed over our bow, misting us with cooling brine.

We threw a wave to a departing Coast Guard cutter. It steamed down the south side of the channel near the Beaufort Inlet. The red diagonal stripes on its bow made the ship look even larger from our vantage point on a tiny sailing craft.

"Eric, did you see the name on the cutter?" Big, black letters displayed her name on the transom.

"The *Yellowfin*."

"What's up with the *Yellowfin?*" Sloan asked.

"It searched for Joey, right after *Wind Rose* sank."

Eric jerked the wooden tiller. Our red sloop pivoted into a huge wake from a sport fishing boat. The wave slammed into our bow, washing over the deck. The green water soaked us.

"I wish we had our crab boat. I'd show that jerk what a boat wake is." Our captain's face hardened as he wrenched the boat back on course.

We cleared Beaufort Inlet, hardening up on a port tack. Eric set a course for the entrance to Cape Lookout, cruising on a beam reach. The jib was eased halfway on the starboard side, drawing nicely. The sailboat heeled, skimming along the electric blue waters of Lookout Bight.

With sails taut, our sloop happily glided along at a steady four to five knots. We cruised in fifteen feet of water along the ivory white sand of Shackleford Banks. The long, vacant beach stretched for miles.

Little clumps of green scrub dotted the rolling sand dunes on this deserted island.

Tom pointed toward the land. "I was reading about this place last night. Shackleford Banks. There is this legend of a bad shipwreck right on this shore in the 1800's. A severe storm, on the order of a hurricane, swept along this coast. The ship was trying to seek refuge in Beaufort Harbor but the waves wouldn't allow it." The fishing captain paused, capturing all of our attention.

"The storm battered the ship for many hours as the crew fought valiantly to save her from the raging sea. When the wind went 'round to the southwest, it was too much for them. The ship ran aground near this spot. The crew struggled ashore in the boiling seas. Waves crashed over the deck, breaking the ship apart. The last of the crew jumped overboard. Some of the bodies were never recovered. Now the island is haunted."

Tom looked very serious. Ashore, a horse sprinted across the beach. A sly smile crept across the tough features of the fisherman. "Some of the crew were reincarnated as horses. The island is haunted by feral ponies that feed on unsuspecting tourists."

"Tom, you're so full of it." Sloan laughed while pushing his hand off her shoulder. "I can't listen to any more of this. Look!" The scientist popped up, crouching under the boom. We followed her pointed finger to the front of the boat. "Dolphins."

The researcher and I crawled to the bow of the scudding boat, hanging our feet over the side. Our swaying figures joined the rhythmic bouncing of the sloop's bow. She blasted off each tiny wave. The sleek gray dolphins, covered with white and gray spots, cavorted around us, only inches from our dangling legs. One dolphin made a game of surfing off our bow wave.

"They're spotted dolphins, look at those markings." I leaned far over the side. The dolphins kept just out of touching range.

"Beautiful. That's a pretty large pod. There must be plenty of food around here."

We hung on to the jouncing bow. The light chop sprayed over us. Slick bottlenose mammals skimmed effortlessly along the hull, rolling on their sides for a better look at us. They didn't even appear to be swimming. What a great escort on this fabulous sail.

We continued romping along for another hour until the dunes of Cape Lookout grew large.

"Where's the entrance to the harbor, Linda?" Tom tugged on the tiller in response to a small puff of wind.

"Straight ahead. It's tough to see from here."

"Would you steer for a moment? I want to check something."

Tom leaned into the small cuddy cabin. He straightened up with a revolver in hand. The firearm was tucked into a compartment on the starboard side of the cockpit.

"Jeez, brother. I don't think we need a gun. We're only going to take a look."

"Remember our first trip to Trinidad? What did I tell you on the jet? 'You can never be too prepared.'"

"Do you think there will be trouble?" Sloan's brow creased with concern.

"Don't worry, fair maiden. I'll protect you," Tom laughed.

The wind eased. We sailed into the protected harbor at Cape Lookout. After passing a sandy bluff, the anchorage came into view. A huge harbor stretched before us. Dotted around the safe haven were pleasure boats lazily swinging on their anchors.

"I remember anchoring here one time with Joey on *Dark & Stormy*. The water in the anchorage was pretty murky. Over by the sandbars, it's crystal clear. We were riding in the inflatable when we stopped to look at a ball of bait fish. No sooner had I commented on how much the swirling mass of shiners reminded me of a television documentary, when a six-foot, black-tip reef shark swam right under our inflatable boat." Tiny shocks of electricity shot up my spine, making me shudder.

A new sight in the anchorage caused my breath to catch in my throat.

There before us, a half a mile away, lay Carlos' dilapidated shrimp boat. The ominous black-steel hull was streaked with rusty red veins scarring the ship to the waterline. The hulking monster appeared to be splashed with blood. My brain flooded with the memories of my imprisonment there. Despite the warm day, I felt ice cold.

"I'll be dammed," said Tom. "How do you think they get the drugs ashore? It doesn't look deep enough for a mini-sub."

"If I remember the chart correctly, there's a small, shallow passageway over by the sandbars, called Barden Inlet. That's where the Harker's Island ferry goes. Behind Shackleford Banks, there are a bunch of little waterways. They could load up a smaller boat, then bring the drugs in at night, as long as they knew the way." My hand tried to block out the sun while I gazed at the bare sand beach.

Tom searched the bay through the binoculars. "Seems like a drug smuggler or pirate haven. We shouldn't get too close to Carlos' boat. He may recognize us. I'm pretty sure we are out gunned. By the looks of the runabout tied astern of his boat, it's a hell of a lot faster than this one."

Eric prepped his crew for a tack. "Ready about." The lazy sheet was made ready to be pulled it in once the jib crossed the foredeck.

"Tom, could you throw the other line off?" His brother pointed to the working sheet.

"Sure."

"Hard alee." Eric pushed the tiller toward the mainsail. We ducked as the boom swept over our heads. The elder brother unwrapped the working line from the black plastic cleat, releasing it right when the sail flapped across the center of the foredeck. Quickly, I tugged it in. The sail filled on the new tack. Our captain steered the little boat for open water.

"Looks like we have company," Tom grunted before our sloop could reach the safety of the open sea. The skiff from the shrimp boat was making way toward us. The coal black tender threw a monstrous wake as it careened in our direction.

"Linda, get below."

Without questioning my husband, I wedged myself out of sight, in the small, dank cuddy cabin. The sailboat heaved and rolled, making the tiny space even more untenable. My elbow wedged against a slimy metal plate. A bolt stuck out, perfectly aligned with my spine. Tiny drops of water slid down my forehead. Since my arm was wedged in so tightly, I couldn't wipe them clear.

The small sailboat rolled as the bigger boat pulled alongside. Tom's gun was hidden in the small of his back.

"Stop your boat!" A heavily accented Spanish voice barked. The rasping grate of his shout sent alarm bells off in my brain. This was one of the men who terrorized me last year aboard the rusty hulk in Trinidad.

"It may be difficult to stop when we are sailing." Sloan voice appeared light and friendly, but I knew her well enough by now to pick up on the tension. "Can you tell us where the horse beach is?"

"I know no horse beach. Why you come so close to the boat?" The voice was less harsh. Good for you Sloan, work the charm.

"We were admiring her. Will you sell us shrimp?" A cute giggle emerged. I pictured the hardened drug smugglers completely enamored by the very pretty lady before them.

"No, no shrimp. Leave us alone. *Vamonos!*" The black tender's motor screamed, leaving us bobbing in its wake. Our pram rocked sharply, jabbing the bolt into my spine.

"Bye, nice chatting with you." Sloan's voice was lost in the roar of the smuggler's engine.

"Whew, that was a close one." Eric reached under the deck to give me a hand back out. "I don't think they recognized us."

Back in the Atlantic, the wind freshened. The jib sheet was cranked in hard. The daysailer heeled over, dipping the worn toe rail into the sea.

Sloan leaned back obviously enjoying the sail.

"I thought the heeling of the boat would make you nervous." Tom's eyes followed the scientist's salt-encrusted hair, streaming in the wind.

"My grandparents were from Bermuda. They invited me to spend a summer with them when I was ten. Everyone sails there. Every day, my grandfather would take me out in his Bermuda dinghy. We'd sail for a hour or so until we were out at the reef. Fishing didn't keep my interest for very long, so we spent the afternoons snorkeling around the coral. I guess that's where my love of the sea came from."

Over the next couple of hours, we rocketed toward Beaufort Inlet. The little boat bounced and gyrated in the rising chop. Spray blasted over the bow. The four of us were like kids on a carnival ride.

The large channel markers came into view. As the young man from the charter company predicted, the tide poured out the inlet. After the main and jib were stowed, Eric had the outboard at full throttle to make headway. A few minutes before five, we swung the pram into her designated slip.

After unloading our gear, we sauntered back to the *Lady Diana*. Our group looked like castaways, sunburned and salt-caked. We climbed aboard the megayacht, sliding open the salon doors. Our salty shoes were kicked off. Gage was stretched out, on one of the couches, absorbed in a book.

"Hey, Eric. Did you guys have fun today?" The Navy SEAL glanced up from the novel. He looked like a cheetah ready to spring on an unwary antelope. His muscles were as tense as his voice. Though the inflection was casual, an accusatory tone rang out. Our group stopped to look at him.

"Yes we did. We went for a little sail."

"Where did you go sailing?"

"Oh, up and down the beach."

The Navy SEAL sprung off the couch. "Come on man, cut the shit."

Gage tensed for an attack, looming over my husband. "What the hell were you doing at Cape Lookout?"

"What makes you think we were at Cape Lookout? And so what if we were?"

Gage's anthracite eyes burned with intensity as he stood no more than an inch from his quarry. Eric backed off a step as Tom slipped by his side. All three men glared in a tense standoff.

"Eric." The SEAL's voice was unearthly growl. Rage dripped off his tough features. "Enough already. I've had Carlos under surveillance since he arrived there two days ago. Of course, he has no idea he is being watched. Imagine my surprise when I find out the four of you sailed into the same bay." His voice was very low, almost a whisper...a very harsh, throaty whisper.

"That is one hell of a coincidence." The lanky man took another step toward my husband. Tom thrust his hand out, flat against the Navy SEAL's chest. He stopped his advance, but only for a moment. The big man brushed the elder brother's hand aside.

"You didn't even have the courtesy of clearing it with me, or letting me know where you were going in case something happened."

"We were armed," Tom said lamely. "By the way, Gage, who the hell died and made you leader of this expedition?"

"I didn't die, but I did put Gage in charge. And the last time I checked, it was my signature at the bottom of the checks, paying your salaries." We turned in unison to see Martin Sanderling enter the main salon. There was a grave look of displeasure on his face.

"I'll deal with this, Martin." The SEAL stared hard at my husband.

"Eric, you are damn lucky you weren't recognized. As far as we know, Carlos knows nothing about this yacht, the mini-sub, or the surveillance we've had him under. Don't you think he would be suspicious to see you, Linda, and Tom sail into the bay he's operating out of?"

The former Navy SEAL paced. He turned around, getting into Eric's face again. "Not to mention the fact you put Sloan in danger."

"I would have protected Sloan," Tom said gallantly.

The ex-Navy SEAL sneered at the crab fisherman. "That makes me feel a whole lot better."

"Gage," Eric said, but was interrupted by a voice behind him.

"What's all the shouting about?" Joey meandered into the room. "Are the boys having a fight?"

"Shut up, Joey."

"Linda, Linda, Linda." Joey smirked at me. "Are you still defending the pretty boy?"

My mouth dropped open to give this irritating man the verbal thrashing he deserved, only to be stopped by the ringing of Eric's cell phone.

"Hello?" His face darkened when he heard the voice on the other end. "You have the wrong number." He snapped the phone closed sharply. Strange.

"Listen, Gage, you must have forgotten I have a score to settle. I don't intend to sit idly by while that animal roams wherever he wants to, threatening my family."

"Carlos has been threatening you?" Gage asked.

"Shit." My husband turned away.

The former Navy SEAL wrenched him back around. "Eric, what the hell are you talking about?"

"It started when we returned to Dallas, right after Linda's rescue from the smuggling boat. Carlos calls my cell phone making threats." Eric looked furious at his own admission. I reached for him, but Gage wedged himself between us.

"Why the hell didn't you tell me? I would have put extra security around you two."

"That's exactly what I don't want. When he gets close, I want my shot at him."

"You are using yourselves as bait? That's a pretty stupid move, in my book."

"Listen, Gage, I'll deal with this my way."

"Eric, was Carlos the wrong number you hung up on?"

"Yes." He shook of his head. The cell phone rang again. We stared as he glanced at the Caller ID.

"Put it on speaker phone."

"Hello."

"Eric, it's Carlos. How very nice to speak with you."

"What do you want?"

"Don't hang up on me again," Carlos hissed into the phone. "I'm so sorry I missed you at Cape Lookout today. You should have dropped by in your sailboat."

"I wasn't at Cape Lookout today."

"Oh, but I heard you were. My source is very reliable. Was Linda with you by chance?"

"Go to hell, Carlos." Gage shook his head furiously.

"Now, Eric you always get so huffy. I would have loved to see Linda. She has such beautiful hair. There are many things I look forward to doing with her when..."

Eric slammed the phone closed. "Gage, I don't want your protection. Stay the hell out of my way."

"Listen, man, I will make you a deal." The big Navy Seal put his hand on my husband's shoulder. He lowered his voice so only Eric and I could hear him.

"First, you must agree to do what I say. We need to work together. I cannot have any member of my team going off like a vigilantly, trying to settle a score on his own. You are only going to get yourself killed."

When Eric tried to interrupt him, Gage raised his hand to stop him.

"Let me finish. You promise never, and I mean never to pull this shit again." Gage's black eyes stared my husband down. "I will make you a promise. When we get close to nabbing Carlos, I'll give you five minutes alone with him. Make it look like an accident."

Chapter 12. Back in the Atlantic

The next morning we were up at dawn, preparing the mega-yacht for an early departure out of Beaufort. We needed to do a few more sea trials, making sure all the systems worked properly. Then we would get down to the business of tracking Carlos and the other drug runners in the Gulf of Mexico. Eric was reading the morning newspaper in the galley. I decided to take my java to the back deck, a great place to view sunrise.

A gentle morning breeze blew across our transom. Gage stood on the dock, talking with three uniformed men wearing U.S. Coast Guard garb. Perched in the center of the group was Mitch wearing plain clothes. After a few moments of chatting with the uniformed guys, the Navy SEAL and the Coast Guard officer came aboard, right when Tom exited the sliding glass doors.

"Morning." Our captain greeted us with his usual gruffness.

"Tom, are we ready to get underway? Mitch is joining us for the final equipment tests. There is a planned rendezvous with a Coast Guard ship to check out the anti-piracy systems." Gage leaned casually against the stern rail.

Our captain downed his coffee in one large swig. "I'm not sure Eric is going to be too thrilled having him on board. You better make sure my brother doesn't get a hold of any guns."

The former Navy SEAL stared hard at me. "No offense to Linda here, but I don't give a damn what Eric likes or dislikes. We have a job to do." It was obvious the ex-Navy SEAL completely missed our captain's attempt at a joke. With a grunt, Tom turned for the wheelhouse. The two military guys went into the main salon.

A moment later, Martin Sanderling stepped aboard. "Linda, I'm glad you're here. There is something we need to discuss."

"What's on your mind?"

"I have amassed a phenomenal group of extremely talented people to complete my research, then implement my own personal war on drugs." Martin paused. "In doing so, I have managed to mix several extremely strong personalities, in slightly too small a space."

Our boss studied me. "Mitch, Gage, and I were discussing another possibility which would make use of your strongest skills." What the heck was he trying to say?

"We are contemplating another platform. It would be useful in tracking the drug boats and the mini-subs. The new one should be less, *hmm*, ostentatious than this yacht. Flo and Jet could keep up more easily with a slower boat. They would be a great asset in the actual search for the mini-subs."

"OK."

"We thought a sailboat would be the ideal choice. Because of your expertise, you are the perfect resource to find a suitable sailing vessel for such an expedition. Not only will you run the boat, but also keep other... strong personalities in check." Martin smiled at me with a curious look on his face.

"The sailing vessel will remain in constant communications with the *Lady Diana*. If a drug smuggling boat or mini-sub is spotted, you can call this boat, a Coast Guard cutter or U.S. Navy vessel to intercept it. There would be little or no danger to you or your crew."

"Let me get this straight, Martin. All we have to do is sail around the Gulf of Mexico, with the dolphins and the Lokator, looking for suspicious boats or mini-subs?"

"Exactly." The boss rubbed his hands together excitedly. "The yacht must have enough room to house a scaled-down model of the Lokator, plus extra radio and satellite communications gear. She must be large enough to accommodate a crew of four to live aboard for a couple of months at a time."

"A crew of four?"

"Yes. I would dispatch you and Eric, of course. Tom and Sloan would be likely crew because Tom is an excellent seaman. He may be disappointed to lose his job as the captain of this yacht. Maybe we could make him the captain of the sailing yacht, but in fact, you would be in charge. Would that work?"

"Tom and I can work together with no problem."

"Excellent. Sloan will to join you, too. She is an obvious choice because of her ties to the dolphins and intimate knowledge of the Lokator gear. The big question is, do you know of a particular sailing yacht adequate for the task at hand? She must not look too out of place, cruising around the Gulf of Mexico."

"A Pacific Seacraft 40 would be the perfect boat. The pilothouse model has plenty of room for all the extra communications gear."

"*Hmm*. I'm not sure I'm familiar with Pacific Seacrafts."

"They are strong, well-built ocean going yachts. Should we run into any bad weather, there is no worry about their ability to handle it. Also, as very sea-kindly vessels, they track well in any kind of sea state. Two friends of ours have one in Naples."

"Linda, you are the expert. The *Diana* will depart when my wife arrives. This cruise, with the Coast Guard, should take two days. Can you get on line, via the satellite gear, to see if you can find a suitable boat to buy?"

"I'll get right on it, Martin."

Our boss stopped me as I turned for the main salon. "Please keep these plans quiet for now. I don't want to upset the balance aboard this yacht during our upcoming trip."

"No problem, Martin."

A short time later, our crew scurried around the deck, preparing the yacht for departure. Diana strutted down the dock in another garish pink outfit, wearing skin tight, rose Capris. Silver high heels with gleaming sequins almost tripped her as a heel caught in a crack on the dock.

Nearly regaining her balance, Martin's wife pried her errant shoe from the dock with her toes. When the woman tried to straighten up, she lurched unsteadily toward the transom of the boat. Could she be tipsy this early in the day?

When the lady of the boat saw me, she straightened her ridiculously frilly hat. Once again, her eyes looked down her nose at me. "Oh, you again. What's your name? Lydia, Lindsey?"

"Linda." My calm answer didn't hide the irritation.

"Well, whatever. I thought Martin was getting rid of you. How am I ever going to tolerate another dreadful trip? With...well never mind. Don't just stand there playing with the rope, give me a hand. I always hate stepping on this miserable boat."

I was about to re-secure the stern line and, oh yes, give Diana a hand. Maybe a little assistance directly into the ocean behind the boat. Before I got my chance, someone walked up behind me.

Joey's grating voice bleated out. "Mrs. Sanderling, could I be of assistance to you? I could help you aboard, seeing as Linda is so busy removing the stern line?"

"Joey, isn't it? What a nice thing to do. Thank you so much. I must put in a good word for you with Mr. Sanderling." Joey smirked while extending his hand to our boss' wife. She flounced aboard. With a flourish,

Martin's wife disappeared into the main cabin, followed by my ex, who was trailing behind like an obedient puppy dog. *UGH!*

"Steady, Linda." Tom's voice laughed, echoing in my headset. "Your body language could be read all the way up here in the wheelhouse. Don't let them bother you. Take up the stern line, now."

The dock hand released our attachment to the pier. The line was retracted with the winch, disappearing into the recesses of the transom. After retrieving my laptop, I took refuge in to the wheelhouse. It was the best place to avoid Diana, the wicked witch of the east.

I sat in a small chair behind the twin helm seats. The laptop connected, via the yacht's wifi, to the internet. Tom and Eric piloted the yacht, out the narrow channels to the Atlantic. We would rendezvous with a Coast Guard Cutter seventy-five miles offshore. The guys were scheduled to test our weapons systems, communications gear and the secret anti-piracy technology.

Mitch and Martin entered. The Coastie stood to one side as our boss watched over Tom's shoulder. The big crab man expertly piloted the yacht out the channel. Eric gave Mitch a cold stare. After slipping over behind me, he watched me flip through the sailboats on the yacht search website.

"What are you looking for on the web? A new sailboat?"

"She's doing a project for me," Martin said evasively.

My fingers continued to pound away on the keyboard as the mega-yacht began to sway with our increasing speed. Long rollers gently rocked the boat. Stretching before us were the broad waters of the Atlantic Ocean.

After traveling for a couple of hours in a southeasterly direction, the yacht slowed to an idle. The Atlantic was relatively calm today with a light east wind ruffling the Gulf Stream. There were no other vessels in sight except for a big, white Coast Guard cutter a mile to the south.

Mitch stood to the left, with a headset on, speaking in hushed tones. I assumed he was in contact with the Coast Guard cutter. Gage and Tom watched the monitors. Eric maneuvered the yacht from the helm. Martin Sanderling was in the middle of it all, scrutinizing every detail.

A small hatch opened up on the foredeck. A long, black tube extended toward the bright blue sky.

"What's that?" I asked in a whisper.

"It looks like a cannon," Eric whispered back.

"It's a high tech, laser guided water cannon, used to repel pirate attacks. With the velocity and huge volume of water this baby can spray out, we could sink most vessels. The laser guide, designed by Martin's company, allows the cannon to lock on a boat. We can follow their movements while dousing them with 10,000 gallons per minute of high-pressure seawater. This provides maximum defense."

Gage grinned like a little boy with a new water pistol. "I wanted to put a real 76mm cannon aboard, but the Department of Homeland Security would not allow so much firepower on a civilian vessel.

"We are locking on the Coast Guard cutter to simulate our defense against pirates or any attacks by the drug runners. Some of the smuggling boats have pretty good weapons systems. We won't shoot, of course, but the Coasties are checking the accuracy and strength of our laser lock."

Throughout the afternoon, our yacht and the Coast Guard went through a series of maneuvers, playing a sort of cat and mouse game. Mid-afternoon, a smaller hatch opened, allowing another piece of equipment to emerge. A rounded metal plate, similar to a satellite dish, popped out of our navigation bridge.

"Gage, what's that?"

"It's a LRAD, Linda."

"It's a what?"

"Sorry. It's a Long Range Acoustical Device. It's like a big megaphone. With the help of the LRAD, we can broadcast very loud messages, in several languages. We'll blast these at approaching vessels. The device is an excellent anti-piracy aid, because it tells the bad guys we're aware they are coming. It also lets the pirates know we are armed and ready to fight. If more of a deterrent is needed, well, we souped up this device, thanks to Martin's company."

Our boss had a self-satisfied smile on his face.

"What else can it do?" Eric asked.

"It can send out ear-piercing, high-pitched acoustic bursts, directly at the approaching vessel. The sound blast is so strong, it can rupture your eardrums. If extreme pain in your ears is not enough, we can switch to an extremely low frequency, way below normal bass sounds. You know how it feels when kids go by, blasting loud music out of their cars?"

"It's really irritating when they do. Jeez, I must be getting old," Tom laughed.

"You know how you can "feel" the low frequency bass?" Gage asked, surveying us like a university professor. We nodded our heads in unison.

"If you crank up the power and drop the frequency lower, you can generate a pulse that can rip apart the internal organs. The pirates have to be pretty close to get the full effect. By the time they are, we better be in full defensive mode."

"Are we expecting this kind of trouble?"

"No, Linda. At least not in the near future, but who knows what desperate drug runners will try. Also, Sanderling Industries is using these 'war games' opportunities to test equipment which may be used in the Gulf of Aden, to combat the Somali pirates."

"Anti-piracy technology would be helpful to the unfortunate yachts in transit to the Red Sea."

"You are right, Linda, but the technology will be pretty expensive. The cost will limit the availability to those vessels who's owners have deep pockets." Gage paused a moment. "We should take this opportunity to discuss our own shipboard emergency procedures."

Joey slipped into the wheelhouse. He stood by the door, listening intently.

"If we come under attack, this is what I expect of everyone. First, we'll be notified by five short blasts on the ship's horn, followed by a message on the intercom. Tom, Eric, and Linda will come to the wheelhouse to manage the piloting of the ship. Martin, you will find Diana and go to the safe room, inside the armament room."

Martin nodded his head.

"Depending on whoever else is aboard, all the ex-military guys will go to the armament room to get small arms. My place will be on the bridge as it is the most important spot to secure. Jake, you'll take the aft area to guard the helicopter. Rick will shield the bow. If we have Mitch aboard, he will secure the engine room, if not, I will bring a weapon for either Tom or Eric."

"What about me?" Joey asked quietly, from his dark corner of the room.

"Joey, yeah sorry. Maybe it would be best for you to come to the wheelhouse to help with communications." My ex glared at Gage. It seemed he was not happy with the former Navy SEAL overlooking his part as an essential crew member during an emergency.

"It's getting dark out. We'll break off the war games for now. Let's begin our regular watches. They are posted on the schedule by the door. In addition to the navigation watches, I want someone manning the bow all night."

"Are we expecting trouble?"

"Not necessarily, Tom. The Coasties are trying to find any weak spots in our defenses. Who knows what they may cook up." When Gage finished his statement, the intercom sounded. It was our chef, announcing dinner was ready. On my way out, I checked the watch schedule to see my assigned time was midnight to two.

After dinner, Eric and I strolled the upper deck. Standing on the dimly lit helicopter pad, the stars burst from the sky. A light breeze, filled with humidity, blew across the ship. Beneath our feet, we could feel the vibrations of the engines slowly making way through the calm sea. The yacht rolled lightly, taking the small amount of chop off the port bow.

"Linda, why were you looking for sailboats on the computer today?" My husband leaned against the rail, watching me in the dim light.

"It was nothing. Just something Martin asked me to do."

"I was hoping for a breakthrough in your stand-off with Joey over *Dark & Stormy*."

"You know, Eric, Joey is being such a jerk over this whole thing. I'm about ready to tell him to take the boat and go. Get the hell out of my life." Before he could respond, his cell phone rang. Even though we were far offshore, our phones worked via the satellite system.

"Eric, it's Carlos." The drug kingpin always spoke loudly, making it easy to eavesdrop on the call.

"What do you want?"

"My sources tell me you're on a cruise, playing games with the Coast Guard. They won't be able to protect you or your precious Linda. I can't wait to have her back aboard my pretty yacht." Carlos' evil cackle made my blood run cold. Calmly, Eric closed the cell phone. His stare was intense.

"How the heck do you think he found out about this trip and this boat?"

"I don't know, but I'm sure as hell going to find out."

We swiveled around to face Gage. "He threatened you again?"

"Yes."

"I overheard the rest. Somebody must be feeding him information. Let's keep this phone call between us. We may need bait to bring out the culprit."

"Gage, did you notice how Joey snuck into the war games meeting in the wheelhouse? Do you think he is supplying the information to Carlos?"

"Linda, he was my first thought. The facts don't add up, considering the way Carlos beat him. Your ex must have bad feelings for those drug dealers. It doesn't make sense for him to help them now."

"Maybe Carlos offered him money. Joey is not in the greatest of financial position since we lost the boat. Delivery jobs are few and far between, especially when the boat you are delivering sinks."

"We'll keep this between us for now. I'll find out who the informant is."

"Keep the boat heading at 120 degrees. We are maintaining a speed of two and a half knots, just keeping steerageway," Tom told me. My two hour watch would start in a few minutes, right at midnight. The wheelhouse was dark, except for the dim green lights on the GPS and radar. Our track zigzagged every couple of hours, closely shadowed by the Coast Guard vessel off our starboard quarter.

"I've got it, Tom. Who is on bow watch?"

"Gage. He may come up to check in with you around one."

"Get some sleep." Tom left the wheelhouse. I settled in for a couple of hours of staring at the sea. I kept an eye out for any other vessels which may cross our path. We were on the eastern side of the Gulf Stream, where the current flowed northeast at about one knot. Any ship traffic was likely to come out of the southwest, heading for Boston or New York. A quick glance at the radar showed no blips other than the Coasties.

After the one o'clock check in with Gage, my feet were propped up in a very comfortable position for the last hour of watch. Things were real quiet when the door to the pilothouse opened. Joey walked in. He strolled over to the navigation equipment. His eyes scanned our position, course, and speed.

"Hi, Linda."

"Joey."

"Listen, I'm sorry about our encounter on deck the other night. I don't know what came over me."

"*Hmm.*"

"Linda, it's so hard to see you with him. I guess we need to move on."

"Joey, what the hell do you want?"

He stared at me in the dim light. A moment later, the door to the bridge opened, allowing Diana into the wheelhouse. Great. Now, I had to deal with two of my least favorite people.

"Oh, it's you up here." Diana walked over to the helm. Her long fingers trailed over the navigation equipment as she approached. "I can't believe Martin trusts you with the boat. Well, whatever. I couldn't sleep because of all the bouncing. Why don't you change course or something to smooth out the ride?"

"Mrs. Sandlerling, I was instructed to maintain this course until two. When Eric takes over watch, we are going to alter course."

"Joey, you are a captain. Why don't you take over and steer us in a better direction?"

"Don't even think about it," I hissed at him.

"I wasn't going to. Mrs. Sanderling, we have to keep our course with the Coast Guard. It's part of the exercises we are doing in conjunction with them. Maybe I could make you a nice cup of tea in the galley? Something hot to drink often helps me to sleep."

"Joey, once again you are such a nice man. Yes a cup of tea, with a shot of bourbon, would be lovely."

My former partner latched onto Diana's arm, leading her to the door. She threw a disdainful glance over her shoulder. Maybe a thank you should be directed to Joey, but why bother?

"Linda, we have a high speed vessel approaching our port bow. It's coming in fast with no lights on. Sound the alarm." Gage's calm voice filled the headset from his position on the bow.

"Stop," I shouted as Joey was exiting the wheel-house. "Get Mrs. Sanderling to the safe room." My finger stabbed at the alarm button on the navigation panel. An ear-piercing clanging sounded through the quiet night. Seconds later, the yacht was a frenzy of activity.

Tom was at the helm in a flash. "I've got command." Our eyes locked on Gage. Rick sprinted across the foredeck, armed with two Ruger semi-automatic rifles. After grabbing a gun, the taller Navy SEAL moved back toward the wheelhouse. Over the bow, we saw the white, frothy wake of the passing boat, very close aboard.

Gage stormed into the pilothouse. "Where is it, Tom?"

"I don't know."

"It circled around the stern." I glanced at the blank radar.

"Hold your fire, unless fired upon. Keep a sharp eye on the rails," Gage said through our wireless headsets.

"Where's Eric?"

"I met him on the way up. He headed for the aft deck armed with a Ruger."

Tom swiveled both deck cameras to the stern. A darkened figure climbed over the rail from the swim platform.

"Eric, we have a tango at the stern rail."

"Got him."

"Cover him. Jake can you get down there?"

"Already on my way."

A moment later, the former Marine hustled to the inky recesses of the stern. A blackened figure dropped to the deck. Jake and my husband materialized out of the shadows. Guns were trained on the darkened invader. He raised his hands.

Instead of a tense standoff, the three men appeared to be engaged in a conversation. A moment went by before Jake lowered his gun. He crept over to the man, then shook hands with him.

"He's a friendly. A special forces dude who says he's a friend of yours, Gage."

A few minutes later, Jake and Eric walked into the wheelhouse followed by a man wearing black fatigues. He removed his hat, allowing bright white teeth to form a big smile on his African-American face.

"Gage, I should have known you would have good defenses up."

The man extended his hand to the former Navy SEAL who still seemed very tense.

"Shit, Hammer, you scared the bejezus out me. What the heck is this, old home week?" The former Navy SEALs exchange a brief handshake-hug.

"Sorry, guys. Let me introduce Master Chief Elton Sanders, better know as 'Hammer'. We served together in the Navy SEALs. He's one tough dude who was injured while fighting in Iraq and Afghanistan."

After introductions, Elton explained how he arrived here.

"Once retirement raised its ugly head a couple of years ago, the missus decided she wanted to live in the tropics. Hell, Miami bored me to tears with all the golf and tennis...all those fancy cocktail parties. I needed to get my hands dirty again and keep up on my skills." He paused to wipe a bead of sweat off his forehead.

"A buddy of mine approached me to start a training facility in the Everglades. We would specialize in tutoring police and security forces. It was opened up for private membership, six months ago, but only to ex-military or police. We do quite a lot of paramilitary work there, along with SWAT team tactical practice.

"Another friend of a friend introduced me to Martin Sanderling right when I was looking for new capital to expand the place. Did you know he was almost killed when a drug lord went after his brother for an unpaid debt? Seems his kid brother had a real bad cocaine problem. The drug lord blew his brains out after nearly beating him to death."

"That would explain Martin's personal war on drugs," I said while looking over this military man.

"Yes it does," Elton said. "After Mr. Sanderling dumped cash into my business, he came out to do pistol training. He told me about the boat you were putting together and this war game. After chatting with a buddy at the Coast Guard, we thought it would be fun to organize a boarding party."

"Did you actually think you could waltz aboard my boat undetected?" Gage asked, with a challenging grin.

"Yeah, and I'd find my way into the galley for a nice cup of joe, after checking out my old pal's new hang out."

"All right, everyone can stand down. Tom, why don't you call the Coasties. Thank them for the present they sent over."

"OK, Gage."

"Elton, why don't you and I go to the safe room to spring Martin and his wife? Once they are free, I'll buy you that cup of coffee." The two Navy SEALS left the pilothouse.

"Eric, do you want to take watch? I need some fresh air, maybe a walk around the deck." Tom rubbed his hand over his tired face. Our captain turned for the door.

"That was exciting. At least it proved we have good defenses."

"Yes, Eric, though it was more than enough melodrama for one night."

Chapter 13. Oriental, NC

After another twenty-four hours of war games with the Coast Guard, we made our way toward the entrance to Beaufort. When our ship was two hours from port, Martin called a meeting in the wheelhouse.

"You are here to discuss a new project I'm working on."

Our boss stood near the helm. From the captain's chair, Tom scanned the horizon. Eric leaned against the navigation console. Sloan and I sat in chairs toward the back of the bridge.

"Tom." Martin paced across the floor, stopped, then placed a hand on our captain's shoulder. "I've been extremely lucky to have such a talented master aboard the *Diana*. Now, there is a new challenge which would suit your skills very nicely."

Tom appeared baffled. The Bering Sea captain turned to face our boss. "What would that be, Martin?"

"Your expertise is needed to engage a new surveillance platform of a more modest size, but also equipped with the Lokator gear. A smaller boat which could stay at sea for a month or two at a time. It needs to be slow enough to allow our dolphins to swim along with it."

"Martin, this is news to me. You want to take Flo and Jet out to sea? For what purpose?" Concern creased Sloan's brow.

"Simply put, the dolphins can increase the range of the Lokator gear with their echolocation. Also, they can be trained to look for mini-subs. This will give the new surveillance yacht much greater range."

"Martin, the dolphins would be at great risk in the open ocean."

"Yes, Sloan, there would be increased peril. If we take the proper precautions, the danger can be minimized. This war on drugs is so important we need to utilize every possible asset."

"Martin, how could you possibly minimize the risk? Any large sharks lurking out there would attack sweet little Jet. He has no idea how to protect himself. I cannot allow it."

"You cannot allow it?" Martin's voice raised. He strutted over to the researcher. "The last time I checked you were not the boss here. If you don't like my proposal, maybe you would prefer to seek employment elsewhere?"

"No, Mr. Sanderling. I didn't mean that." Sloan stumbled over her words. Our boss cut her off in a very stern voice.

"Well, my dear, a unique challenge awaits you. While we are preparing the new yacht, you need to teach the dolphins about the wild ocean and all the dangers there.

"After completing this task, you will accompany Tom, Eric, and Linda aboard the craft to keep an eye on your precious cetaceans. Your goal will be to ensure the Lokator gear is functioning properly. In addition, Linda's team will assess any contacts the yacht encounters."

The researcher looked like she was about to argue again when Tom's head shake silenced her. Martin turned to me.

"Linda, why don't you tell everyone about the boat you've found?"

Eric's arms were folded against his chest as his blue eyes stared into mine. He knew I hadn't been forthright with this information about the new yacht.

"Well, the new boat is a sailboat...a Pacific Seacraft 40. The one we are going to look at is in a place called Oriental, NC."

"A sailboat?" Tom lurched out of his seat, heading for Martin. "You want me to skipper a sailboat? You've got to be nuts. That's like riding a horse versus a Harley, which is not something I'm interested in doing. Why not have Linda skipper the boat?" The big crab fisherman towered over our boss, who stepped back. Martin regained his composure after wiping his face with a handkerchief.

"Tom, you are correct. Linda is very capable of skippering the yacht. She needs enough skilled seamen aboard to enable long range forays into the Gulf of Mexico."

"Let me get this straight, Martin. I'm leaving a job as skipper of a 150 foot mega-yacht to become crew aboard a measly forty-foot sailboat? I don't think so. No offense, Linda. I'll head back to Alaska."

"Tom." Our boss started to speak but I interrupted him.

"Martin could I try, please? Tom could we discuss this later? Once I've explained everything, you should be happy with the situation."

"I doubt it." The elder brother turned back to piloting the yacht.

"This meeting is over." Martin seemed miffed as he turned to Eric. "I assume you have no problem with this."

"Not having heard the whole proposal, there's no guarantee I'm going to agree. The early stages seem interesting enough, but I would like to see my brother happy."

"Linda, it appears you have your work cut out for you. Good luck." The boss marched out the wheelhouse.

Tom turned on me. "Linda what the hell is all this about?" I had never seen my brother-in-law so pissed off.

"A couple of days ago, Martin approached me with his vision of buying another boat to track the mini-subs and drug boats in the Gulf of Mexico. He thought the four of us should go because of our close ties, and Sloan's expertise with both the dolphins and the Lokator equipment."

"The dolphins aren't going. It's a ridiculous idea to put them in such danger."

"Sloan, you know Martin better than I do. He doesn't appear to be the type of man to take no for an answer."

"Linda, you should have discussed this with us before agreeing to do this." Eric glared at me from across the pilothouse.

"What the heck? Is everyone against me on this? Do we or do we not want to get Carlos? If you were subjected to the same terrible abuse and indignities that I was, you'd be damn glad to have someone with Martin's resources help you get the stinking drug dealer. Shit!" My tirade was directed at the three of them, though the focus of my anger was the two brothers.

"You should try being slapped around, tied up in a dirty cabin, and forced to pee in a bathroom full of cockroaches. How would you like to be dragged into an ocean full of sharks on a pitch black night? Would those indignities be enough to make you check your stupid male egos at the door and help me? Not to mention the fact, the stinking bastard stole my engagement and wedding rings. I intend to get those back from the son of a bitch."

My breath came out in gasps. Tears pooled around the corners of my eyes. I would be damned if I was going to allow these men to see me cry. The brothers jaws dropped. Before they could respond, I stormed out the wheelhouse.

At the stern rail, the inky blue waters of the Gulf Stream comforted me. My pounding heart quieted down. Fury frothed right below the surface.

"Why do men have to be such idiots?" The empty ocean didn't respond.

Gage appeared. "We're not all idiots." His hands gripped the stern rail. The SEAL's eyes locked on our bubbling wake.

"Martin told me about his discussion with the four of you. I was coming up to try to explain, when...

your tirade blasted straight through the door." The Navy SEAL shrugged his shoulders. He was trying to help, but the smile on his face aggravated me more.

Gage laughed. "You really gave it to Tom and Eric. I can picture those two big fishing captains cowering in front of you."

"They were hardly cowering." Was this man trying to irritate me with his airy appraisal of the situation? "I don't want to discuss it."

"Oh, but I do." Gage became very serious. "Linda, you never talked about what happened aboard Carlos' boat. Knowing what a strong woman you are, everything he did must be eating you up inside."

"Gage, I don't want to talk about it."

The big Navy SEAL slipped his arm around my shoulders.

"Linda, sooner or later you'll have to let it out. It's not good, keeping all the negative energy bottled up inside. When I was in the Navy SEALs, we were locked up in solitary confinement, sometimes for days, in nasty conditions. Even though it was a part of our training, you couldn't help being pissed off at the guys who dragged you out of bed, in the middle of the night. It usually took a big group to force you in." Gage turned me toward him.

"Do you know what happened when we were finally released?"

My gaze returned to the sea behind us.

"The guys who dragged us in would take us out for a couple of drinks in a local bar. We'd blow off steam getting drunk and exchanging stories of just how bad the experience was. One of the instructors, who was imprisoned in a tiny cell in Vietnam for several months, told me our training was a piece of cake compared to reality. He also taught me to channel my anger against the bad guys, not the guys on our side."

When I didn't respond, Gage put his hand on my face, turning me back toward him. The big SEAL raised my chin until our eyes met.

"Linda, you need to let us in on what's hurting you and what you intend to do about it. I had no idea you were so angry. You never told me about your plan to go after Carlos. We're supposed to be a team here. We have to work together, while trusting one another, completely.

"How well do you think the Navy SEALs would function, if each member of the team went off on their own vigilante mission? I'll tell you what would happen. They would all be dead. Poof. The bad guys win."

Gage grabbed both of my shoulders when I attempted to turn away.

"Linda, listen to me dammit. Here I am trying to organize a mission to get the man who hurt you so badly and what do I have to work with? Your husband wants to go after Carlos, but doesn't want to let me know about the threatening phone calls from the drug dealer. Instead, he sets off on his own mission. Carlos' goons spot him at Cape Lookout. You have no idea how lucky the four of you were. My bet is the druggies were armed to the teeth.

"Eric is pissed off at Mitch, because Mitch didn't call about Joey's rescue. This makes our Coast

Guard friend less effective, because your husband won't confide in him or hardly even speak with him. Your brother-in-law, Tom, is so worried about his stinking tough guy ego and his brother, he's not willing to work with our Coastie friend either. What's the solution?

"If we send you guys in a different direction, maybe the hostility aboard this boat will diffuse. A great plan until Tom announces he won't work on a sailboat. Since Sloan is now involved with him, her cooperation is in doubt. Also, the lady scientist doesn't want her precious dolphins injured, so I bet they are up there now plotting a way to escape with the stupid fish."

"Mammals." The former Navy SEAL's eyes blazed.

"To top it all off, you and you ex are continually squabbling over a trivial sailboat. Martin's prima donna wife parades around bitching about seasickness. I haven't even mentioned the traitor among us, who is passing along our every move to Carlos. This puts our lives in extreme danger. I'm nearly fed up with all of this and all of you. It's like a stinking soap opera. We should call it 'As the Anchor Drags.'"

"Gage, what do you want us to do?" A voice from behind the ex-Navy SEAL made him release his hold on me. He pivoted around. Tom, Eric, and Sloan stood on deck behind him. All three looked embarrassed.

"Stop acting like a bunch of spoiled rotten kids. You'd better realize, very soon, how dangerous this is. When you guys get on the sailboat, you will have no one to protect you. All of you need to get serious. We need so start working together or else I'm done with this project."

Eric walked over with his hand extended. "You're right, Gage. We've let our personal feelings get in the way of our jobs. As far as I'm concerned, we should get down to business. Let's go get Carlos."

After our arrival in Beaufort, we spent the rest of the afternoon cleaning up the mega-yacht. Around five, we did exactly what Gage suggested the Navy SEALs did. Our crew went to the Dockhouse Restaurant for a light dinner and drinks. The ex-Navy SEAL's buddy, Hammer, joined us for a little bonding. Or could he be playing the role of referee?

"Are you guys on board with the sailboat thing?" Gage scrutinized us while swirling his Jack Daniel's on the rocks. His elbows rested on the table, supporting the drink. Black, cat-like eyes flashed back and forth as if trying to decide which of his prey he should attack first.

"Yes, Gage." Eric finally answered, after giving the former Navy SEAL an intense stare.

"OK, if we're going after this joker, you guys need to do some training, together as a team. Maybe these four won't get into any trouble on the sailboat, but what if they do? They need to have a defensive plan. Each one needs to know what the other one will do." Elton tipped a glass of bourbon to his lips while eying all of us.

"Is that an offer to use your facilities?" Gage asked his old friend.

"Absolutely. I don't normally allow civilians in, but considering their ties to Martin, I can make an exception. I'll check the schedule. We'll get these sissies in shape in no time." Elton chuckled pleasantly, but the deep void in his eyes told me he was a serious executioner.

From the look on the elder brother's face, the "sissies" poke bothered Tom. The tough fisherman remained silent. My guess was, he didn't want to provoke the hardened Navy SEAL.

"Excellent, thanks, Hammer. We have to get both boats down to West Palm for fine tuning in the boatyard. After that, we'll be available for a couple of weeks."

The six of us spent the rest of the evening enjoying cocktails, allowing much needed camaraderie to infuse our tattered spirits.

The next morning we were up early, ready for our trip to Oriental. Some say this sleepy North Carolina town on the Neuse River is the sailing capital of the southeast. Years ago, I spent time there, during a trip up the Atlantic Intracoastal Waterway. It was a relaxed place with a ton of sailboats. Our hope was, the boat we were looking to buy would be in good shape.

After renting a sporty convertible, Tom burned up the narrow back roads, driving us on a wild ride to the yachting mecca. Rock and roll blasted on the car stereo. When we arrived, both my hair and Sloan's looked like we'd spent a full day under one of those old-fashioned hair dryers. The scientist examined herself in the rear view mirror, laughing off the tangled mess.

"I look like a hedgehog with an Afro." She giggled while trying to smooth her disheveled locks.

"You look OK," Tom said gruffly, under his breath. Eric smirked, resisting the opportunity to rib his brother. It was a moment I couldn't pass up.

"Well isn't this the compliment of the century, Sloan. 'You look OK.' Why I just wish Eric had such a silver tongue." The two of us giggled at Tom's expense.

Tom grinned, grabbing me by the arm. "Watch it, Li'l Sis, or I might have a better one for you." Our captain led of us to the multitude of docks before us.

Standing at the entrance to "A" dock was a nondescript man wearing a nice, collared shirt, starched pants, and Sperry Topsiders. My usual opinion of someone wearing fancy deck shoes is a wanna be sailor. *Hmm.* We'll have to see.

"You the broker?" Tom asked the man.

"Yes." After introductions, we strolled down the dock. The salesman halted us in front of slip number twenty-four.

Before us was a very pretty Pacific Seacraft Pilothouse 40. Her hull was dark blue, but the gelcoat looked hazy from oxidation. "Linda, ignore the cosmetics," I told myself. The mechanics of the boat needed to be sound.

We jumped aboard. The guys checked over the electronics. A casual walk along the hull brought me to the rigging, mast, and deck fittings.

"There's lots of great space on deck to sun yourself." The yacht broker directed this at me. *Ugh.* Another male chauvinist needed to be dealt with today.

"Thanks."

"The bathroom is really nice, too, though it could use a woman's touch."

"Easy, Linda." Sloan giggled. We slipped below to check out the V-berth. Drawers and lockers were examined.

"I'll give him a woman's touch."

The guys came below. My husband occupied himself at the navigation station. His brother opened the engine compartment. Tom bent over to check the oil. Peeking over his shoulder, I saw a clean motor. Behind me, Eric looked over the machinery.

"I have this great memory of you checking the oil in your nighty aboard *Dark & Stormy.*"

"That's a vision my imagination could run with."

"Tom, you are dating one gorgeous, very smart woman. Are you happy? No. You have to fantasize about your brother's wife. Unbelievable."

"Who says Sloan and I are dating? Besides, I've fantasized about you since the day we pulled you out of the water." Tom turned his head toward me with a mischievous grin. There was a sparkle in his eyes.

"Eric, are you going to stand here listening to this rubbish or are going to defend my honor?"

"Linda, you play with fire you're gonna get burnt."

In an attempt to extricate myself from this situation, I tried to squirm past the fisherman behind me.

He shifted his weight, blocking my path with his knee. I was wedged against the elder brother's back with the younger brother behind me.

Tom spun around. "Li'l Sis, it looks like you own me an apology for the 'silver tongue' comment earlier." My husband backed off as his brother playfully grabbed me by my shoulders.

"Eric, help. Rescue me from this horrible cad."

"Nope. Sorry, Linda. Blood is thicker than water."

"Now, now boys. Gage was right. This is like a soap opera." Having finished her V-berth inspection, Sloan walked up behind Eric.

"Tom, what did you mean when you said, 'who says Sloan and I are dating?' If we're not dating, what would you call it?"

"You go, girl." My retort distracted the elder brother enough to allow me to squirm out of his grasp.

"We better get this boat inspection done." If I was not mistaken, Tom's gruff reply was accompanied by a touch of scarlet around his checks, though it was tough to see through his beard.

After another ten minutes of examining the boat, we had a private conference in the main salon.

"Linda, what do you think?" Eric asked from across the polished teak table.

"She looks good. Some cosmetic work is needed, but the rest seems sound."

"Tom?"

"The engine looks good. If we make an offer it should be subject to a sea trial."

"Right. Sloan?"

"There is enough room to install the Lokator and the other equipment. I say we go for it."

My husband made a brief call to Martin Sanderling. He agreed to purchase the yacht on our recommendation. We found the broker on deck.

"We're ready to make an offer," Eric said much to the broker's surprise. "The deal is subject to a sea trial. We'd like a response right away. Can we take her right out for a ride this afternoon?"

"Yes, sir. We'll go to my office to write the offer. Do you have a check with you?"

"Is a thousand dollars in cash sufficient? The new owner will wire the balance to your bank account."

"OK. It will only take a little time to complete the sales agreement."

We followed the man to his office to go through the formalities of bidding on the yacht. Per Martin's instructions, we didn't haggle too much. The yacht's owner agreed to our price.

Soon, we untied the dock lines. The broker backed the boat out of the slip, heading down the narrow channel to the Neuse River. The brown waters were relatively calm today with only a light chop out of the northwest.

"I assume you guys know how to sail?" The broker asked while Tom played with the GPS-chartplotter. He grunted in response.

"Yes," Eric said. Having unzipped the stack pack sail cover, he was sorting out the lines running back to the cockpit while I checked out the roller furling jib.

"I'll turn her into the wind, if you'll hoist the main. There's an electric winch right near the halyard." The broker steered the yacht head to wind. My husband wrapped the halyard around the winch. With a push of a button and a whirring sound, the mainsail slid up the mast.

"Want a hand with the jib, Li'l Sis?" Tom reached for the starboard jib sheet.

"Thanks, big brother."

"You have to let the blue rope out slowly," the broker said.

"Thanks so much, jerk," I said under my breath.

Tom laughed. "Easy, Li'l Sis. You can beat him up once the deal is complete."

After setting the sails, the salesman leaned back from the wheel, motioning to Eric or Tom to take it.

"Linda?" My husband nodded. Without a word, my right hand gripped the wheel, steering the yacht for the open water. We heeled slightly on a beam reach, quickly sliding across the river.

"We'll need to change course soon, because the water's shallow up ahead. Would you like me to take it?" the broker asked.

"Yeah, Garbacon Shoal. We'll be all right for a few more minutes. Guys, you want to get ready to tack?"

Tom and Eric sprang to the winches. The elder brother unwrapped, but held the leeward sheet while my husband wrapped the lazy one.

"Hard alee." The boat eased into the wind. Once she nosed across the wind, I spun the wheel farther.

The yacht responded nicely, cruising off on the new tack. The brothers did a great job handling the jib sheets, like we'd done this a million times before. The sloop dug in, then accelerated. The broker was agape at our smooth handling of the maneuver. We sailed the short distance back to the channel. I returned the wheel to the salesman. After stashing the sails, we motored back toward the dock.

About the same time, a small twenty-something-foot sailboat tacked back and forth across the channel in front of us. We tried, but had difficulty getting enough room to pass the small sloop. As soon as they tacked away, the broker throttled up to make our pass.

The small boat tacked again, heading straight for us. When they were ten feet away, the young male sailing instructor jumped into his cockpit. He wrestled the tiller away from his student. They tacked a mere five feet from our bow. Their starboard side nearly grazed the left side of our yacht.

The young man hollered. "Don't you know what the hell a sailboat is? We had right-of-way."

Tom casually strode on deck. "Yeah, but you should avoid a collision, among other things."

"We had right-of-way. I did avoid a collision. You should have gotten out of the way."

"Whatever," Tom said. The visibly upset broker remained silent.

"Stupid kid doesn't even know rules of the road. I bet he wouldn't have tried that if we had our big steel crab boat."

"Easy, Tom," Eric said. We returned to the dock with no further incident, to finish the deal on Martin's new yacht.

"The paperwork and financials will take a couple of days. You guys are sending a surveyor to check the bottom at the haul out tomorrow?"

Eric shook the broker's hand. "Yes. Once the survey is complete, we'd like to pick up the boat as soon as possible."

"I'll be in touch." After leaving the office, we strolled to the car.

"Why don't we get a bite to eat at the restaurant over there?" Tom asked.

"Great idea," Sloan agreed. On our way to the restaurant, we were stopped by a young, sun-bleached blond kid in his early twenties. His hand held a copy of the maritime rules of the road.

"Hey, you guys were on the sailboat that almost hit me. You see this?" He opened the book. "Sailboats have the right-of way." He pointed to the page emphatically.

"Son." Eric tried to place a calming hand on the agitated young man's shoulder. The kid shrugged it off. "Why don't we buy you a beer. We can discuss this calmly."

"Yeah, maybe you'll learn something," Tom said under his breath.

"There's nothing to discuss. You owe me and my class an apology."

"Son. There may be a couple of rules in play which you violated. Not to mention the fact, if there was a collision, someone might have been hurt. The Coast Guard would have yanked your license, not ours, because you had passengers on board."

As Tom started to speak, the kid cut him off.

"Listen, I altered course to avoid a collision. You should have stayed behind me."

"Hey kid," Tom said not able to keep his cool any longer. "What kind of license do you have, one from a gum ball machine?"

Red flashes blazed on the young man's cheeks. "I have a fifty tons captain's license, for your information. What the hell do you know about captain's licenses?" The kid puffed up his chest. He took an aggressive step toward Tom who outweighed him by at good fifty pounds.

Eric edged between them. "Son, I don't feel compelled to tell you this, but it may save you future problems. My brother and I both have 200 ton Master's licenses. Linda has a 100 ton Master's. As for Sloan, she's forgotten more lessons from the sea than you've learned. Why don't you have a beer with us, and discuss this?"

The kid squinted his eyes at Eric, studying his face. "Where do I know you from? No way. No way are you the guy from TV. The captain of *Denali*."

"No, actually Tom is the captain." Sloan giggled not able to resist teasing the fisherman.

"I'm so sorry. I didn't mean to almost hit you. Geez." The kid blubbered on.

"Son, let's get a beer." Eric took the young man's arm, leading him into the restaurant. After we were comfortable seated, with drinks in front of us, Eric spoke again.

"What's your name?"

"Steve."

"Steve. When we were coming up behind you, we were overtaking. Right?"

"Yes, sir."

"When you tacked away, you established a new course, right?"

"Yes, sir."

"When you tacked back toward us, you altered course."

"Yes, sir"

"You violated the rule which says the boat with right-of-way must maintain his course."

"Right, but I was under sail."

"Even though you are under sail, you must maintain your course and speed, so we can safely pass. You didn't do that. Also, a small sailboat can't force another boat outside a channel if the other boat has to remain inside, because of the depth."

"If I stayed on starboard tack, we would have run aground."

"Better to run aground, then risk a collision. It looked like you had ample room to make a short tack, followed by another quick tack, giving us plenty of time to get beyond you, with no yelling." Eric allowed the kid time to think about it. My husband threw Tom a stern look.

"Darn, maybe you are right." The young man stood, extending his hand tentatively to Eric. "I gotta go clean up the boat." My husband shook his hand.

"Sorry." He muttered under his breath as he walked away.

"Eric, you really handle the situation well. You taught the young man something without making him look stupid."

"Yes he did, Sloan," Tom said. "I sure as heck wouldn't have wanted to be that kid if he argued with my brother much more. Eric has a long fuse, but when it blows, look out."

Chapter 14. West Palm Beach

We waited several days for the new boat to be surveyed. Martin purchased the yacht the following day. Finally, our foursome was back in Oriental, prepping the sailboat for the day trip down the Intracoastal to Beaufort.

"Linda, can I hand down this water?"

"Sure, Tom."

"Are we ready to shove off?" Eric stood by to fire up the engine.

"Yes, let's go." Martin Sanderling joined us for this motoring session down the narrow channels to the coast. A couple of days would be spent in Beaufort, provisioning and adding safety equipment, such as a life raft before leaving for Florida.

My husband backed the yacht out of the slip, steering us down the narrow channel to the Neuse River. It was flat calm this morning. There was little wind ruffling the brown, muddy surface of the broad water before us. Luck was with us as the weather conditions were unusually fair. The Neuse was notorious for treacherous conditions.

I made the crossing in the past, with the wind howling out of the northeast, kicking up fierce waves in the twenty-something-foot depths. Hours were spent, banging into the short, nasty chop. Every nerve in the crew was jarred. This foul weather was often accompanied by a wet, miserable chill.

During other trips, the mighty Neuse greeted me with wicked thunderstorms and waterspouts. The river was only a few miles wide, giving you little sea room to dodge the fluid twisters. You never knew what was lurking in this very dynamic area of the Outer Banks.

Today we were in luck, with sunny and warm conditions. Our new boat motored quietly toward Adams Creek, with the boss at the helm. Thank goodness his wife, the wicked witch, wasn't here to spoil things. Sloan and Tom lounged on the foredeck, soaking up rays. Eric was seated to Martin's left, carefully watching the chart plotter in the cockpit aft of the pilothouse. We dodged around a multitude of sandbars, dotting the edges of the channel.

"This is a very pretty area," Martin said as we puttered into Adams Creek.

"Yes, I love the houses along this section. When we get to Core Creek, the dwellings are painted all sorts of bright colors, like they are trying to re-create either Bermuda or the Bahamas." My concentration focused on the channel markers in front of us.

"See those two fixed markers up ahead, Martin? The black and white ones? They are range markers."

"What do I do with them?"

"You want to line up the lower, front marker with the taller one in back. Steer the boat to make the black lines align. See how the lower marker is off to the right? We are off course to the left. If you turn the boat to starboard a few degrees, the markers will line up. When the Army Corp of Engineers deepens the waterway, the dredge follows the range markers, not the buoys."

"I see." Martin corrected our course a few degrees to the right, soon aligning the signs. "These range markers are a clever system."

The rest of the trip, along the winding waterway, was uneventful. Near the end of Core Creek, we were visited by dolphins.

They frolicked in the muddy waters. Sloan leapt up in an instant, hovering over the bow pulpit while encouraging the mammals' play. She always seemed ready to jump into the water with these aquatic acrobats. They reacted to her by squealing and jumping with delight.

Once we were secured to the dock at the Beaufort waterfront, we rinsed down the yacht. The water tanks were filled. The air conditioning cooled the crew off as we relaxed for a few moments. Eric divvied up the remaining tasks on his list.

"Linda, why don't Tom and I tackle the engine stuff? We need to change the oil and the filters in both the engine and the transmission. Do you and Sloan want to go to the store?"

"Sloan, would you prefer to help the boys with the dirty old engine stuff or go shopping? There's a great boutique up the waterfront with cute swim suits in the window."

"Hey, that's not what Eric was talking about. You two need to go to the grocery store to get provisions for the trip," Tom said gruffly.

Sloan wrapped her arms around his neck from behind. "We know, my captain. Linda was just kidding you. She got you again." The researcher planted a kiss in front of the startled captain's ear. This was her first public show of affection. The tough guy fisherman was none too pleased by it.

"Whatever. Hey, knock that off." After pushing his girlfriend away, Tom stared at me. "You didn't learn your lesson the other day, when we were checking out the new sailboat, did you, Li'l Sis?"

Instead of behaving myself, I couldn't help but tease the rugged fisherman. When he looked away in disgust, my arms slipped around his neck, exactly where Sloan's were a moment ago.

"Sorry, big brother. I didn't mean to upset you." My coquettish voice aroused a groan of displeasure from the crab man.

Roughly, but playfully, he pushed me away. "Get away from me, women, I'm trying to work. Geez, Eric if they keep this up, it's going to be one hell of a long sail to West Palm."

"Yeah, but it could be great fun, too."

Sloan and I jumped off the boat. We went to the dock master's office before getting into any more trouble. The old, beat-up station wagon was the courtesy car for the marina. It bounced and jounced its way down Live Oak Street. The radio blasted.

"Linda, we are like a couple of teenagers getting ready for a date."

"More like a couple of middle-aged Thelma and Louises."

After finding a parking spot, we went inside the grocery store. Our cart soon brimmed with good, healthy food. That was one other aspect of Tom's lady I had recently discovered. She had very little tolerance for junk food, except for the occasional Corona. With groceries bags bulging, we made our way back to the marina. All the guys, including Gage, helped us lug food aboard.

The former Navy SEAL hefted a few bags over the lifelines."Wow, look at all this yummy stuff you ladies bought. Bean sprouts, apples, salad...where the heck are the steaks?"

"They're in there, Mr. Carnivore. Don't worry."

"Good, because I need my guys tough and well fed when they get to port."

"What about us ladies?"

"Linda, there's no doubt you can take care of yourself. Have a safe trip, OK?"

"You guys, too. We'll wave when you pass by."

"We won't be leaving for a couple days. This will give me time to keep Carlos under surveillance, making sure he doesn't find out about the sailboat. We don't want him following it or...."

"Or what, Gage?"

"Don't worry about it. We'll keep an eye on him. Eric has a new satellite phone Martin bought for your boat. Make sure you keep in contact with us."

After loading the groceries, our crew made one final check around the sailing yacht before heading over to the *Diana* for a farewell supper. The entire crew gathered around the large dining table, including the wicked witch.

As dinner was served, our boss raised his glass of wine. "Here's to my new sailing yacht and her crew. May they have a safe voyage down to Florida."

We clinked glasses, enjoying our last scrumptious meal while seated at a table which didn't bounce around. After dinner, our crew partook in only a couple of drinks before retiring to the sailboat. Tomorrow would be a busy day.

As we climbed into the V-berth for much needed sleep, my guy's cell phone rang.

"Eric, it's Carlos. I'm sorry we haven't had a chance to chat the past few days. I've been very busy making plans to pay you a little visit."

"Carlos, what the hell do you want?"

"Eric, you are always so impatient. You need to be taught patience and civility. It has come to my attention you too have been very busy, with a new sailboat, no? You and the Navy SEAL think you can defeat me. I need to send you a message showing you how far reaching my grasp is. A little revenge, no? A reminder of who you are dealing with."

The phone went dead. Eric exhaled. Our eyes met.

"Honey, you should call Gage."

With a shake of his head, he placed the call. Afterward, my husband recalled the conversation for our two shipmates.

"Gage wanted to come along on the sailboat, but I told him we'd be fine." Eric looked very tired as he explained the call to Tom and Sloan, who curled up on the port settee.

"The Coast Guard will be tracking us. They will fly helicopters over us, daily. Mitch said they are always looking for things to do on training missions. Also, Jake is going to fly over us a couple of times a day. They discussed an idea to have the mega-yacht shadow us much more closely than originally planned."

"How the heck did Carlos find out about the sail-boat?"

"I don't know, Tom." Eric left it at that. His look told me the conversation was over.

One long night ensued. We both tossed and turned uneasily. Sometime, during the wee hours of the morning, my mind finally relaxed enough to ease into sleep.

Drifting, drifting, drifting. The water's cooling embrace felt great. Long ocean swells lifted my body up and down, rhythmically, like a wonderful massage. The sun was rising with a burning red glow in the east. What's the old saying, "red sky in the morning, sailors take warning?" A dreadful, uneasy feeling infused my senses. I was alone. Adrift in the ocean.

Spinning in a frantic, 360 degree turn, I searched for the boat. Directly behind me, afloat with the tide, was a boat. Not the boat I was look-ing for. Looming a mere fifty yards away was Carlos' rusty shrimp boat. Standing on the stern was none other than the dirty drug dealer himself. His face twisted in a nasty sneer.

"Linda, the ocean has brought you back to me." His echoing cackle made my skin crawl. The swift ocean current pulled me closer. Closer. My arms lashed out. Swim. Swim. Swim. Oxygen rushed in and out of my lungs in short gasps.

A shadow flicked by. Was there something in the water? I hesitated. My eyes strained. A huge fin erupted. The current dragged me. Closer, closer toward the rusty hulk. A double dose of fear paralyzed me. I was dragged to a spot a few feet from the transom. Carlos stepped onto the swim platform. A bullwhip. The leather wrapped tightly around my wrist. No! He dragged me closer...."

"No!" My body jerked me awake. Only partially conscious, I tried to sit up. Bang! My head smashed into the headliner.

"Linda." Eric grabbed me. Since I was not fully awake, my hands lashed out at him. A light came on. He tried to deflect my blows. The door to the V-berth thumped open.

Tom rushed in. "What the hell happened?" The big fisherman's fists were balled.

"Nightmare." Eric pulled me against him. My breathing took a few seconds to return to normal. "She' OK. Go back to bed."

"Damn. I didn't think she was still having nightmares."

"It's been a long time." The squeaky voice, filling my ears, didn't sound like mine. "Sorry, Tom."

The elder brother put his hand on my quaking shoulder. "It's OK, Li'l Sis. I'm glad it wasn't what I thought it was." He closed the door behind him.

"You want to talk about it?" Eric frowned.

"Not now. Maybe in the morning. I'm sorry I woke you."

The next morning dawned quickly. Eric was curled up, sound asleep. My ribs twinged when climbing out of the V-berth. The same ribs injured the night the fishermen dragged me from the sea after *Wind Rose* sank. Strange. They hadn't bothered me in a long time.

In the main cabin, Sloan sipped coffee. The wonderful aroma swirled around the salon. With cup in hand, I took a seat near the researcher. She watched me for a few minutes before speaking. "Linda, you look tired this morning."

"It was a long night. I'm not sure either of us slept much. Did we keep you awake?"

"No, I slept well. Tom told me you had a bad nightmare."

"Sloan, I can't wait to get offshore. It's the only place I ever feel safe, except when we're at the ranch."

A short while later the guys joined us. The boat became a flurry of activity. Dock lines were cast off. Eric motored the yacht toward the open sea while the rest of the crew rechecked the security of the gear. Tom and I rigged jack lines. These strong webbing lines, strung between the bow and stern, provided a safe point of attachment for our safety harnesses, during rough weather.

After clearing Beaufort Inlet, my husband steered us in the direction of Charleston, SC. This course led us outside the dangerous shoals off Cape Fear, inside the strong current of the Gulf Stream, flowing against our vessel. The wind was a brisk fifteen knots out of the northwest. The breeze filled in behind an end of spring cold front.

Eric set the autopilot. "You want a reef in the main?"

"OK, though this boat should be able to handle the wind." My hubby and I made a team effort out of hoisting the large aft sail.

With the main trimmed, the motor was doused. Tom and Sloan rolled out the jib and the staysail. The new yacht dug in as her white sails filled the clear, blue sky. We cruised at a comfortable six knots in the light chop.

The land slowly faded from view. An look over my shoulder ensured there was no rusting shrimp boat stalking us. Eric saw my glance off the stern.

He shook his head. "There's no one behind us. Relax. You know the old sailor's superstition...it's bad luck to look back at port once you've left."

"I never heard that before."

"Looking back to port implies you are not truly ready to brave the seas."

"It's not the seas I was worried about."

"I know. Don't worry about Carlos. Gage will keep an eye on him."

"I hope so." Our eyes locked. Would this nightmare ever be over?

Tom and Sloan perched on the bow, their legs hanging over the side. The greenish-blue water on the Stream's edge spritzed them. They looked like two kids riding a roller coaster. The bow rose on the face of the next wave, then slid off the back, dipping the twosome close to the bubbling foam. The next wave yanked them skyward. Bubbles tickled the bottom of their feet.

Sloan raised her face toward the warm sun, giggling like a young girl. Tom's serious demeanor relaxed under the scientist's playful influence. His hoarse laughter drifted back to the cockpit now and again.

"Those two are having fun, Eric."

"Yes. Sloan is good for Tom. He tends to get too serious about things. If she wasn't here, he'd be in the cockpit checking our course or going through the engine. It's nice to see him relax."

The four of us quickly adjusted to the shipboard routine. We decided to split watches into three hour shifts, with Tom and Sloan keeping night watch together. This allowed Eric and I six hours off at night. The schedule was a luxury compared to the four hour on, four hour off watches during past trips with Joey.

Our new yacht soared across Onslow Bay, heeling slightly, bouncing in the small waves. The afternoon flew by. There was a poker game in the main salon. The winner would have no afternoon chores. The losers had to cook dinner and clean up.

The game came down to the final hand. Sloan and I were out of chips, so we handed in our cards. Eric and Tom were involved in a serious brotherly duel. The boys acted like a million dollars was riding on this victory. Each brother tried to out bluff the other.

"Little bro, the time has come for your defeat. Why not give up now and admit I am one hell of a great poker player?"

"Maybe you're right…. Let me ask you this. Is it good for all the cards to be the same color?"

"Yeah, but all the suits must be the same. Do you have to be taught how to play before I whip your butt?"

"Just shut up and make a bid, old man."

Tom folded his cards into a small stack, setting them face down on the table. He entwined his two fists together, allowing his eyes to peer over the knuckles. His younger brother grinned back at him.

The wily older fishing captain pushed his chips to the center of the table. "I'm all in."

The tension in the cabin was palpable. Sloan sat in the companionway, keeping watch. She had a great view of their hands from her spot high up in the cabin. Eric glanced at her, but the researcher managed a good poker face. My husband turned his attention back to his elder brother with a cold stare.

"What have you got?" Eric pushed an equal number of chips into the big pile.

Tom slammed his cards on the table.

"*Ha*, I never thought a pair of red deuces would beat you." Eric leapt up with delight, slapping his brother on the back. Tom had nothing.

"Thought you could bluff your little brother? *Ha!*"

"Knock off the gloating before I beat your ass." Tom looked at Sloan. "What the hell are you smiling about?"

"Nothing." The lady attempted to stifle her grin. "Tom, does this mean you are cooking dinner?"

"What?" The tough fisherman strode for the pilothouse. "Cook dinner? That's woman's work. I don't even cook dinner on the crab boat."

"Maybe we should ask the captain." Eric looked to me.

"Watch it, Li'l Sis." Tom glanced in my direction. The temptation to bust the elder brother's chops once again was nearly overwhelming.

I decided to play it safe. "I'll cook dinner if Tom helps Sloan clean up."

Days slipped into nights as we cruised easily down the coast with no harassment from Carlos. The weather stayed favorable, with only an occasional rain squall passing by.

On the morning of our fourth day at sea, we made visual contact with the *Diana*. For the past two nights, we spied the glow of her running lights, off to our east. It was a comforting gleam on the horizon.

We were adjacent to St Augustine, motor sailing in a light southwesterly wind. At this rate, we should be in West Palm Beach the following morning. Eric checked in with Gage on the satellite phone, with the speaker engaged.

"Hi, Eric. How's it going?"

"Great. Everyone is fine and happy."

"Excellent. About an hour ago, I received a call from Daniel at the ranch. He said it was no emergency, but to call as soon as you can."

"Thanks, Gage." Eric pressed the end button. A moment later, my husband dialed his horse trainer's cell phone. Once again, he engaged the speaker phone.

"Hello, Eric. I was waiting for your call."

"Hi, Daniel. Gage said you called."

"Yes, sir. I've been over at Jeb's ranch most of the past week and a half. Don't worry, I got all my chores done here, too." My husband smiled without comment. There was never any doubt Daniel would get his work done, even if he had to work all night.

"I've been working with Ace. Boy, is he the spitting image of Blackjack, ornery and headstrong. Gee, he can run a blue streak. Jeb thinks it's time for him to come to your ranch. He's pretty much weaned from his mom."

"Excellent news, Daniel. Thanks for all the extra time you've put in with him."

"He's an awesome horse, Eric. I've loved every minute of it. Is it OK for me to go to pick him up with your horse trailer?"

"Daniel, we are offshore, delivering the new sailboat to West Palm Beach. Let me check with our boss to see if he can spare us for a few days. The three of us can pick up Ace together."

"OK, Eric." There was a twinge of disappointed in the young man's voice. Did he want the baby horse in his domain sooner?

"Son, keep up the good work. We'll call you in a day or so."

My husband turned to me after disconnecting the phone call. "That young man is busting to get his hands on our new horse."

"It's so nice to hear joy in his voice. He's been so down since the Derby."

A shout was heard from on deck. Eric and I sprinted up the companionway steps. Surrounding us, was a huge pod of spotted dolphins.

"Let's stop the boat. We can jump in to swim with these guys."

Concern creased Tom's face. "Sloan, do you think it's safe getting in the water with all these wild animals?"

"Absolutely. What do you think, Linda?"

Fear cramped my gut. There was no fear of the dolphins, but my mind flashed back to the night *Wind Rose* sank. I'll never forget the terror as the sailboat drifted away from me. Damn, this thing could not control me forever.

"Tom, would you drop the main please?"

Sloan dashed below for her mask and fins. After rolling up the jib, I lowered the swim ladder. Eric tossed in the life sling.

"Are you sure you want to go through with this? It's a pretty big step."

"Yeah. It will be good for me. Do me a favor, though, keep an eye our for sharks."

The lady scientist was over the side in an instant. I sat on the cabin top, slowly slipping my fins on. Tom was at the bow watching the spectacle.

The mammals paused as they swam by, curling their bodies toward the drifting researcher. She kicked her fins, gliding along with the yacht. After my giant stride entry into the clear, blue water of the Gulf Stream, my mask filled with the gray smiling face of a passing dolphin.

Capt. Marlena Brackebusch

All around me was a wonderland. I always wanted to jump in with a huge family of marine mammals, but was never brave enough. As the boat drifted away, there was no time for fear. Completely surrounding me was a whirling, circling mass of adorable, spotted cetaceans all very curious to see the creatures who invaded their paradise.

They darted toward us, stopping inches away. Squeaks and squeals resonated as they communicated in a language we knew nothing about. When they directed their echolocation at us, it felt like an electric buzz in the water.

"Having fun, Linda?" Sloan asked after surfacing, her face aglow with delight.

"This is an amazing experience. It is helping me get over my fear of the water."

The sea around us boiled with one dolphin wave after another. Unfortunately, no slow moving objects kept their attention for long. The last stragglers cruised over to gawk at us. With a flick of their tails, they disappeared.

"Sloan, let's get back on board." A few quick strokes took us to the waiting boat. The hot transom shower felt great.

"The wind is light. I'll start the motor." Eric fired up the engine. "By the way, Gage called while you were swimming. He wasn't too pleased to stop the boat for a dolphin encounter."

"He'll get over it," Sloan said glibly.

The remainder of the trip to West Palm was uneventful. We arrived the following afternoon. After cleaning up the boat, we joined the crew of the *Diana* for dinner.

Seated at a large table in the chic restaurant our team chatted over cocktails. We enjoyed a great meal on a stationary table. During a lull in the conversation, Eric leaned toward our boss. "Martin, I have a favor to ask you."

"What can I do for you?"

"I've told you about my new foal who was born at a friend's place. He is weaned from his mom and ready to be transported back to our ranch. Would you mind if Linda and I take a few days off to make sure he settles in?"

Diana leaned toward her husband, listening intently to Eric. "Horses are such lovely creatures, not that I would ever get near one. They are too smelly. Everyone knows they bite and kick, but they are pretty to look at. Darling, why don't we buy the little horse from Eric? If he is any good at running, we can dabble in thoroughbred racing. It's quite fashionable you know." She stared down her nose at me.

Eric mustered up a most charming smile. "I'm sorry Mrs. Sanderling, but Ace is not for sale. You are always welcome to join us at the track, once he is old enough to start racing."

"Eric, everything is for sale." Our boss' wife gave my husband a cold stare. "We simple need to discover what your price is."

Martin tried to distract his wife. "My Kitten, maybe it would be better to wait until we see if Eric's horse has any racing ability."

"*Hmm.*" Rebuffed, she turned her attention to Joey. The wicked witch immediately began gabbing with my ex.

Martin leaned toward us. "Go ahead and take a few days off. We aren't scheduled to start tactical training until next Monday. I'll call my pilot to fly you to Dallas."

"You're very generous, Martin. Thank you very much, but we can fly commercial."

"Nonsense. The plane is just sitting around. Take my jet."

The next morning, the boss' jet whisked us away to DFW airport. Ricardo picked us up. During the ride back, he filled my husband in on all the ranch business.

Back at the house, we took a few moments to unpack before heading down to the barn to check on the horses. They were such amazing animals. Whenever I was in a bad mood, they lifted my spirits.

As we entered the barn, Sonny poked his head out of the stall, whinnying with delight. He leaned his golden head, flecked with gray, over the gate. Fuzzy lips searched for the carrot always hidden in the pocket of my jeans.

During the early stages of my recovery from the sinking trauma, nightmares plagued me. A combination of exhaustion and anxiety were often soothed by spending quality time stroking Sonny's head or combing out his mane. As much as he enjoyed the attention, my debt to him for his calm acceptance would be difficult to repay.

The moment we entered the barn, all the horses reacted to Eric's presence. He took his time, checking the steeds, giving each one a reassuring pat on the neck. Daniel poked his head out of the tack room. His eyes lit up when he saw us.

"Eric and Linda, welcome home." The young man strode over to shake his boss' hand. After a brief hug, I was glad to see the old sparkle in his eyes.

"I was cleaning some tack. All the horses are fine."

"So I see, Daniel. How's everything with you? I'm surprised to see you here. After our phone conversation, we expected to arrive home to find you working for Jeb now."

"No, sir." Daniel looked perplexed. "I would never leave this job."

"I'm only kidding you, son. You've spent so much time over there, lately, I thought Jeb lured you away."

"No, sir. There were a whole bunch of things to do with your new foal."

"I know, I know. What's the news with Ace?"

"He's awesome, Eric. The little guy runs like the wind and has his father's spirit."

"I'll call Jeb to arrange his pickup. We'll allow a few days to let Ace settle in before you continue his training. Which stall will you put him in?"

Daniel seemed nervous with this question. This was a big decision for the horse trainer. My husband relied on the young man to take more responsibility around the ranch. He stared at Eric for a moment, shifting his weight back and forth, from one foot to the other.

"If it's OK with you, I'd like to put him next to Daisy. Being Blackjack's mom and all, well she's still pretty down, since, well, you know. It may cheer her up having a new foal around."

"Excellent idea. Linda and I will be at the house if you need us."

"Yes, sir. *Um*, Mr. Eric? I mean Eric? Could I ask you a big favor?"

"Sure, Daniel, what is it?"

"*Um*, well I *um*, am going to spend a whole bunch of time here in the next week or two with Ace." Daniel hesitated, his old shyness coming through. He looked to me awkwardly.

"What is it, Daniel?"

The young man's cheeks flushed. "Well, sir. I'm supposed to take Tina out to dinner tonight."

"Good idea, son. You probably need a break."

"Well, no, sir. I mean yes, sir."

"How is Tina?"

"She's doing fine, ma'am, thanks for asking." His face darkened a couple of shades of red. "Anyway, well maybe, if it's OK with you, could I leave a little early, so there's time to get...cleaned up?"

Eric did a wonderful job suppressing a grin. "Why don't you go home now? Everything looks under control."

"Oh no, sir. I'd never leave this early. The horses still need to be fed."

"Daniel, go," my husband insisted. "Linda and I will feed them."

The young man looked to both of us shyly. "Thank you, sir." He hurried from the barn.

"He's such a great kid. Let's head up to the house. We can feed the horses later on," Eric said with a grin.

The next morning, the ranch was a flurry of activity. My husband was on the phone last night with Jeb, arranging to pick up Ace mid-morning. Daniel and Ricardo were up early, prepping the horse trailer. Eric backed up his big green pickup to the trailer hitch. When everything was hooked up, we drove to the southwest part of Dallas.

Daniel rode up front with Eric, while I reclined in the back seat, enjoying the scenery.

"Should I ride in the trailer with Ace on the way back?"

Eric chuckled. "Daniel, I don't think it's necessary. We'll adjust the stalls so he can't hurt himself." The young man sighed like a worried father, bringing home his newborn son.

We arrived at Jeb's ranch. Eric spent a few moments in the paddock with Ace and his mom before trying to separate them. Both horses sensed something was going on. Every time Eric tried to grab Ace's halter, the young horse trotted around the other side of his mom. The mother's confidence was gained by talking to her. The cowboy gently ran his hand down her neck.

Ace responded to him. The foal came over, allowing my husband to put a lead on his halter. Mother and son were coaxed to the gate.

The little horse reared up when Eric tried to guide him out of the pasture. It only took a moment for the new horse to calm down enough to be led into the trailer. Daniel spent a few extra minutes getting the young foal settled before we drove back to our ranch.

During the next couple of days, we watched the new foal sprint around the pasture while getting to know the other horses. It was no surprise he spent most of his time with Daisy and my favorite old boy, Sonny. As the senior horse at the ranch, the golden palomino was a gentle, calming influence on the boisterous new addition to the herd.

Later in the evening, we relaxed in front of the fire. Eric's phone rang. He frowned when looking at the Caller ID.

"Hello?"

"Eric." The unmistakable voice of Carlos hissed from the phone. "Did you remember my promise to you? A show of revenge, no. Keep your loved ones close. The time is very near."

The line went dead.

"Shit." Eric looked at me with a mixture of anger and agitation. "Thank goodness he doesn't know we are here. In case he finds out, you make sure you stay close to me."

My husband walked to his gun cabinet. He pulled out two holsters with a couple of handguns. "I'm not going to wait for Gage's tactical class. Tomorrow morning, we will practice shooting. You are to wear a holster and keep this gun with you at all times."

"Eric."

"Linda, the threat he made was his most serious one to date. I'm not taking any chances."

After going to bed, we tossed and turned. The minutes ticked by like hours. A glance at the clock on the nightstand showed three A.M.

The front door to the house banged open, followed by the frightened holler of Daniel. "Eric."

"What's the matter?" My cowboy's feet almost caught in his jeans as he pulled them on, dashing into the hallway. After struggling into clothes, my hand closed around the gun at my bedside.

"It's Ace. Something's really wrong with him."

The three of us tore out of the house, running hard to the barn. We slipped on the wet grass. Eric yanked open the heavy barn door. We rushed into the foal's stall. He lay motionless in the hay. The cowboy stooped over him.

"He's breathing. Linda, give me your cell phone." Eric made two phone calls, one to Ricardo and the other one to our vet.

"The vet will be here in a few minutes. What happened?"

Daniel shook so hard he could barely speak. "Mr. Eric. I was at home and couldn't sleep. I kept thinking about Ace. Something didn't feel right."

A couple of tears escaped from his eyes.

"Daniel, tell me what happened."

"I got in my truck and drove over here. I thought I saw something outside the barn. When I rushed in here, Ace collapsed on the ground, like he passed out or something."

Eric eyes rose to meet mine. My cowboy noticed the gun clutched in my hands.

"Give me the gun, Linda. Both of you stay here." He strode out the back side of the barn. A moment later, Ricardo came in the front, carrying a rifle. He handed the gun to me, before leaning over Ace.

"We should cover him with a blanket." The few minutes it took the vet to arrive seemed like an eternity. The doc rushed in the front door of the barn just as Eric returned from the back.

"Ricardo, keep watch outside." All eyes were on the small foal, who was still unconscious. The vet checked him over while listening to our story.

"This is really strange. His pulse is very rapid and his breathing shallow. See how the coat is covered with sweat?" Our little horse started twitching. Spasms overtook his body. The vet struggled to hold his airway open. The convulsions subsided a moment later. Our small horse lay very still.

"Eric, he may have been poisoned. I want to check his blood sugar."

The vet pulled out a small needle with a little machine. He pricked our horse's skin. A drop of blood was collected on the strip attached to the meter.

"His blood sugar is extremely low. It looks like hypoglycemia is causing the unconsciousness. I'm going to give him intravenous glucose." The vet started an intravenous line. It took a few minutes for our baby horse to stir. His eyes blinked open.

"Is he all right?" Daniel's voice cracked. He squatted next to the weakened foal, gently stroking his neck.

"He's coming out of it. The question is how did this happen? Did he eat his dinner?"

"Oh yes, sir. He ate all of his grain. I even gave him an apple." Daniel looked fearfully at Eric.

"Son, you didn't do anything wrong. We need to figure out how this happened so it doesn't happen again." Eric placed his hand on the younger man's shoulder.

The vet stood up. "There's only two ways the blood sugar would have plummeted quickly enough to drop a horse so fast. One possibility is Ace is an extremely sick horse, suffering from an infection or disease." When the vet said this, Daniel turned away.

The young man slammed his fist against the barn wall. "He's not sick. He can't be."

"Daniel, let the man speak. Take it easy." My husband turned his attention back to the vet. "What would the other cause be?"

"I agree Ace is not sick from disease or infection. I examined him myself only two days ago. He was fine. I know it's hard to believe, but I think someone injected him with insulin, a very high dose. A fast shot of insulin, in an extreme case, would kill a horse. Also, it leaves no trace."

"Carlos."

Eric gritted his teeth. "Son of a bitch."

"I saw someone coming out of the barn. The shadow. It did look like a man."

"If Daniel startled the intruder, he may have dropped the syringe. Let's look around." The four of us fanned out around the barn. Daisy seemed highly agitated. She pawed at the ground with her hoof.

"Eric, look at Daisy." My husband entered the stall. He attempted to calm Blackjack's mom. We sifted through the hay behind her. My cowboy bent down to pick something up. He exited the stall, carrying a small hypodermic needle.

"That's an insulin syringe. We need to call the police."

"Not yet. I can get it analyzed much quicker. Paul, please keep this quiet for now."

"Eric, you need to watch Ace closely for a couple of days."

"He's going to be OK?"

"Thanks to your quick work, Daniel, we were able to give him the glucose in time. Your horse should be fine."

Chapter 15. The Florida Everglades and Paradise

After removing the intravenous line, the vet bid us goodbye.

"I'll come by to check on Ace later. Get him up in a couple of hours. Make sure he eats a good breakfast and drinks lots of water."

"Thanks, Paul. Ricardo, you and Daniel stay here. Call me if you see anything suspicious." After walking back to the ranch house, Eric and I plopped on the couch. We were exhausted after the night's tribulations. Despite the early hour of the morning, my husband called Gage to update him on the near disaster.

"Eric, I will call you right back with an address to send the syringe to. Jake and Rick will be on the next plane to the ranch. They will gather a couple of friends to keep an eye on the place. You and Linda need to come back here."

"We'll be back as soon as the security is in place."

By early afternoon, our two military friends arrived. A couple of hours later, several more men filed into our house carrying black leather bags. It was pretty obvious what those bags contained.

Jake met with our new security crew in the living room. "Here's the situation. The perimeter security is in place. One of you will be stationed in the barn at all times. A repeat attack on Eric's horse is doubtful, but we should make sure he is safe."

Daniel sat on a chair, over by the window. He raised his hand tentatively as if he were in school.

My husband acknowledged him. "Yes, son."

"Eric, since all this security is in place, I would like to go with you to get the bastard who hurt Ace."

We were shocked at this statement since the young horse trainer never cussed. His face was a mixture of determination and hatred.

"Daniel, you are needed here to supervise the care of the horses." The young man's face shifted to a look of frustration, though he remained silent.

"If there are no other questions, we need to get back to Florida. Are you guys ready?" Jake asked us.

"Let's go get the bastard."

Back in West Palm Beach, we were seated in the wheelhouse of the *Diana*, along with Gage, Tom, and Sloan.

The former Navy SEAL spoke first. "We need to figure out how Carlos found out about your trip to Texas."

My husband gave Gage a warning glance, nodding toward Tom and Sloan.

"Eric, I already brought them up to speed on our informant."

"Yeah, you would think you could trust your brother," Tom said.

The Navy SEAL ignored him, refocusing his attention on my husband. "Eric, who did you tell about the trip?"

"Only Martin and Ricardo. Of course, the pilot knew where he was flying us to."

"The pilot is not a suspect. Linda, did you tell anyone?"

"No. You know, Gage, I've been thinking about the night at the restaurant. Do you remember what Diana, the wicked witch, said?"

"She wanted to buy Ace."

"Yes and guess who else was within range of the conversation?"

"Joey?" Gage asked. "His involvement with Carlos doesn't make sense."

"What about Diana?" Tom asked.

Gage sighed, looking at all of us in turn. "Diana's involvement doesn't make sense. Why would a bubble-headed woman, who has everything she wants, turn against her husband? Damn, he dotes on her every time I see them together." The tall man turned for the door. "I'll call my contacts at the FBI to have her vetted, but my bet is, someone else is squealing to Carlos."

The next morning, we were up early, loading our gear into two minivans. Gage took the lead, while Tom piloted the second vehicle. We cruised down I-95. Our caravan turned west on the Dolphin expressway through Miami to the Florida Turnpike.

After exiting at Homestead, our car bumped along a winding back road through the southern Everglades. Swamp after boggy swamp passed by our windows. We came to a stop at a tall fence topped with barbed wire. Inside the fence, Hammer stood by his Humvee.

"It's about time you got your butts down here. I'll open the gate once the electricity is turned off." Elton spoke into a radio. When the gate slid open, the ex-Navy SEAL motioned us inside.

"Welcome to hell." He laughed, while leaning into our minivan. "Follow me."

The guys followed the Humvee down a rutted dirt road to a building sprouting from a clearing in the jungle. The structure was dark green with a sheet metal roof. We climbed out of the car into a humid Florida spring day.

"This building is one of three back here." Elton motioned to the edifice behind him. "The colors camouflage it well from the air. We have a helo pad in the back. This building houses the offices and the classrooms."

"The one in back is the barracks, where all of you will sleep at night, assuming you get any sleep. This encampment is surrounded by an electric fence, so no one can get in...or out." He laughed an eerie laugh.

"Why don't I take all of you to your rooms? After y'all are settled, we can meet in the rec room to discuss our training schedule." We hopped back into the minivans to cruise the short distance to an identical building directly behind the first one. My hubby hoisted our bags through the heavy steel door into a large central room.

"This place used to be an immigration detention center, back when all the Cubans were escaping Castro on anything that floated. When I bought the place it was a real mess. It doesn't take long for mother nature to reclaim anything down here in this swamp." We turned down the right hand hallway, stopping in front of room number five.

Elton motioned to us. "Eric and Linda, why don't you take this one?"

We entered the sparsely decorated room. A queen-sized bed, covered with crisp white sheets topped by a green army blanket, dominated the room's center. The walls were cinder block painted an olive hue. A large, drab utility closet sat next to a desk and chair.

"Well it's not luxury, but it should suffice." There was uncertainty in Eric's eyes. After hanging our clothes, we strolled down the hallway to find the group gathered in a big room furnished with a couple of couches. The left wall was covered by a bookcase chock full of books. A muted television had images flashing across it.

The walls in this room were bare cement painted bright white. A couple of photos of army warriors, patrolling thick jungle in remote parts of the world, was the only artwork. Elton stood near one of the couches, talking with Gage. "Have a seat you two. We'll chat about our skills, before discussing our training. Who hasn't shot a gun before?"

Sloan tentatively raised her hand.

"OK, you will be my star pupil. In past training sessions, I've found the best shots are women with no prior gun experience. At least, I don't have to fix all your bad shooting habits.

"Here's the deal. My job is to get you all in fighting shape. No matter what situation these bad guys throw at you, you'll be able to react to defeat them. Every morning, we will do physical training on the ropes course. This will tone up your sissy bodies.

"Next, we'll go to the classroom building for breakfast. Classwork will be followed by a couple of hours of shooting practice. After lunch, we'll work on tactical strategies and teamwork. You need to know exactly what the other will do given a situation you are likely to encounter. We'll even practice hand to hand combat training. Any questions?"

No one said a word.

"I'll go easy on you today. Y'all can take a couple of hours off. Enjoy the pool out back. One thing though, no one goes on the shooting ranges without an instructor. I'll see you at dinner." Eric and I spent the afternoon looking around the grounds. The swimming pool lured us into a quick dip.

"Eric, doesn't this place strike you as kind of spooky, like a military base or something?"

"Yes. I get the feeling this guy, Elton, is all business. It should be an interesting week."

The following morning we were up at dawn. Our uniforms consisted of drab olive T-shirts with long green pants, like army pants, with lots of pockets. These were issued to us yesterday afternoon. We assembled at the ropes course.

"Let's see how tough these Bering Sea captains are. Gage, do you want to show them how it's done?"

"You've got it, Hammer." The Navy SEAL loped toward the first rope which was hung vertically off a metal structure ten feet of the ground. The thick rope had a series of knots in it. Gage jumped up, grabbed the rope, then pulled himself up to the horizontal bar. He paused, looking to Elton.

"Give me ten, I feel generous today." The tall man easily did ten pull ups before climbing back down the rope.

"Eric." My husband glanced at me before imitating the former Navy SEAL's jump onto the rope. He struggled, but managed to reach the top. After five pull ups, he dropped to the ground.

"Tom." Hammer didn't miss a beat. The elder brother repeated the maneuver, managing only three pull ups before hitting the ground.

"Jake." The ex-Marine had no trouble accomplishing the task. Neither did Rick.

"Joey." My ex didn't even make it halfway up the rope.

After dropping to the ground, he turned on Elton. "This is ridiculous. I don't expect to be climbing ropes aboard the *Lady Diana.*"

Elton ignored him. "Linda." I managed to make it close to the top before dropping to the ground.

"Sloan." Much to the guys' surprise, the scientist struggled to the top. She grabbed the bar, managing three pull ups.

Sweat dripped off us by the time we crawled, ran, and pulled our way through the ropes course. The final hurdle was a towering wall. A rope dangling over the side, only a couple of feet from the top.

"OK, kids, here is the toughest challenge you will have today. Gage, why don't you show them how it's done." The tall Navy SEAL broke into his cheetah lope. He planted his foot three feet up, grabbing the rope. Using his momentum, the tall guy vaulted easily over the wall. After Jake and Rick repeated the ex-Navy SEAL's performance, Elton turned to the rest of us.

"Linda, why don't you try it next?" My run at the wall wasn't bad, but I could not get enough height to grab the rope. Even if the rope was reached, there was no way I had enough upper body strength to hoist myself over.

"Hey, crab men, I thought you guys were a team. Eric get your butt up the wall. Hang on at the top. Lean over and give your wife a hand. Tom, give her a boost up."

The younger brother made a run at the wall, barely grabbing the rope. It was a darn good thing he was a Bering Sea fisherman with great upper body strength. He struggled, barely managing to top the barricade.

My husband straddled the wooden planks, leaning over to assist me. Tom interlocked his fingers into which I stepped. The elder brother hoisted me up. Eric grabbed my wrist, yanking me up enough so I could grab the top. I hung there unable to pull myself up any farther.

"Dammit, Eric, grab her belt and get her over. If someone was shooting at you, she'd already be dead." My guy's hand reached behind me, yanking on the belt loop of my pants, finally pulling me over. Gage helped to break my fall on the other side.

"Good job." The ex-Navy SEAL encouraged me. The two brothers repeated their performance with

Sloan, who managed to pull herself over the wall. Finally, Tom leapt up, joining us on the other side. We all stood panting in the scant shade of the monstrous blockade.

"Not bad." Elton joined us near the obstacle. "Let's get breakfast before our class on gun basics."

During our classroom session, the Navy SEAL taught us shooting maneuvers. Next, Elton led us to the gun range for firing practice. There was another man there, fixing paper targets to the mounts.

"Meet Victor. He's an former special forces sniper. This guys is the best shot of anyone I've ever had the pleasure of working with. If there's a man to teach you shooting accuracy, you just met him."

We looked over this thin, lanky young man, who looked like he was in his mid-twenties. He was medium height and build with a friendly smile radiating from the neatly-trimmed mustache and goatee. His dark brown hair was cropped very short and covered by a Miami Dolphin's cap.

"We're going to shoot at stationary targets from ten feet away. All of you need to learn to fire from a four-point stance. First, you want to bring your left hand across your chest. Make sure you keep your fist tight to your breastbone."

"Why are we doing this?" Sloan asked.

"In case you are attacked while drawing your gun. You can use your left fist to push the assailant away, while still getting off a shot with your shooting hand." Victor went through all the steps of drawing the gun and positioning us for the proper shot.

"It's all about the muscle memory. You need to train your muscles to react to what your brain is thinking."

Soon a barrage of blasts rang out as we refined our shooting techniques. The two instructors worked on our stance, posture, and aim. We re-loaded quickly. At the end of our first couple of hundred rounds, we all managed to hit the targets.

"You all are doing pretty well. Tomorrow, we will work on accuracy."

The next several days flew by as our sailboat foursome, as we were been dubbed by our instructors, melded into a team. My muscles ached due to all the physical exertion and the hand to hand combat the military guys taught us.

"It feels like my bruises have bruises," I said to Eric one afternoon.

"Yes, it's been a while since I've been challenged this physically. This is like slinging crab pots around only it's more like catching crabs in an inferno."

On our final day of training, we managed to whip through the obstacle course, with Sloan and I needing only a small amount of help over the wall. Joey, on the other hand, never made it over the top. Due to his physical disabilities from the shark bite, Elton cut him some slack on this.

Later in the afternoon, Martin's helicopter arrived to pick up our sailing foursome, whisking us away to the Paradise location. Sloan had her work cut out for her the next few days. She needed to train the dolphins how to protect themselves in the open ocean. Tom, Eric, and I accompanied her. We needed to be sure the dolphins would respond to all of us, in case the researcher was busy should an emergency arise.

After our arrival back on the island, we held a meeting in the lounge area to discuss the dolphin training.

"The most important part of the training will include teaching you how to get the dolphins to do whatever behavior is necessary at the time. We all need to be consistent with our hand signals, whistles, and tone of voice."

"Sloan, how do you teach a dolphin to avoid sharks?"

"Good question, Tom. We'll use a method called operant conditioning. Basically, we will reinforce the positive behaviors. Think about your childhood. Didn't your mom give you either positive or negative reinforcement when you did or didn't do your chores? It's the same with the dolphins. We need to accentuate the positives and restrict the negative reinforcement to life threatening situations, such as the presence of big sharks."

"How are we going to see the big sharks at sea?"

"We may not see them. The dolphins need to be taught to return to the sailboat if they encounter anything potentially harmful. Let's head down to the pen. We'll start with basic commands."

Down at the beach, Flo and Jet rushed over. They seem delighted to see Sloan. The four of us waded into the water to get reacquainted with the pair of slippery mammals.

After allowing a few minutes of play, Sloan blew a high-pitched whistle. She raised a finger, like she was asking for everyone to pay attention. Both dolphins stopped what they were doing. They raised their heads above the surface of the water with their eyes on the scientist.

"The whistle gets their attention. When I raise my hand, they know I am about to ask them to do something. Search," she said to the dolphins while lowering her palm downward with a sweeping motion of her arm.

The two dolphins swam off, side by side, around the enclosure. When they returned, Jet brought a rubber ring to Sloan. She blew the whistle again, then rubbed his jaw in praise.

"Good boy, Jet. See how easy the basic maneuvers are? The most important signal you need to learn is the recall signal, so you can get the dolphins to come back. It's easy. Just blow the whistle, then put your finger up like I did. Once the dolphins are paying attention, wave your arm in the air, like you are motioning them to come back."

The scientist blew the whistle again. Both dolphins poked their heads out of the water. As soon as the researcher waved her arm, Flo and Jet swam over, stopping next to her. She rewarded each one with a small fish.

"Food rewards are useful to reinforce the most important behaviors, like the recall signal. We want to make sure the dolphins don't swim too far away. They may lose us, especially if we encounter rough weather."

"How are we going to be able to store enough fish to feed them?"

"Martin is having a new freezer installed in the sailboat. It should be able to hold enough fish for a couple of months. Though, once they are out in the wild, the dolphins will be able to forage for food."

"How far away will the whistle be effective?" Eric asked.

"Good question. I don't know how the wind and sea conditions will affect their hearing above water, so Martin's company devised an underwater recall sound. It's a very high-pitched sound, above human hearing, so using it will not give away our location. Also, the sound will travel several miles beneath the sea."

We spent the afternoon working with the two mammals in more of a training session for us than them. Soon, we were all proficient at recalling the pair and sending them on a search.

The next day, we took the skiff to the dolphin pen. Flo and Jet rushed over, eager to play with the powerboat.

"Linda, make them stay inside the pen, until we open the gate. Don't release them until I tell you. After you give the release signal, blow the whistle and give the follow command. They should come along with us."

I stood near the bow, holding up one finger while blowing the whistle. The two mammals stopped to look at me. My palm thrust forward, telling them to stay put. Both dolphins remained stationary as Eric opened the gate. After a moment, I lowered my hand, blew the whistle, then motioned for the pair to follow.

Flo and Jet swam fast alongside the planing skiff. We stopped the boat on occasion as each of us practiced recalling the dolphins. It was early afternoon before we returned the mammals to the pen and the boat to the dock.

The rest of the afternoon was spent constructing a crude mock-up of a shark. The model was waterproofed and painted with a non-toxic paint. Tom installed a remote controlled, battery operated motor. We hoped to condition our mammals to avoid anything in the shape of a shark.

"The shark training will occur outside the pen. I don't want them to think anything bad could invade their home. We'll start by launching the fake shark from the beach, so they don't associate the predator with the boat. It could interfere with their recall instincts."

The resplendent sun marched toward the Gulf. Our foursome reclined in the mangrove retreat with a couple of beers. A ringing cell phone disturbed the silence of sunset.

"Eric, it's Carlos. How are you, my friend?"

"Carlos, you are a dead man. What the hell do you want?"

"Eric, do you really think I'm afraid of your threats? How is your little horse? Remember this, if I had wanted to kill him, he'd be dead, no? The next time we meet, it will be your turn, cowboy. I will have Linda all to myself." The phone went silent.

"Damn." Eric ran his hand through his hair. "Linda, we need to be extra careful."

"Don't worry, little brother. Sloan and I have your back."

The next morning, one of Martin's employees was stationed on the beach with the remote control shark. The dolphins followed us over.

"When the shark comes over, I will whistle for the dolphin's attention. A harsh vocal command will let them know it's a bad thing. Once they respond, you guys recall them. Make sure you give them a food reward."

Eric piloted the power boat toward the small beach with the two mammals swimming alongside. Sloan donned her mask and fins, sliding into the water. Flo and Jet were elated. The three swam around until the fake shark approached. The new object caught Jet's attention. He darted for the shark. Sloan blew the whistle. The young male dolphin looked to her for guidance.

"No, Jet," Sloan yelled harshly. The small male looked back at the shark, circling tantalizingly close. Tom activated the recall machine, sending out a sound only the dolphins heard.

"Did it work?" Jet turned toward the boat, then decided to play with the shark instead. Flo turned for our skiff when her son blasted off in the direction of the toy and Sloan. The researcher again blew the whistle. The little male dolphin stopped a few feet from the fake predator.

"No, Jet," Sloan shouted. The sound of my whistle distracted the young mammal's attention. He swam halfway back to the boat before his youthful curiosity got the better of him. He pivoted, swimming back toward Sloan and the model. Tom repeated a blast of the underwater recall sound as I blew on the whistle.

Jet stopped again, looking at me. My hand swept in the arc of the recall signal. The little guy reluctantly returned to the boat. He was greeted with a fish and a rub on his head.

"Good boy."

Sloan climbed back aboard. "It didn't look like he was going to swim back to the boat. He's going to need a bunch of work on this behavior. Another useful lesson would be to teach them to jump out of the water, if they encounter a shark. This is a natural behavior in the wild. The dolphins leap out of the water to gain some distance away from an approaching predator. It also confuses the electrical signals the shark is receiving. When they jump, we will be alerted to the possibility of danger.

"Let's take them back to the pen. They've had enough work for one morning."

After cleaning up the skiff, the four of us went to the research building for lunch. The cool air conditioning felt great after the morning's humid heat. A few minutes later, Eric's cell phone rang. "It's Martin."

Our boss' voice boomed through the speaker. "Here is the update on the progress of the two boats. The yachts are ready to head to the Gulf, to start tracking the drug boat's activity. There is disturbing news, though. The Coast Guard has lost track of Carlos' shrimp boat. The villain's last known position was offshore on a tack toward the Caribbean. In case he made a course change, we all need to be most vigilant. Eric, I would like you and Linda to fly here to bring the sailboat to the Paradise location. How is the dolphin training going?"

"It's going well, Mr. Sanderling. Though, I still don't like the idea of taking the dolphins to sea."

"Sloan, once again your concern is noted, but we need to get busy, breaking up this drug smuggling ring. You have one more week to work with the dolphins alongside the sailboat, before the four of you head to sea. The *Diana* will be in Naples waiting to rendezvous with you. Eric, the helicopter will be in Paradise in two hours."

My husband returned the phone to his pocket. "I guess we'd better pack. It sounds like Martin is getting impatient."

After tossing our clothes into our suitcases, we walked over to the helipad with Tom and Sloan.

"Bro, make sure you and Linda take good care of yourselves. Have guns loaded on the entire trip over here. Are you going to stop in Key West?"

"No. We'll cut through Marathon."

"Don't let anyone know which way you are coming, not even Gage. Call me when you're departing."

After the brothers shook hands, we climbed aboard the helo. Soon we were back at the West Palm Beach boathouse.

Chapter 16. Naples

My husband and I spent the remainder of the afternoon checking out the new equipment on the sailboat. Martin's crew did a great job of fitting in the new GPS and chartplotter. We switched on the Lokator gear, a cutting-edge radar, and the satellite communications equipment. All seemed in order. The newly installed separate refrigerator and freezer were inspected. Frozen herring and mullet along with people food filled the new cold box.

Eric closed the freezer lid. "Everything looks good."

"It better look good. We've been working our butts off while you two played with the dolphins." Gage climbed down the steps to shake my husband's hand.

"Hi, Linda. How did the dolphin training go?"

"Pretty well. They need more work on the shark avoidance, but overall the two dolphins are ready."

"Great. Eric, what time do we shove off in the morning?"

"We?"

"Yes, I'm your special security detail. Did you tell anyone about the trip?"

"Only Tom and Sloan. Who else knows?"

"Just Martin. I asked him not to tell anyone, not even his wife."

"Was he suspicious?"

"No, he laughed saying his wife didn't care about the boats. Why don't we have dinner? We should make it an early night."

"Great. I want to leave by six A.M. so we arrive in the Keys in daylight. Tomorrow night we can push through getting us into Paradise early Thursday morning."

We were up bright and early the following morning. By five forty-five, Eric fired up the sailboat which Martin named *Island Time*. Gage was busy checking guns and ammo. A loaded rifle would be kept in the pilothouse along with two nine millimeter Springfield pistols. The former Navy SEAL was not taking any chances.

My cowboy slid the forty-foot yacht out of the boathouse. We turned south on the ICW. The wind was light from the northwest, allowing us an easy motor to Hawk Channel.

As we entered the protected shallows inside the reef, the water beneath us turned crystal clear. It was like motoring through a swimming pool. The boat passed over an abandoned crab pot. It looked so close, like you could reach in the water and pluck it out. The only trick was, the water was fifteen feet deep.

Island Time cruised at six knots. A few hours later, we reached the turn for Moser Channel, beneath the Overseas Highway. The channel zigged around many sand bars. It would deposit us in the Gulf of Mexico.

My feet were propped up on the console in front of me. The autopilot steered the boat. We were about to pass under the US-1 bridge, so I reached forward to disengage the autopilot.

The current ran hard behind us. The throttle to the engine was adjusted until the right amount of speed was achieved to keep control in the swirling water beneath the Seven Mile Bridge. This sixty-five foot steel pass through to Florida Bay was tricky because of the narrow tunnel through the massive girders along with swift tidal action.

After popping through, we weaved around the sand banks for another hour, before breaking out of the shallows into the comparatively deep water of the Gulf. A fair breeze from the southeast greeted us. We hoisted sail, then headed north.

Our pretty white sails were eased out, allowing the yacht to reach along at a gentle pace in the fifteen feet of pale, green water. The new yacht rolled slightly, completely at ease on her watery home. The red sun dipped into the emerald waters of the Gulf of Mexico.

"Eric, we will run without lights tonight, just in case. If there is a radar target within three miles of us, let's turn inshore. The mangroves will help to scatter any electronic signals."

"Gage, I don't think we can get close enough to hide in the weeds. The water is pretty shallow along this coast."

"Yeah, Linda, you're correct. I'm hoping an abrupt course change will tell us a whole lot. If the other boat alters course also, there may be trouble."

The next few hours slid by until one A.M. A small target appeared, then disappeared on the glowing green screen. With the autopilot on, I ducked my head outside the pilothouse to see if my eyes could pick up the lights of the other vessel.

The night sky was brilliantly clear, with the stars twinkling overhead. There was no moon to brighten the total blackness. My eyes should have picked up the signature red and green lights of the approaching vessel. The Gulf of Mexico was smooth. Hardly a ripple reflected off the mirror-like surface. Looking to the northwest, I didn't see any running lights. My stomach flipped.

"Gage." The man, resting on the settee, sprang to his feet. He grabbed the loaded rifle.

"There is a target on the radar, about three miles to the northwest. It's moving fast in our direction. The size of the boat is difficult to judge because it doesn't have lights on. Due to the faint radar blip, my guess is a small vessel."

"Eric." The former Navy SEAL poked his head out of the pilothouse. "Linda, make a big course change to starboard."

The autopilot was tweaked forty degrees to the right. The target altered course for us.

"What can I do?" Eric watched the radar.

"Go below. Grab another Ruger. Cover the back. I'll take the bow. Linda keep the nine millimeter close to you. Damn."

The former Navy SEAL poked his head out again. "One of you get on the satellite phone with Mitch, we may need help."

The small target continued to close with us. The ghostly outline of a small motorboat stalked a mile away. It was difficult to see any details of the little boat, though it looked like a center-console fishing boat. The former Navy SEAL crouched down while scrambling to a position on the bow. He was in a good position to track and intercept the intruder from there.

"Linda, Coast Guard Station Ft. Myers Beach is scrambling a helo. They should be at your location shortly." Mitch's voice came through the sat phone. Even though our relationship with the Coast Guard officer was strained, it was good to hear a friendly voice.

Eric crept aft with the other loaded rifle to a position behind the pilothouse. He crouched in the shadows. All eyes locked on the silhouette of a small powerboat a hundred yards away.

Tense minutes passed as the boat motored around our stern. Gage tracked the boat by moving aft. Eric crept forward. A spotlight grazed our stern, lighting up the yacht's name and hailing port. Why did they look at that?

A second small motorboat appeared on radar. It blasted toward us until it reached the perimeter of the first vessel. The second boat took a position aft of the first vessel.

"Gage, we have a second boat. It's heading around the stern."

"I've got it, man."

When the second boat arrived, both vessels closed with us. The first aimed for our starboard quarter.

"Guys, hold your fire. This doesn't feel right. I don't think it's Carlos' gang."

A blinding spotlight focused on our wheelhouse. The searing white light destroyed my night vision. My eyes squinted in the painful glare.

"Police. Stop your boat." The first boat pulled within fifty feet of us. The second lingered behind.

"Stay back, we're armed. The Coast Guard is on its way."

"Stop your boat, now. Drop your weapons and show me your hands," a harsh voice said.

"Guys, keep your weapons on them. Hold your fire unless they shoot first. My name is Gage Stevens. I'm a U.S. Naval Reserve officer. We are delivering this boat for the Defense Department. I'm ordering you to stay back. The Coast Guard is sending a helo from station Ft. Myers Beach. You can check this with your dispatch." The spotlight continued to illuminate our boat, though no further attempt was made to approach us.

My nerves were on edge. I struggled to focus, remembering the words Gage drummed in during our tactical training. "Linda, if you draw a weapon, you better be mentally prepared to shoot someone. Go through the four steps we taught you. The training will take over when you need it."

The uneasy standoff continued. Chatter from what sounded like a police radio drifted across the void between our vessels. An eerie silence enveloped us. A moment later, the quiet was broken by the loud thump, thump of helicopter blades.

The helo flew in fast, lighting up the waters around the two small boats with another blinding light. Both vessels were dark gray in color, with no official markings on them. Each was manned by several figures clad in black, bulky clothing. We overheard voices, talking to the intruders. I was pretty sure they were police officers, though Gage maintained his defensive posture at the stern.

The red and white bird hovered over us. A voice boomed from a loud speaker. "Sailing vessel at twenty-five thirty north, this is U.S. Coast Guard helo six. We have confirmed the identity of the two motorboats in your vicinity. They are Florida Fish and Wildlife officers. We have instructed them to not engage with you at this time."

Gage's sigh of relief was heard all the way from the stern. "Stand down." He remained crouched down as he made his way back the pilothouse.

"Sailing vessel, this is the Florida Fish and Wildlife officers. We are coming alongside." The first powerboat sped to our starboard side. One of the officers tied a line around our stanchion.

"Put your weapons down and step away from them. Keep your hands where I can see them." A harsh voice ordered from the lead vessel. "Face forward. Move slowly up to the bow." Even though I knew these were officers of the law, my frayed nerves made me hesitate to leave the pilothouse. Several assault weapons were trained on me. My instinct was to stay at the helm.

"You in the pilothouse, come outside now." A tall, heavily built man climbed aboard our vessel. His gun pointed in my direction. "Let me see your hands."

With a few tentative steps, I advanced into the cockpit with my hands over my head.

"Walk up to the bow."

My path to the bow led me to my husband and Gage, who both faced the sea, with raised hands.

"Which one of you is special ops, Stevens?"

"That's me."

"Turn around. Show me your ID."

Our Navy SEAL friend pivoted around, pulling his wallet from his pocket. He showed the police officer his navy credentials.

"Are you part of the GOM marine task force?"

"Yes, though this vessel is not at operational status at this time."

"You crew can put their hands down."

With relief, my arms dropped to my sides. Gage patted my shoulder. "Relax, Linda. You can turn around now."

"What the heck were you doing, running without lights?"

The ex-Navy SEAL walked over to the officer cautiously, with his hand extended. The two men shook hands. The officer appeared much more relaxed as he chatted with our friend. Several other officers looked around the boat.

"Guys, we have positive ID. These folks are friendlies."

"This vessel is a surveillance boat which will be engaged in tracking drug trafficking boats here in the Gulf. We are working with the U.S. Coast Guard," Gage said when the officer again looked to him.

"We've already had a few encounters with one very nasty drug lord, Carlos Sanchez. Unfortunately, all of our intelligence on him has gone cold. Since he's made serious threats against the crew of this boat, we thought it best to sneak into the Gulf as stealthily as possible. There is a good chance he may be stalking us."

"Our office is well aware of Carlos. There is an active warrant for his arrest. He shot and killed a civilian in West Palm Beach. We didn't have any information about your boat. We even called dispatch after checking the name and hailing port on the transom. Since no lights were visible, we are obligated to come over to investigate. At that time, the vessel must be stopped and your weapons lowered. You are lucky we didn't shoot you."

"Officer," I said. "We couldn't be sure you were law enforcement officers. You have no idea how scary it is to be approached by another vessel, at high speed, in the middle of the night. There was no way of identifying you, other than calling the Coast Guard. If you were drug runners, we all could be dead."

"Yeah. I'm sure they would have no problem shooting you. You did the right thing." The officer removed his black ball cap, then scratched his head. "I wish the task force had informed us. We didn't need this kind of encounter tonight."

Gage grinned. "Neither did we."

"After the Coast Guard confirmed our identity, why did you still board our vessel? You guys scared the heck out of me." My knees finally managed to stop shaking.

"Sorry, ma'am. We are trained to confirm the situation, even though the Coast Guard cleared you. There is always the chance your vessel was stolen or hijacked. There is no way of knowing, whether or not there is a hostage situation without investigating the scene.

"If I didn't board your vessel and ask for ID, I wouldn't be doing my job. Your murders tonight isn't something I want to hear about six months from now. We'll keep an eye on your boat and the other traffic tonight. Where are you headed?"

"We're going to a small island near Everglades City."

"Is there any way we can assist you?"

"No, we'll be fine. Thanks for your help."

"If possible, could you guys give us a heads up about your future activities here in the Gulf so we can not only coordinate with you, but make sure we have no other encounters similar to tonight's."

"You've got it." Gage shook the officer's hand. "I'll make sure the task force gives you a full briefing, once we near operational status." The officers climbed back aboard their vessel.

"Let's get out of here." The former Navy SEAL patted my shoulder. "Good job you two."

The rest of the night was quiet, but none of us managed any sleep with all of the adrenaline surging through our veins. As the sun peeked over the tree tops, we weaved our way through the unmarked, dredged channel through the mangroves. At nine A.M., we arrived at the Paradise location.

Our anchor dropped in the clear water off the sandy beach near the dolphin pen. After launching the dinghy, we went ashore for breakfast and much needed sleep.

Bright sunlight streamed through the window of our thatched-roof hut when my eyes struggled open. Eric reclined in a chair, reading a magazine.

"Eric, it's one P.M. You shouldn't have let me sleep so long."

"You needed the rest. Tom and Sloan have the dolphins out with the sailboat, getting them used to it. Tomorrow we'll go on a trip with both the dolphins and the powerboat to get them used to following the sailboat."

The rest of the afternoon, we relaxed around the island. Our group rendezvoused with Gage in the mangrove sitting area, at sunset. Eric's cell phone rang.

"Cowboy, it's your friend Carlos. I heard you went sailing. My sources tell me you had a encounter in the Gulf, no. It doesn't matter how many guns or Navy SEALs you have. We will meet shortly. After I kill you, I get my prize, no? Your pretty wife."

Eric had no chance to respond before his phone grew silent.

A look of frustration crossed Gage's face. "How the hell did he know about the sailing trip?"

"Mitch?"

Eric rose from his seat, seething with anger. "That bastard."

"Hey, man, take it easy. Mitch is a United States Coast Guard officer who is trying to catch Carlos. Why would he feed him information?"

"Maybe to bait him."

"No, no way, Tom. Mitch would tell me," Gage said quietly.

"Just like he told us about Joey's rescue? I don't trust the bastard."

"Do you think Martin slipped, telling Diana about the plans?" Sloan asked.

"No, I still don't think it's her."

"What about Martin himself?" Tom asked. "He seems to be getting impatient. What do you think the chances are he's trying to draw Carlos out? Also, the welfare of the dolphins is no great concern to him. We all could be expendable as long as he gets what he wants. Why is he so intent on catching Carlos anyway?"

"It has to do with his brother," Gage said thoughtfully. "He started out buying cocaine from one of Carlos' dealers. After his own money ran out, the brother started leaching off Martin. When our boss found out what his brother was doing with the money, he put a stop to the funds. The guy's next stop was rehab."

"Like an intervention?"

"Exactly, Sloan." Gage looked off into the distance. "Martin's efforts were too late. The brother was hooked. He sneaked out of rehab only to start dealing to support his habit. The younger brother made the mistake of not paying for a big drug drop. When Carlos came after him, the brother tried to hide out at Martin's home in West Palm Beach. After the drug lord broke into the house, in the middle of the night, there was a struggle. Martin was badly injured trying to protect his brother."

"The scar on his forehead?" Eric asked

"Yes. Our boss was knocked unconscious and his brother was murdered. It certainly explains Martin's drive to capture or kill Carlos. As long as the drug runner is on the loose, the man's family is at risk."

Tom rubbed his hand over his beard. "It sounds like our boss wouldn't have any qualms putting all of us at risk."

"I don't know. We'll need to keep an eye on him. When someone is desperate, you never know."

A beautiful sunrise followed a night of uneasy sleep. A short wander along the beach brought me to my husband who was sloshing his feet through the shallow water while nudging a shell with his foot. His hands were buried deep in the pockets of his shorts.

"Eric."

"Morning." He tried to smile, but his brow was creased with concern.

"Are you hanging in there? You didn't sleep much."

"I'm trying not to let this Carlos thing get to me."

"Eric, I'm sorry. This is all my fault. If we hadn't tried to find Joey..."

"Linda."

"I wish we never tried to find him. Look what good it's done. He's being such a butt head."

"You always have a way with words. Let's have breakfast."

After picking our way through the food, we cruised on the sailboat with the dolphins in tow. They quickly adjusted to the slower pace of the sailing yacht.

The marine mammals seemed to enjoy ducking under our keel, only to pop up on the other side.

After a few more days spent teaching the dolphins how to identify and track the small motorized model submarines, they were ready to go. The Lokator equipment provided great data as the computer program learned to differentiate the cigar shaped submersibles from other objects found in the depths of the sea.

Early one morning, we left Paradise with Flo and Jet following along. We turned the sailing vessel north. Our destination was Naples. The wind blew a brisk fifteen knots out of the east. A reefed main and full genoa billowed out to port as we cruised along. There was only a light chop close to the shoreline, making this an easy trip. Our dolphins escorted us for the first few miles, before Jet started acting strangely. Suddenly, he turned back south.

"Sloan, something's wrong with Jet," I called to the researcher who was working below. As she came on deck, Eric grabbed the ship's wheel, spinning the sailboat through the wind. *Island Time* hove to, quickly stopping, before drifting to the southwest. Flo circled the boat, clicking loudly. She was very agitated.

"Do you think there is a shark around?" Tom surveyed the water with binoculars.

"No." Sloan whistled, giving Jet the recall signal. He swam a few feet in the direction of our boat before he again turned south. "He's confused. The little guy wants to head back home because he's never been so far out into the Gulf before. I'll jump in to reassure him."

"Keep an eye out for sharks."

Eric fired up our motor as we doused sail. The sailboat closed with the small male dolphin. His mom swam to her son. Sloan jumped in alongside the young mammal. She tread water while stoking his slick gray skin.

"It's OK, Jet."

After some encouragement and a couple of fish, the little guy tentatively joined up with us. The rest of the trip to Naples went smoothly. We pulled the sailing yacht into the slip directly aft of the *Diana,* behind Martin's home in Port Royal. The two dolphins circled nervously around the murky bay.

"Flo, Jet, come over here," Sloan called to the pair. They swam over, looking very agitated. Jet kept tossing his head out of the water while clicking very rapidly. Flo swam close circles around her son as if to protect him. The researcher decided to put the two mammals into a small enclosure between the dock and the seawall.

"It's not the largest temporary home, but at least they'll be safe."

"Martin, I'll say this again. I don't like putting these two mammals at risk. Look how upset they are." We watched the dolphins circle around the small pen.

"Sloan, I understand how worried you are, but they will be fine. They are two very important assets who will be crucial in tracking the drug runners."

"Is that all they are to you, Martin? Assets? They are living, breathing animals with real feelings, for goodness sakes."

"Sloan, I've noted your complaint. The dolphins' involvement is the search for drug boats is non-negotiable." He walked off the dock, signally an end to the protest.

"Hey, lady, why don't we head down to the Cove Inn Chickee? We all could use a cocktail," Tom asked.

The scientist turned back to her mammals. "No thanks. I'll stay here to be sure they settle down." Once the lady sat down on the dock near the dolphins, Flo came over, resting her bottlenose on the researcher's crossed legs. Tom shook his head. Our threesome left the dock.

Eric slid behind the wheel of the Volvo. Martin dedicated the car for the crew's use. Once at the Cove Inn, we strolled to the Chickee bar. The first person spotted was probably the last person I wanted to see, Joey. He sat at the far end of the bar, engrossed in a conversation with Jan, one of the bartenders. Cindy, the bar manager, worked the near end of the bar. The three of us grabbed seats as far away from my ex as possible.

Joey glanced at us without acknowledgment. He was engrossed in telling a story. Jan beamed as she listened. Her shift had to be ending as she gathered up her belongings. The two of them walked near us on their way out. At least Jan had the class to say "hello".

"Hi, guys. How's it going?"

"Hi, Jan." Eric answered for all of us. "We're great. How about you?"

"I'm just fine. It's great to see you." To our surprise, the duo walked arm-in-arm in the direction of *Dark & Stormy*.

"Well there's an interesting development," Tom said while watching the departing couple climb aboard my beloved yacht.

"How dare he bring another woman aboard our yacht?" My blood pressure soared. Eric laughed. "Linda, excuse me, but did you forget about the other man you brought aboard your yacht?"

Blinking, my eyes focused on my husband.

"Do I get the feeling you are a tiny bit jealous, Li'l Sis?".

"Jealous? Tom, are you nuts?" The two brothers shared a laugh at my expense.

"I guess I'm glad for Jan. Maybe she can tame the savage beast. It's best to forget about it. Why don't we head over to the Dock for dinner?"

After paying our drink tab, we strolled along the waterfront, to one of my favorite restaurants--the Dock at Crayton Cove. As we approached, Bobbi, one of the owners and a good friend, was speaking with the hostess. She turned to greet us.

"Eric and Linda. What a nice surprise. It's great to see you."

"Hi, Bobbi. This is Tom, Eric's brother." After introductions, she was kind enough to show us to a great table by the water. We invited her for a drink to catch up on all the news around Crayton Cove. Tom studied the multitude of decorated paddles, hanging around the rafters of this rustic restaurant.

"What's with the paddles?"

Bobbi gazed up at the ceiling. "They are the broken paddle awards from previous Great Dock Canoes Races."

"A canoe race, huh. Sounds like fun."

"Tom, the race is next weekend. It's not too late to enter, if you like. You and Eric could enter the VIP race. It's a great race which benefits local organizations."

While Bobbi, Eric, and Tom discussed the details of the brothers' entry into the race, a pictured formed in my mind...a picture of two big, strong Alaska fisherman dumping a canoe in Naples Bay. This was one race I was not going to miss.

"I need to get back to work. See you guys later." After Bobbi left for the kitchen, we enjoyed scrumptious margaritas with our favorite appetizer...Rock Shrimp Nachos. We dined on yummy grouper fixed just right by the Dock's excellent chef. Stuffed to the gills, we returned to *Island Time* to meet up with Sloan.

The next several days were spent in the company of the *Lady Diana,* the mini-sub, and the dolphins as we taught the mammals how to track an actual mini-sub off the coast of Naples. The murky water in this part of the Gulf added quite a challenge to our duo's echolocation, but they quickly proved they were up to the task.

On Friday evening, Martin hosted a dinner, at his home, to celebrate all of our hard work. Early next week, our team would launch the first in a series of expeditions into the Gulf of Mexico. Eric and I stood by the pool, enjoying a drink with Tom and Sloan. Joey arrived with Jan at this side.

"Hi, Linda." Joey smirked at me.

"Joey." My response was filled with cool indifference. When my ex went to the bar, is seemed as though Tom couldn't resist stirring up trouble.

"Hi, Jan. It's a surprise to see you here with Joey."

"Well, yes. He's a fun guy to be with." The bartender grabbed my arm, pulling me aside. "Linda, I hope you're not angry with me."

"No, Jan. Why would I be? There's nothing between Joey and me anymore."

"Good. I didn't want it to affect our relationship." My ex returned a moment later, making a show of handing Jan a drink. They wandered off to admire Martin's estate.

A short while later, our boss came over to chat with us. "Linda, I was hoping you could help me."

"Yes, Martin. What can I do for you?"

"It is my understanding you have quite a few associations with artists in town. I wanted to have a painting done for Diana's birthday, maybe a nice landscape of her vacation home in upstate New York. Do you know of an artist I could approach to help me with this project?"

"Yes, absolutely. There are two very talented artists who have a great gallery in Crayton Cove called the Art Gallery of Old Naples 2. We can go there tomorrow, if you like."

"Thank you, Linda. I'll drop by. Would you mind if I use your name as a recommendation?"

"Of course, Martin. Not a problem at all. You'll love Karen and Lynne's work."

Once our boss was out of earshot, my husband turned to me. "Let's get some sleep. We have a big day tomorrow."

Chapter 17. The Gulf Of Mexico

We went to bed anticipating the Great Dock Canoe Race. Considering the guys had all of three practice sessions aboard a borrowed canoe, from the Naples Ship Store, my expectations of a victory were not high.

We approached the Dock restaurant and the canoe staging area, mid-morning on Saturday. There were many participants readying their boats for the races.

Several were decorated with the tropical theme of the event. One pram looked like a miniature atoll with palm fronds jutting off a makeshift tree trunk. On one branch perched a fake parrot, colored with red, blue, and yellow plumage. A tiny pirate hat sat atop the bird's head with a skull and crossbones patch covering the left eye. It squawked commands to its human crew.

"Row, stroke, paddle this boat. Come on, put your backs into it. *Arrgh.*"

My husband grinned at the stuffed bird. "A pirate parrot. We could use him on *Denali* to keep Tom in line."

My guy was dressed in his typical cowboy dress, wearing cut-off jeans, a flannel shirt, and his black cowboy hat. We decided flip-flops were much safer than cowboy boots, should the canoe flip during their sprint. His brother dressed as a crab fisherman, sporting a yellow slicker with the sleeves removed.

A close likeness of the brothers' crab boat was hastily sketched upon the back of the rain jacket earlier this morning. Tom also sported a *Denali* cap. The local press did not miss the opportunity to film the famous crab duo. When the brothers waded out to the race announcers' float to chat with Vin and Bobbi, the owners of the restaurant, the television crews filmed away.

"We have special guests paddling in today's race," Vin announced. "Eric and Tom Iverson from the fishing show, 'Crabs From the Deep'." The crowd on the city dock erupted in applause. The brothers waved to their fans.

"Nothing like adding pressure to our performance," Eric said while shaking our hosts' hands.

Race time neared. Sloan and I hurried over to the Chickee Bar, to cheer our guys on. We noticed Joey and Jan aboard *Dark & Stormy*.

"Nothing like flaunting his new relationship. What a jerk."

"You know what girlfriend? I'm completely fed up with Joey and his antics. The real problem is, it's so hard not to be able to enjoy my yacht any longer. He's made it extremely difficult for me to even go aboard. Maybe I need to let them both go."

"Come on, Linda, let's get a drink. The race is about to begin." We found a place at the Chickee Bar rail. The bar was halfway down the VIP sprint course between the Cove Inn and the City Dock. Vin counted down to the start as the crowd echoed him... three, two, one. They're off!

Our guys made a good start. Paddles flew. The competition was stiff. The half dozen VIP canoes flew in our direction. One of the paddled boats nearest the brothers lost control, careening in our guys' direction.

Tom dug his oar in, making an impressive turn. The crab boys' small canoe yawed dangerously. Somehow, they managed to miss the out of control boat. Despite the violent rocking, the Alaska duo salvaged their balance. Their course and speed was regained.

Sheets of water drenched the competitors. A barrage of water cannons doused the small dugouts from all directions. Other spectator boats, along with the many guests lining the City Dock, took wild aim with all sorts of water weaponry. When the guys reached the turning point, they were drenched but enjoying a sizable lead on the competition.

The brothers cruised around the buoy. Looming, nearly out-of-control canoes made the boys alter course toward the Chickee. Two oncoming dugouts tried to force them into the dock. A barrage of cocktails and ice was poured over them from the Chickee revelers.

Sloan and I cheered them on. "Come on, Tom and Eric. Go! Go!"

A three way wrestling match ensued between our guys and the four other paddlers. Whoosh! All three boats upended, flinging the six contestants into the bay.

Cheers and jeers erupted from the crowd. A mass of arms and legs grappled to regain their crafts. They struggled to keep heads above water. Eric grabbed the dock. His legs righted the sodden canoe. They scrambled back in with my husband on the aft seat. Two other dugouts managed to round the mark unscathed. The sleek crafts streaked for finish line.

"Bail out the boat," Eric yelled while wildly paddling to intercept the other boats. Tom grabbed Eric's cowboy hat. The elder brother frantically bailed the sinking craft. The crowd cheered them on.

"This is a crazy comeback from the crab boys," the announcer hollered. The crowd roared with delight. Equipped with only one paddle, Eric dug in. Their little boat zoomed alongside the lead canoe. Tom doused the other team with the cowboy hat full of water.

With a mere fifty yards to go, the elder brother rescued another paddle. The Alaska duo thrashed through the final few yards, neck and neck, with the competition. The crowd cheered them on..."stroke, stroke, stroke."

The bows of the two canoes darted under the finish line rope at exactly the same time. From our vantage point at the Chickee, we couldn't tell who won. Sloan and I dashed back toward the Dock Restaurant.

Two wet, bedraggled Alaska crab fisherman toasted the paddlers from the other canoe who happen to be a couple of local fireman.

"Great race, guys," Eric said to the pair. They clinked bottles of beer.

"Who won?" Sloan asked breathlessly as we waded through the sand alongside the restaurant, beneath the canopy of a huge sea grape tree.

"I think it was a draw." Tom grinned at the two local men, not wanting to steal their thunder from the cheering crowd.

We hung around for a good dose of revelry while the rest of the races were run.

It's amazing how big a crowd of locals and tourists amass for this truly unique event. After the final awards were handed out, we opted for the Dock's awesome burgers before heading back to *Island Time* to prep her for our upcoming foray into the Gulf of Mexico.

On Sunday evening, Martin held a meeting of the troops aboard the *Diana*. The plan was to head out early the next morning.

"Here's the game plan." Gage stood before a large chart of the Gulf of Mexico. "Our recent intelligence shows increased activity along the west coast of Florida. Tom, why don't you guys head northwest toward Panama City? You may have an encounter offshore of the big bend, somewhere to the northwest of Tampa. It seems as though the druggies are trying to utilize the lesser populated areas around Apalachicola to sneak their drugs ashore. Our crew will take the *Diana* south toward the Keys."

"Do you want us to head on a direct course?"

"Yes. Our intelligence points to the drug boats releasing the mini-subs farther offshore as their technology improves. We would love to catch one in the act."

"OK. We'll head on a direct line to Panama City, looking for any suspicious contacts, especially shrimp boats."

"Yes, but do not attempt to make contact or to intercept them. Have the dolphins look for submarine activity. Track any subs with the Lokator gear. We have plenty of Coast Guard and Navy assets in the vicinity. When you have a firm contact, give Mitch a call. He'll send in the troops."

Eric sighed. It seemed he was not pleased with the more passive role assigned to our vessel. "Gage, are you telling me we are only to track the bastards with no chance to engage them?"

"Eric, I remember the promise made to you in Beaufort. If Carlos is on the boats you track, I'll make sure you have a chance for a private chat. Will you do me a favor, cowboy? Do not even think about any vigilante stuff."

My husband's response was a grunt. From the burning look in his eye, there was no doubt he would have trouble sitting on the sidelines while the federal officials boarded any of our quarry's vessels, especially one particular black shrimp boat.

Monday morning dawned bright and clear. There was a light but steady breeze out of the northeast. Flo and Jet seemed ecstatic to gain the freedom of the open seas. We hoped all the training of the past several weeks kept them safe from any predators lurking nearby.

With sails set, the autopilot steered our ship on a course of 330 degrees magnetic. Our crew settled into watch keeping routines as we checked and re-checked all of the equipment aboard. Everything seemed in order.

Our vessel crept offshore, as the green coastal water gave way to lovely shades of aquamarine. Around midnight, we were abeam of Sarasota, thirty miles off the coast. The distant glow of the Ringling brothers' home reflected in the eastern sky.

"Check out the stars." Tom reclined next to Sloan in the cockpit. Eric and I were about to head below for some off time and a quick nap.

"It's so pretty out here. Look at the dolphins. There is so much phosphorescence in the water, it's leaving trails of light behind them." We gazed off our port quarter to see two streaks of light. The dolphins' motion through the water disrupted the microorganisms floating all around us.

The tiny phytoplankton responded by lighting up in a most amazing glow, lining the path of our two cetaceans through the water. There was even a small trail of silver, emerging from the silent wake of our sloop.

"The wind has eased," Tom said, looking at the wind meter which read ten knots. This slowed our progress to a mere three knots.

"It's good for Flo and Jet. The slower speed will allow them to rest." They cruised alongside us, undulating their tail flukes in a rhythmic beat. The rigging creaked and groaned while the autopilot whirred away, driving us into the dark abyss of the night.

My midnight to three A.M. watch went by quietly. Several contacts appeared on my radar, but all seemed to be vessels on innocent passage to their destinations. The Automatic Identification System lit up my screen with the target's name, speed, type of vessel, and destination.

In the upper part of my screen, three miles away, was the cargo ship, *Mauru,* steaming along at fourteen knots bound for the Port of Tampa. Another was a small motor yacht, making his way out from the coast probably on a sport fishing trip.

These were not the targets we were looking for. No, the drug smugglers won't have an AIS system on board, or if they did, it would transmit false information. The fake would be difficult to decipher. If we were in close proximity, I could distinguish a large steel shrimp boat from other types of traffic. Pleasure boats gave a much fainter, less crisp, radar return.

Another good indicator of illicit activity would be the speed of the vessel. In order to launch a mini-sub, the ship would heave to. Once the ship stopped, the submarine would be dropped off their deck. If we saw a vessel's speed decrease, this would be the boat to investigate.

No such activity occurred during my shift. The wind picked up to a nice breeze. Eric climbed on deck to relieve me. After a quick check of the dolphins, he settled down next to me while sipping a cup of hot tea.

"Everything quiet?"

"Yes. All went well on my watch. I jotted all the radar contacts in the logbook. Most of it was commercial traffic, heading into Tampa."

"I suspect there will be a bunch of boring watches, staring at the sea. This is very different from crabbing, where you're working all the time."

"The payoff will be worth it. I'm going to bed."

The next morning, we hove to while feeding the dolphins. Sloan jumped into the water to reassure our aquatic duo. They seemed to be settling in well, but appeared confused, cruising around with no apparent purpose. The scientist engaged them in a game of Frisbee, to keep them from getting bored.

The wind built throughout the morning to a stiff twenty knots.

"Eric, let's put a reef in the main." The depowered boat careened northwestward at a steady six knots. A couple of hours later, the wind backed to the east, sledding our craft down the white foam. Our target search area was now only a hundred miles to the northwest.

The dolphins had a blast, cavorting around in the rolling seas. They body surfed alongside the sloop, submerging right under the bow, only to pop up again at the starboard quarter.

Later in the afternoon, the wind eased. Sloan and I shook out the reefs in the mainsail. The guys were below, preparing to grill dinner. The mainsail slapped back and forth, with the boom held in place by the preventer.

"Sloan, this is sure a turn around. Here we are taking care of the sails while the boys get dinner ready." We shared a laugh over the role reversal with the men.

"I overheard them discussing the gourmet meal they are planning...grilled sausages with veggies. Yum!" Sloan stopped a moment to glance at our dolphins.

"At least the Flo and Jet will be eating healthy tonight. We have lots of nice mullet for them. Look over there." Sloan pointed to an area of intense splashing off our starboard bow. Small flecks of silver popped out of the shimmering sea.

"Bait fish. I'll bet there are many delicious treats over there for our mammals. It will interesting to see if they head for the school." Her observations were interrupted by Tom coming on deck, carrying a plate of food.

"What's wrong with grilled sausages? You should be damn glad I'm handling this woman's work."

Without further comment, our captain went to the back deck. After tweaking the valve for the propane grill attached to the rail, puffs of smoke wafted astern. Flo and Jet rotated their heads to have a better view of the human's activities. The sausages and veggies sizzled away. The smell of cooking meat was irresistible.

The yacht rolled in the leftover swell. We meandered to the northwest. Eric, Sloan, and I lounged comfortably while Tom tended to our dinner. The sun morphed from a bright yellow orb to a burning red fireball, sinking slowly into the western sky.

Our captain reopened the lid to the grill, right when a strong roller hit the side of the boat. The yacht slammed to the port, then back to starboard.

The dinner sausages lurched. The elder brother made a stab for them with his metal tongs. An errant link careened toward the edge of the grill.

The meaty delicacy hung in mid-air, for just a moment. Time was suspended. In slow motion, with a perfect end over end flip, our savory link plunged over the rail into the sea.

Not a sound was heard in the cockpit other than the banging of the mainsail. Tom leaned over the rail with his hands over his head. A series of salty expletives emerged from beneath his black beard.

"Shit, damn boat. Why the hell did it have to roll?" The other crew members, sprawled around the cockpit, were reduced to fits of laughter in response to the look of outrage on our captain's face. I giggled so hard, I almost missed what happened next.

A loud squeal erupted from alongside the boat. Sloan leapt to her feet to see what her dolphins were all riled up about. Joined by Eric and me, the three of us were consumed by fits of hilarity.

Jet tossed the escaped sausage into the air, catching it on the down slide. He seemed quite pleased with the new toy his uncle Tom sent over the side.

"Give me that damn thing," our captain shouted. He leaned far over the rail in an attempt to snatch the oversized wiener from the crafty mammal's mouth.

Just like a kid, Jet did not give up his prize. He continued to taunt the elder fishing captain, keeping the sea sodden link out of Tom's reach.

"Oh, to hell with this." Our captain regained his feet. We were silenced when he turned to face us.

"What the heck are you laughing at?" This question brought a new peal of hilarity from his crew, whose eyes dripped with tears of merriment.

"Eric, do you think this is funny, our damn supper going over the side?"

My husband did his best to straighten out his face. He tried to look serious when he put his hand on his brother's shoulder. "At least you won't need a roll to put that sausage in."

Even Tom couldn't help but laugh at this quip. Before our captain's mood deteriorated further, I slipped below to fish out a cold beer from the fridge. Back on deck, the frosty can was handed to our chief.

"Tom, why don't you take a break. I'll finish up."

The rest of our supper was very enjoyable. A great camaraderie was building between our crew members. Sloan was accepted as if she had always been a part of our lives. It would be interesting to see how far their relationship went. Tom had never been the "settle down" type of guy.

The rosy dusk gave way to a clear night. The light breeze off our stern quarter drove us ahead at a couple of knots. The violent roll from the earlier swell died off to a gently sway.

The constellations of twinkling stars swirled through the endless sky above us. There was no moon. The horizon turned black as the full blanket of night descended over our ship.

Chapter 18. Searching the Gulf

My watch was from nine to midnight. Tom and Sloan retired to the main cabin for a nap while Eric kept me company on deck.

"Another beautiful night." My husband glanced at the radar from across the cockpit. "What's up? What are you looking at?"

"There is a weak contact two miles ahead. It's not very consistent. The blip is only showing up on every two to three sweeps of the scanner."

The younger brother slipped behind me, leaning against my back. He eyed the green rotating beam on the glowing screen.

"See this blip."

"Yeah, it's not a strong return. What do you think it is?"

"I'm thinking a pleasure boat, but it's not moving. Strange."

"It could be a sport fish, drifting with lines out."

"There aren't any lights. You would think they would want to be lit up, so no one runs into them." Getting to my feet, I squinted into the darkness. I attempted to restore my night vision, which the bright radar screen destroyed moments before.

We stared off the starboard bow for the few minutes it took our eyes to adjust to the darkness. No red or green lights invaded the black horizon to our northwest.

"Nothing. I'll wake up Tom and Sloan. Turn on the Lokator and send the dolphins for a look."

"OK, Eric. I'll shut off our running lights so the other boat won't see us."

Moments later, our full crew was on deck. All eyes scanned the water. We were under sail, creeping toward the phantom blip on the radar screen. The Lokator remained blank. The dolphins disappeared into the darkness, responding to Sloan's hand signal to search.

Our sloop inched closer to the green splotch. The return was growing stronger on our navigation aid. The screen was dimmed so no light was visible to our foes. The target was one mile ahead. A splash next to our starboard beam announced the return of our mammalian lookouts.

"Flo, Jet is there a boat out there?" Sloan asked the aquatic duo. Jet responded by flipping his head up and down, while squealing noisily. He leapt into the air a couple of times before settling alongside us.

"There may be a boat out there, but neither the Lokator nor the dolphins are indicating the presence of a mini-sub." Tom rubbed his beard hard while staring into the blackness.

"The radar target isn't right for a big, steel shrimp boat. I would bet it's a small cabin cruiser or a sailboat. Why are they just sitting there, with no lights on? Let's get the sails down. We'll drift while we try to figure this out."

Eric and I doused the mainsail. Tom and Sloan rolled up the genoa. We bobbed back and forth, drifting with the current. Since the wind died down, the silence was nearly complete. A seagull screeched in the distance. Even though we were less than a mile from the other vessel, no lights or reflections were seen. A big, black void separated the two vessels.

"This is spooky," Sloan whispered. We drifted through the night.

"I'm not going to sit around wondering what the heck the other boat is doing all night. Why don't we launch the r.i.b (rigid inflatable boat) and head over for a look?"

I reached for the satellite phone. "Eric, shouldn't we call Gage and Mitch to let them know what we are doing?"

"No!" Eric grabbed my arm. "Not until we know what's going on."

"Easy, bro. You don't have to bite her head off. I'll grab a couple of guns while you launch the dinghy. Linda, we'll go take a peek. Listen for a call on the radio. If we find something, you notify Gage."

"You guys are going to leave us here...alone?"

"It will be fine, Sloan. You have a loaded mini-14 and two more Springfield's right here at the nav station. Nothing will happen. Eric and I will be right back."

After exiting the pilothouse, my husband climbed into the small dinghy. He reached up, accepting a pistol from his older brother. Tom joined him in the small rubber boat. We tossed their lines off.

"Let's use the electric outboard. I don't want to make any unnecessary noise."

"Guys, be careful."

The black inflatable emitted a low rumble while carrying our two men into the night. Flo and Jet tried to follow, when I gave them the recall signal. Reluctantly, they returned to our side, swimming lazy circles along our starboard quarter. The minutes ticked by like hours.

My eyes tried to see any movement through the pair of high-powered binoculars. The blackness was too complete.

"Do you think they're OK?"

"Sloan, they'll be fine. I bet the boys will be back any second." My attention was distracted by a light flashing on the console of the pilothouse. Our satellite phone rang in silent mode.

"Hello."

"Linda, my darling. What a surprise. It's Carlos." My throat closed.

"My dear, can you hear me? It's such a pleasure speaking with you. Where is Eric? He usually answers my calls."

"How did you get this number?"

"Oh, how soon you forget. My sources among your ranks are very good. They tell me everything I need to know. Even your present location is no secret to me. I'm coming for you, Linda. Once you are back aboard my yacht, I have many lessons to teach you.

We'll have plenty of time together, because you will never escape me a second time." The phone went dead.

"Oh, my God. Was that Carlos?" Sloan asked. Her hand gripped mine tightly.

"The son of a bitch. We've got to help Tom and Eric." Panic infused me. My hand pounded on the engine start button. The satellite phone blinked again.

"What?" I yelled into the receiver. I jammed the yacht's throttle forward. The diesel engine whined. Our sailboat leapt ahead.

"Linda, it's Gage. What's wrong?"

"Sloan, talk to to him. I need to watch the radar."

"We found a boat adrift with no lights on. Tom and Eric took the dinghy to check it out. Carlos called moments later. I think he's going to kill them."

"What? Why the hell didn't anyone call me? Where are you going now?"

"Linda's heading for the radar target at full throttle."

"No way. Sloan listen very carefully to me. I'm ordering you two to break off and get the hell out of there. Do not approach the other boat. There are military assets on the way."

"Sorry, Gage, the satellite phone is breaking up. I can't hear you." My eyes burned with concentration. The distance to the radar contact decreased rapidly.

"Linda, dammit. Get the hell out of there."

"Sloan. Either hang up the phone or I'm throwing it overboard."

I yanked back on the throttle. A hundred yards separated us from the target. With revolver in hand, my knees shook as I made my way to the bow. Our yacht slid through the water toward the now visible white hull.

A few yards away was a forty-foot sailing catamaran, drifting with the tide. No lights were visible. There was no sign of life aboard. The black inflatable dinghy bobbed alongside, empty. Where the heck were Eric and Tom?

The unmistakable beat of a helicopter's rotor broke the silence of the night. The bow of our boat bumped against the catamaran. A spotlight, from the chopper, inundated the scene with blinding white light. My feet hit the deck running. Two men jumped out of the helicopter's door. We were less than fifteen feet apart. They aimed their huge carbines at me.

"Drop it." One of the men growled viciously. "Drop your weapon. Get down on the deck, face down!"

"Don't shoot." The unmistakable voice of my husband penetrated my terrified brain. "Linda, drop the gun, it's the Coast Guard."

The pistol slipped from my grasp. It clattered on the deck as the two men, dressed in dark fatigues, descend upon me. One of them snatched my gun away. The other twisted my arm behind my back. A rough hand gripped the back of my neck, forcing me to my knees.

The man holding my firearm turned to Eric. The guy's weapon pointed at my husband. "Are you armed?"

"Yes, I have a pistol in the holster behind my back."

"Cuff her first," one Coastie said to the other. "You, turn around and keep your hands in the air."

"Please don't handcuff her. Did you talk to officer Mitch Connolly from the Drug Interdiction Unit?"

The Coast Guardsman snarled at my husband. "We were ordered to secure this vessel. Turn around. Put your hands on your head."

The other uniformed man pushed me roughly to the deck. "Get on the ground." My right check pressed against the cold fiberglass. A sharp click of metal stabbed against my now bound wrists. He yanked me to a half-sitting position.

The dark figure barked. "Stay here." He helped his partner cuff Eric. Carefully, they removed the gun from his holster. My guy was forced to his knees.

"Is there anyone else on board?"

"Yes, my brother is in the cabin."

"I'm right here, bro." Tom advanced out of the shadows with his hands in the air. The Coasties swung their weapons toward him.

"I'm unarmed. My gun is on the table below."

"Turn around. Put your hands on your head." The elder brother complied. One Coast Guard guy covered him as the other one patted the fishing captain down.

We looked skyward as a second helicopter approached, flying in fast. It hovered a few feet off the deck. Two men hopped off the skids to the the catamaran's deck.

The men appeared to be civilians with no uniforms visible. Because the night was so black, their faces remained a mystery. The taller man, who looked very familiar, walked directly toward me. He hauled me to my feet. I was about to sigh a huge sigh of relief when I recognized Gage. The infuriated look on his face made my blood run cold.

"What the hell do you think you were doing?" The Navy SEAL towered over me. His voice was a low, unearthly growl. One of the two Coast Guard guys stepped toward me. I cowered when Gage reached for me.

The other man from the second helicopter intercepted the Coastie, stopping him in his tracks. Gage and I were left alone.

"You didn't answer my question, Linda." The man's anthracite black eyes burned so hard, they nearly glowed. Out of the corner of my eye, I saw Eric attempt to come to my aid, handcuffs and all, until the other man in plainclothes grabbed him.

"Gage, leave her the hell alone."

"Mitch, can you have your guys take those two back to the cutter? Put them in the brig. Leave me here to deal with Linda. Alone."

"Gage, if you are trying to scare me, you're doing a damn good job of it."

"Dammit, Linda, I told you to break off and get the hell away from this boat. I should have the three of you arrested and thrown into jail for interfering with law enforcement." The infuriated man turned away for a moment, running his hands through his hair. His shoulders rose and fell as we watched the Coasties drag Tom and Eric in the direction of the hovering chopper.

The elder brother wrenched himself free, launching himself at Gage. The former Navy SEAL and Mitch struggled to control the brawny crab boat captain.

Tom's fist glanced off Gage's jaw. "Leave her alone."

"Stop it!" Sloan's voice shrieked through the night, from the sloop only yards away. "Tom, stop it."

The two Coasties who guarded Eric, swiveled around. They looked uncertain as to what to do.

The elder brother came to my side. He eased his bear of an arm around me. "You OK, Li'l Sis?"

"I'm fine."

Gage stalked toward us, staring the crab captain down. "You have no idea how close you just came. Tom, get on the sailboat with Sloan. I need to talk to Linda for a minute."

It appeared as though the big Navy SEAL regained his composure.

"It's OK." A quick shrug of my shoulders removed the crab captain's arm from around me. "Go give Sloan a hand."

Eric's older brother glanced at Gage before heading back to the sailboat. Mitch turned for the waiting chopper, grabbing my husband by the arm.

"You still want him locked up?"

"Absolutely. She'll be right behind him. You two," Gage said to Tom and Sloan, "set a course for Tampa. The Coast Guard will intercept you to escort you in. This project is done."

Eric spun out of the Coasties' grasp. "Gage, you've got to be kidding. What do you mean this project is done? You have no authority to do that."

The former Navy SEAL strode over to my husband. "Eric, you've violated my orders one time too many. I spoke with Martin before coming out here. You can consider yourself fired. Now you have legal matters to attend to. If I'm feeling generous, maybe I'll keep you locked up aboard the Coast Guard cutter for a few weeks until this whole mess is settled."

"Dammit, Gage, we had a deal."

"You blew it crab man. Get him out of here."

The two Coasties and Mitch dragged my husband over to the chopper, forcing him inside. The helicopters departed, buffeting the nearly empty deck with a vicious wind.

When the blast subsided, the ex-Navy SEAL slinked back toward me. Complete silence shrouded the gently rocking sailboat. Gage stopped in front of me. He frowned without breaking eye contact.

"Linda, I'm sorry to have to do this to you, but you and Eric can no longer work with me. I understand your passion, wanting to go after the man who hurt you so badly. I can no longer trust you. Make no mistake about it, I will get Carlos."

The former Navy SEAL's face was a stone mask. He stepped back. His eyes burned into mine. When Gage edged behind me, my skin prickled with fear. The hair rose on the nape of my neck. The only sound was the lapping of the water against the hull of the catamaran.

His hand seized my arm. After a click, relief flooded my wrists as the handcuffs fell away. Circulation to my lower hands was restored. I felt too frightened to rub my sore arms.

"We're going to keep you aboard the cutter for a few days until we decide exactly what to do with you. It would be great to send you back to the ranch, but you are too big a target. Our intel, along with the phone call you received tonight, leads me to believe Carlos is getting desperate. We still don't have an exact location for him."

"On top of this, your husband is too big a wild card for my liking. I can't have him going after Carlos on his own." The tall Navy SEAL again stared hard at me.

"Linda, what should I do with you?"

My lips closed because I didn't have a good answer for his question. A moment later, the tall Navy SEAL's powerful hand grasped my arm, leading me over to the now hovering second helicopter.

Chapter 19. Deep in the Everglades

My stomach was nearly out of my throat, back where it belonged. The helicopter circled the huge, white Coast Guard cutter steaming through the water below us. Twin plumes of white water exploded from the bow. A long tendril of wake trailed far behind the huge ship.

The aircraft bumped to a stop on the big "x" painted near the stern. Two men wearing crisp, white uniforms approach the bird, armed with big carbines. Mitch stood at the edge of the circle, surrounding the flight deck.

"Let's go," Gage growled as we stepped out of the chopper. He kept a light hold of my arm.

"We'll take her to the conference room first. I'd like to de-brief her before we stick her in the brig." Mitch told the former Navy SEAL as if I wasn't present. They led me to an interior room, with a long conference table surrounded by chairs. A man sat in one of the chairs. His age was close to fifty. A stern, unfriendly look framed his face as his eyes rose to glance at me. Gage and Mitch stood very straight, leading me to believe this guy was a big wig aboard the ship.

The man returned his gaze to the paperwork splayed on the table in front of him. "Have a seat."

Capt. Marlena Brackebusch

Mitch applied enough pressure to my shoulder to force me into the chair. The Coast Guard officer settled across from me. Gage folded his lanky frame in the seat to my right.

The Coastie placed a tape recorder on the table between us. "Linda, why don't you tell me what happened?"

"I have nothing to say other than you have no right to imprison an American citizen without a trial. I demand to be released immediately."

The man farther down the table raised his eyebrows, then lifted his head to look at me.

Mitch sighed. "Linda, you are not in prison. You are being held in protective custody. We're not even sure whether or not a crime has been committed by you or your husband this evening. So, yes we can legally hold you until this mess is sorted out."

"Gee Mitch, it seems like sorting out this mess may take quite a long time."

My eyes diverted to Gage who had a cocky smile on his face. "Mitch, this is ridiculous. We've not committed any crimes. Take me to see the captain."

"Linda, you are not in a great position to be making any demands right now."

"I want an attorney."

The man sitting down the table stared intently at me. "Why don't you answer the questions? Things will go much easier for you if you do."

"Who the hell are you?"

"Jesus, Linda, he's the executive officer aboard this ship."

"Mitch, I don't care if he's God, I'm not saying anything more."

The executive officer smirked. He returned to reading the papers in front of him.

"Linda, aboard this ship, he is God." Gage looked to the man studying the papers.

"What would you like us to do with miss uncooperative, sir?"

"If she's not willing to talk to us, lock her up. Keep her separated from her husband." The man didn't even bother to look at me.

My voice cracked. "You can't do that."

The former Navy SEAL pulled me to my feet. "Let's go. Don't make this situation any worse."

We walked down a series of corridors, with Mitch in front and the ex Navy SEAL behind me. The stark white walls of the passageways were lined with big pipes topped by many wire conduits. After descending a flight of stairs, we entered a new area of the ship. Finally, the Coast Guard officer stopped in front of a door with a small cutout containing steel bars.

The Coastie unlocked the door to the room, motioning me inside. "Home sweet home. There's a toilet in there if you need it. Don't even think about hollering for Eric because he won't be able to hear you. Keep in mind, we have video surveillance on you all of the time."

"Gage?" My final appeal to the Navy SEAL fell on deaf ears.

"Linda, it's been a long night. Go inside and try to rest."

Capt. Marlena Brackebusch

When the lock clicked in the closed steel door behind me, my brain flooded with memories of my imprisonment on Carlos' boat. Tears filled my eyes. I wouldn't give the video camera, mounted above the cold, white door, the satisfaction of seeing me cry. Instead, my eyes scanned the small room, taking stock of the sparse surroundings.

There was not much, except for a toilet, partially hidden from the camera by a white curtain. Along the wall, hung a pair of bunk beds adorned with only a thin mattress. There were no sheets, pillows, or blankets. A long sigh escaped after sitting down on the lower bed. Five A.M. blinked on my watch.

A few moments later, the lock clicked. Gage walked in, carrying a bottle of water along with bed linens and a pillow.

"Are you all right?" I detected a little warmth in his voice.

"Why are you doing this?"

"Linda, you're exhausted. Drink this water. Get some sleep. I'll talk to you in a couple of hours." Without another word, the former Navy SEAL exited the room, locking the door behind him.

A loud banging woke me from a dead sleep. Struggling off the bunk, I searched for the light switch. The door opened. Gage stood in the doorway.

"Did you get some rest?"

"A little. What time is it?"

"Zero-eight-hundred. Let's go to breakfast." The ex-Navy SEAL lead me through a series of corridors, up a flight of stairs. Another nondescript hallway lead to a white, steel door. He opened the door to a room containing a few small tables and chairs.

Off to one side stood a coffee urn with several white cups surrounding it. Seated at one of the tables was the man from last night, Mitch, and best of all, my husband.

"Eric." The urge to run over and throw my arms around him was nearly overwhelming. Before I had the chance, Gage nudged me into a chair at the opposite end of the table.

"Coffee?"

"Thanks." Eric eyes locked on mine. His silence persisted.

"Why don't we have a nice chat during our breakfast?" Mitch stared at me for a moment before turning his attention to my husband.

"Eric, you were pretty cooperative with us last night which is more than I can say for your wife." A knowing smile crossed my husband's face.

"Now the big problem is, what the heck are we going to do with you? Gage?"

"My immediate concern is for your safety. There is no doubt Carlos will kill you, Eric, at his first opportunity."

"Only if he gets the first shot off."

"Precisely the attitude we don't need at this time," Gage continued. "Which leads us to one definite fact. We cannot release you at this time."

"You have no grounds to hold us."

"Oh yes we do. Eric, did you have the owner's permission to board the catamaran last night?"

"No. What was the deal with the boat anyway?"

"It appeared to be abandoned. At this time there is no link between the sailboat and Carlos. This doesn't negate the fact you trespassed aboard the boat."

"Give me a break, Gage. We weren't trespassing. We were trying to find out if anyone aboard needed help."

"Trespassing can be interpreted as attempted piracy, a very serious charge," said the executive officer. Again, he stared intently at my husband. "This gives us plenty of grounds to hold you until an investigation can be completed. The investigating officer will likely revoke your captain's licenses, pending the outcome of the investigation."

"You can't do that." My ire rose. Eric shook his head "no" slowly.

"Mrs. Iverson, you may want to listen to your friend's proposal, before getting all upset. Gage."

"The captain of this vessel has generously allowed me to come up with an alternative solution to this situation. Before implementing my plan, the two of you must agree to my proposal." Gage leaned back, surveying my husband and me.

"Your first choice is to remain aboard this vessel temporarily losing your captains' licenses. The charges against you will include, at the very least, trespassing. Or you can accompany me off the ship. We'll head over to Elton's training facility, where we did the firearm's training. You will remain there until we've caught Carlos."

Eric looked to me before speaking to Gage. "We'll go to Elton's facility."

"Great. One more thing, cowboy. If you're thinking of trying to sneak out of Elton's camp, forget it.
Remember, a tall electric fence encircles the property.
The perimeter is surrounded by some of the most
impenetrable swamps in the Everglades. Your best
move is to relax there, enjoying my good friend's hospitality."

"No problem, Gage. Linda and I could use a little
down time." Eric smiled at the look of confusion on
my face. What was he thinking?

After breakfast, my husband and I were locked in
the brig together. Once the door closed, he surrounded
me with his arms.

"Eric, what the heck is going on?"

"I guess Gage is really pissed off at me. You're
getting caught up in this mess."

"Why did you agree to go to Elton's facility?" My
husband pulled me onto the lower bunk. He lay with
his arms surrounding me. The scene reminded me of
a night on Mark's fishing boat, so very long ago. The
night he convinced me to allow him to drive me back
to Naples.

"Let's not talk about it now. Trust me. Try to get
some sleep."

Eric shook me awake later in the day. Gage and
Mitch were huddled with my husband in a discussion.

Gage turned his attention to me. "Linda, if you're
awake enough, we're out of here."

"Where are we going?"

"The Coast Guard is nice enough to fly us to
Naples airport where Jake and Elton are waiting for us.

From there, we'll head over to my buddy's place where you guys will be on ice for a while."

"Sounds good to me." Eric seemed so agreeable. Strange.

The Coast Guard officer and ex-Navy SEAL led us to the flight deck of the ship. My stomach did a couple of flips as we walked to the white and red helicopter, warming up on the tarmac in front of us. Mitch climbed in first, followed by my husband, who turned around to give me a hand.

The chopper cruised along the bright blue Gulf of Mexico, soon landing in the general aviation section of the Naples Airport. Standing beside a black van were Jake and Elton, who casually strolled over to our helicopter.

"OK, kids, now behave yourselves. We're going to get out of the chopper, then walk over to the van. Don't try any funny stuff." The former Navy SEAL frowned at us.

"No problem, Gage." Eric said amiably.

My husband and I sat opposite one another in the back of the car. To my right and left were Jake and Gage. Mitch and Elton flanked my husband. Jake squeezed my hand.

"Are y'all looking forward to being guests at my fine facility?"

Eric smiled at our host. "Elton, we really appreciate your hospitality." His attitude baffled the heck out of me. Gage's eyes narrowed. He looked equally surprised.

After the four hour drive to the southern Everglades, we were relieved to finally exit the van. The four ex-military men escorted us into the sleeping quarters.

"I'm giving you two the best room in the house." Elton motioned us into a bunk room similar to the one we stayed in before.

"I'm not gonna lock you in or anything, seeing as you can't escape my security. There are a few ground rules you two must follow. One, neither of you will have a weapon on you at any time. Two, do not go within one hundred yards of the fence. Three, you will personally check in with me every evening at eighteen-hundred hours. Other than that, feel free to enjoy the facilities."

"We took the liberty of bringing your clothes here." Jake's sheepish look softened his tough features. "Tom and Sloan got your things together. They're in your room."

"Thanks, Jake." Eric extended his hand to our old friend. Gage shook his head, then marched over to my husband, standing chest to chest with him.

"Eric, I don't want any problems."

"Neither do I."

My husband led me into the room, closing the door behind us.

"Eric what the heck is going on?" His finger on my lips silenced me.

"Honey, why don't we put our stuff away. We'll go for a nice stroll around the grounds. It looks like a beautiful day outside."

An old cypress tree gave us little protection from the hot summer day. We were drenched in sweat. The sky turned black as the typical afternoon thunderstorms swirled overhead. The wind buffeted us. Angry clouds squeezed out huge raindrops.

"Eric, what the heck is going on?"

"I didn't want to have a conversation in the room. We have no idea how much surveillance they have on us. The room is probably bugged."

"Why did you agree to come here? They can't keep us here. Those charges of piracy are ridiculous."

"Linda, we know that and they know that. They were threatening us so they could keep an eye on us. I have another plan."

"What plan?"

"We are going to break out of here. There is no way we could have escaped from the Coast Guard cutter. This place gives us our best chance for liberation. Once we are out of here, I will get you to Key West to stay with your sister. Then I will go after Carlos."

"Eric, wait just a minute. First of all, how do you expect to get out of here? There's a twelve-foot electric fence surrounding this place."

"I haven't figured it all out yet. Make sure you are ready when the time is right."

"There's another problem with this plan. Have you forgotten we are miles and miles deep in a swampy jungle? How the heck are we going to get out of the Everglades?"

"The same way the Native American's did—walk and maybe canoe."

"Are you nuts? The swamps are full of alligators and snakes."

"Linda, don't worry. Remember, I'm an Alaskan fisherman. I've been in very tight fixes in the wilderness."

"Eric, you've never dealt with a jungle like this before." A huge bolt of lightning streaked out of the sky. It exploded close to the old cypress we hunkered under. The thunder was deafening.

"My dear, I may have found our way out." My husband grinned as he led me back to the shelter of the buildings.

Chapter 20. Escape from the Everglades

Over the next couple of days, Eric scrounged various items from the grounds and buildings of the encampment. He stashed them in a nearly invisible slit in our mattress. In the wardrobe, an old backpack, a metal canteen, and two water bottles were concealed.

"We need to break out of here soon," my Alaska fisherman confided later in the afternoon, beneath the old cypress tree. Another round of severe thunderstorms brewed in the distance. The crackle of thunder grew loud as dusk approached.

"I have no idea how long we have until my stash of supplies is discovered. It's almost six. Let's go check in with Elton."

We walked to the main office building. Our host reclined behind his desk. A light rap on the door caught his attention.

"Hi, Elton, can we come in?"

"Sure, come have a seat." We settled into chairs across from the lanky black man.

"Eric, I have to say I'm pleased with you two. I sure thought y'all would be more trouble than you are."

"Thanks, Elton. The rest is good for us, especially for Linda. She's been so stressed out recently."

"Yes, I feel safe here."

"Good. Is there anything I can get for you two?"

"No, thanks. We're doing just fine."

After our check in with the boss, we hustled back to our room. Eric gathered up our few stolen possessions. "Linda, let's take a walk."

Once back under the protection of the cypress tree, the skies let loose with a deluge of rain. Thunder and lightning boomed, igniting the sky around us.

"Shouldn't we get inside?"

"Linda, keep watch. I'm going to climb up the tree. We'll stash the backpack in the split limb half way up. Tonight may be the night with all of this bad weather."

After changing into dry clothes, we had dinner. After supper, we doubled back to our room. Eric pointed silently to the two pair of boots he confiscated from the supply room. He laced up a pair when a huge bolt of lightning struck outside. Our room plunged into darkness.

"The power's out. Hurry, this is our chance."

After cramming my feet into the boots, we sprinted back to the cypress tree. It was a good thing we knew the way, because the sky was pitch black. The only light came from the occasional flash of the storm. After retrieving the bag, Eric shepherded us away from the buildings.

We scampered through the dense brush. Branches whipped our faces. The looming fence halted us in our tracks. My eyes rose to look at the towering wire mesh. How the heck were we going to get over this?

"This is it."

"Eric, stop. What about the electricity?"

"The power is out, but who knows for how long. They must have a backup generator. We need to get over the fence. Think of it as the wall we climbed during training. I'll go first, to help you over."

A swarm of mosquitoes besieged my head, buzzing and biting me mercilessly. Swatting only made it worse.

"Come on, let's go."

My husband extended his hand, brushing the fence with his fingertips. I cringed. He scaled up the mesh. With one leg over the top, he straddled the apex beneath the sharp barbed wire. Lightning crashed around us.

"Linda, give me your hand." He reached down a few feet over my head. "Come on. We have to hurry."

Fear flooded my body. Adrenaline kicked in. Hand over hand I wrestled up the slick wire. My foot skidded off nearly sending me back to the ground. My arms trembled from the exertion. A few second later, I perched alongside my husband.

With a gloved hand, he thrust up on the barbed wire, allowing me to wriggle beneath the razor-edged spikes. The sharp prongs gouged into my back through the thin shirt. Once I was clear, he squeezed through the narrow gap. We slipped down the other side of the barricade into knee deep water.

"This way." He dragged me into the thigh-deep swamp. My imagination ran wild thinking of all the creepy crawlies, lingering behind every tree or in every puddle. We blindly sloshed, trotted, and scrambled as fast as we could over the next couple of hours. The rain pelted us mercilessly. Mosquitoes gulped our blood. Out of breath, I wrenched my guy to a stop.

"Eric, I need a break." We paused on a patch of more or less dry ground beneath another huge cypress tree.

"Get up the tree." He cupped his hands together to hoist me to the first branch. My arms screamed in protest. I dragged myself up. We clambered over a few branches. The light drizzle contributed to the misery. A dull half-moon peeked out from behind the thick cloud cover. The incessant buzzing of blood-thirsty bugs, rang in our ears.

"We made it." My husband grinned at my dirt-streaked face. I was miserable, wet, and scared. Fighting my emotions, a smile formed on my face.

"You really know how to show a girl a good time."

With a laugh, he brushed back a couple of errant strands of hair away from my forehead. My soaked T-shirt clung to my back.

"We have to keep going. There's no way of telling when they will notice we are gone."

"Which way do we head?"

"Northwest. We need to keep the moon over our left shoulder. We'll try to put as much distance between us and them by dawn. After first light, we'll find a place to hole up in."

We scrambled down from the tree, making our way across the relatively dry area of a large hardwood hammock. For the next forty-five minutes, our feet trudged along until we reached the edge of a big pond.

There was only a thin strip of land visible in the early morning light. We paused to consider our options, when we heard dogs, howling behind us.

"They sound like bloodhounds," Eric whispered. "They can only mean one thing. Elton and his men are right behind us."

"What are we going to do?" My question was interrupted by a voice coming through what sounded like a megaphone.

"Eric and Linda, give yourselves up. You won't be harmed. If you continue on, you will die in the Everglades. Why not stop now? Let's be smart about this."

"Like hell I'm going to give up. Linda, we have to go through the water. Otherwise, the dogs will be able to smell our tracks."

"I'm not going into the pond. There are snakes and alligators..."

My husband stopped the rant with a finger on my lips. "Don't you trust me?"

"Of course I do, but this is the Everglades." My husband handed me a large stick. A knife, nearly the size of a machete, was drawn out of his backpack.

"Take this stick. Beat on anything which comes too close. You can use it to test the depth of the water. Stay close behind me." He waded into the chest deep water. After a second's hesitation, I slid into the water behind him. My hand clutched the back of his shirt.

The faint hint of dawn lit up the murky brown swamp around us. Debris floated by, including decaying plants and leaves. Underwater snags scratched our legs.

A thick area of reeds gave us a challenging passage, but also provided good cover from our foes. We followed a very narrow path. The swamp grazed the underside of our chins. Something slimy glanced off my leg. The razor-sharp sawgrass slashed our skin when we brushed against it. Suddenly, movement flashed by the corner of my eye.

"Snake." The shriek stuck in my throat. The black serpent slithered by, on the surface of the water. Only two feet separated my head from the nearby reeds.

"Stay still. I think it's a coral snake." The ugly striped reptile undulated only a foot from my face. The forked, pink tongue flicked out. We struggled on, wading through the swamp, until a patch of dry ground appeared. A six foot alligator dominated the bank.

"This little trek keeps on getting more and more exciting," Eric whispered. "We'll head right to see if we can get around him."

We waded to our right. The prehistoric monster slid into the water behind us.

"Let's get out, now." My husband jerked on my hand, wrenching me from the swamp. We rushed over to the protection of a large strand of trees.

"Whew! It looks like we lost them for now. There's a nice big tree up ahead we can hide in. Come on." Eric led me into the forest. The sun peeked over the horizon. We paused in front of a large tree with peeling red bark.

"This looks good."

"It's a gumbo limbo tree. The foliage up high is very thick."

"Linda, stay here. I'm going to cut up bamboo stalks to make a platform to sit on. This tree should give us great shelter."

He was gone a few minutes before returning with an armful of hefty limbs.

After dropping them at my feet, my cowboy climbed a few branches into the red tree. One by one, I handed the poles up to him. They were carefully wedged between a couple of large limbs ten feet off the ground. Eric weaved vines around the ends to hold them in place.

"Linda, come on up." With the last of my strength, I clambered to our makeshift shelter. "Sit down here. I'm going to gather palm fronds."

Eric returned a short while later carrying a huge bunch of fronds. He spread several on base of the bamboo logs. Others were weaved over our heads to help shade us.

"Come here." The fisherman leaned against the big trunk of the tree with his arms extended. My body nearly collapsed against his chest.

"Drink some water." With his left arm around me, he held the bottle to my lips. We split the precious ration of lukewarm liquid.

"Eric, it feels like there's something on my back."

"Let me take a look." With my back turned to him, he raised my shirt.

"Linda, take it easy." His hand tightened on my shoulder.

"What is it?"

"Relax, it's OK."

"Eric, what the hell is on my back?" I squealed a little too loudly. My husband reached around to cover my mouth.

"Calm down. Don't yell. There's a leech on your back."

"What?"

"Stop struggling. I'll get him off you." When I complied, Eric withdrew a cigarette lighter from the backpack.

"Hold still." The flame singed my back. A moment later, my husband drew me against his chest. He held the wriggling worm in front of me.

"Get it away from me." I tried to squirm out of his grasp. He laughed, tossing the beast away from the shelter.

"Of all the frightening things out here, a little leech scared you. Tough Linda, huh? Let me look over the rest of you." After a few minutes of checking, no further parasites were located. My husband drew me against his chest.

"You need to sleep." He didn't have to ask me twice. Even though wet, hot, and miserable, the exhaustion won out. My mind drifted away to the constant buzzing of blood-sucking flying teeth.

The sun rose high overhead when my eyes struggled open. The soggy, dirty clothes clung to my skin, rubbing it raw. The heat of the day had to be close to ninety-five degrees.

"You're awake, sleepy head." Though Eric was as miserable as I, he tried to keep our spirits up. "Let's get a move on. It's better to travel in the daylight."

"Do you think they are still looking for us?"

"It's hard to say. We need keep moving. We'll stop again near dusk. I'll build another shelter for tonight."

We loped into another hardwood hammock forest, keeping the sun to our left. A steady stream of sweat trickled off us. Not a hint of breeze offered any relief from the searing humidity or the constant assault from the bugs. After a couple of hours, we devoured the last bottle of water.

"We'll need to start a fire later to disinfect water."

"Won't Elton's men see it?"

"It's a chance we'll have to take. There should be Native Americans and hunters out here. With any luck, our fire won't look suspicious."

We trod on for another two hours before my husband called a halt to our journey. Another gumbo limbo tree stood only twenty-five yards from an area of water. This time we both gathered bamboo and palm fronds for our new home. After an hour of back breaking work, a nice platform stood ten feet above the ground.

Firewood was gathered. Eric squatted over the dry kindling with the cigarette lighter procured from Elton's compound.

A nice fire blazed away. He strained water through a bandana into the metal canteen, placing it in the coals to sterilize it.

"Keep an eye on the fire. I'm going to try to find our supper."

An agonizing forty-five minutes elapsed before my guy returned to camp. He came out of the brush dragging a dead snake. With the amazing skill of a fisherman, he skinned it. A skewer, made from a tree branch, was inserted though the long body. The lifeless serpent sizzled over the fire.

"Dinner is served. Python on a stick." He grinned while picking some of the seared white flesh off the carcass. Eric handed me a small chunk. A surprised look crossed his face when I swallowed it down.

"Linda, you never cease to amaze me. After the leech incident, I didn't think you'd eat snake so easily."

"It tastes like chicken." Despite our misery, we laughed.

After the interesting dinner of serpent and swamp water, Eric stoked up the fire. The smoke from the blaze kept most of the mosquitoes away. From the vantage point of our overhanging platform, we had a good view of the surrounding area.

"Eric, this isn't a bad shelter. Where did you learn how to do this?"

"I grew up on the edge of the wilderness in both Oregon and Alaska. My brothers and I would endlessly wander around the woods, building forts in trees. My dad would take us hunting and camping, when he wasn't fishing."

"Thank goodness for your dad."

The next morning, a few sips of water was breakfast. As we packed up, a surprise was pulled from our knapsack.

"Linda, have some of this." Eric handed me two squares of chocolate.

"Where did you find this?" The sweet, dark candy melted in my mouth. "Oh my God this is good."

"I grabbed it at Elton's place. We'll ration it to make our energy last."

We hiked into the thick underbrush. After thirty minutes of trudging, a very important discovery was made. On the path ahead of us sat an old, beat-up canoe. There was no one in sight.

"There's a small hole in the hull. If we can patch it and make a couple of paddles, our travels will be much easier."

"Eric, maybe we could tie palm fronds around the outside. They will slow the leak."

"Good idea. I'm going to fashion a wooden plug from this gumbo limbo tree. Between the two, the leak shouldn't be too bad."

During the next hour, we sweated while repairing the small boat.

"There are no paddles, but it looks seaworthy enough. I'll see if I can make oars." Eric led me over to a cypress tree. "These two branches look good."

He hacked off a couple of five foot pieces. It took a few minutes to roughly carve a couple of paddles.

"Come on, Linda. Let's give it a try." We tentatively launched the rickety canoe. Soon, we paddled along at a pretty good clip.

"This is much better than swimming through this swamp."

After another night of swatting mosquitoes in my sleep, the next day brought hour after hour of paddling along the interconnecting waterways. Every few miles, we paused to bail out the boat. Fortunately, our makeshift repair seemed to be holding.

My head drooped from the scorching sun.

"Let's take a break." Eric steered the canoe for a dry patch of ground. We scrambled out of the little boat.

"Sitting in the shade sure feels good."

"Linda, drink more water. You need to stay hydrated."

We finish the last bits of chocolate, washed down with swamp water.

"Your face is getting sunburned." His hand gently cradled the edge of my jaw. "Let me try something." He edged over to the river bank, returning with a handful of mud. He smeared it on my face.

"*Ugh*, that stinks."

"Hey, most women would pay a ton of money for a swamp mud facial."

Without much rest, we continued paddling into the afternoon. Up ahead, we saw a clearing. A dirt road ran alongside the canal. Eric scrambled out of the canoe, then extended his hand to help me up the bank.

"This road leads north. It should lead us to US-41." We trekked through the hottest part of the day, sweltering and dripping wet in the blazing sun. Storm clouds formed overhead. Rain pelted us. We slipped and slid along the now muddy road.

"This feels like walking through a sauna."

"Linda, we should be at the highway soon. Keep going."

Around the next bend, the dirt road joined the blacktop. We crouched alongside, trying to come up with a plan. The sun peeked out from the clouds.

"Eric, I'll stand by the road and try to hitch a ride. When they stop, you come on over."

"Sounds like a plan to me." Only ten minutes passed before an old, rusty white pickup slowed down in response to my outstretched thumb. There were two rugged looking men inside. The driver was a gray-haired grizzled old guy. My husband crouched by the guardrail.

"Do you need help, miss?" The passenger said in a very thick southern accent.

"Yes, my husband and I had a boating accident. We need a ride."

"Well come on in little lady. Bring yer feller, too."

The man on the passenger side climbed in behind the seat, allowing me to squeeze in between Eric and the driver. One could not miss the rack full of guns bolted across the back window. The old man stomped on the accelerator. He glanced at us out of the corner of his eye. "Where y'all headed. I can drop yer at the ranger's station."

"No," Eric said a little too loudly, then lowered his voice. "We're trying to get to Ft. Myers."

"Well young fella, my cousin and me are headin' back to the homestead in Immokalee. You welcome to come by and rest for a stretch, iffin' you want to."

"That's so sweet." My muddy face lit up with a most charming smile. "Mr...."

"There ain't no mista' here. My friends call me Cooter." The old man grinned through his missing front teeth. "My cousin's name is Travis."

"Miss, we don't rightly know yer names?" Travis asked from the back seat.

"Eric and Linda." My husband pivoted in his seat to shake hands with the man behind us. The old truck rumbled and bounced along until we made a right turn on state road twenty-nine.

An hour later, Cooter made another right on a rutted dirt road, soon coming to a stop in front of a broken down ranch-style house. Laundry hung off a frayed line strung between two trees.

Chapter 21. Deliverance

When we climbed out of the truck, two half-naked young kids ran over accompanied by a white pit bull.

"Don't let the dog scare ye'. She's mor' in likely to lick ya', then bite ya'." We followed Cooter to the porch, where an older woman sat on a rocker She swayed back and forth while snapping the ends off beans.

"I wonder if that is Mrs. Cooter," I whispered to Eric.

"*Shh*. This whole scene reminds me of the movie *Deliverance*."

"This is ma wife, Mae. She's the granny to the young uns. The older one's Susie May and the younger one is Sara May." The little bare-footed girl ran to her granny's side. Her little fingers grabbed a hold of the old lady's apron. The thumb, on her right hand, slipped into her mouth. Two adorable baby-blue eyes stared warily at us.

"Mae, these are my new friends, Eric and Linder."

"Pleased to meet y'all. What the heck happened to you child?" The old woman struggled to her feet. She shuffled over to squint at my face. "You got chicken pox or somethin'?"

"Mosquito bites," Eric explained.

Capt. Marlena Brackebusch

"My gosh darn, they ates you alive. Come with me child we'll fix you on up." Granny grabbed my arm, leading me into the house. "Susie May! You run over and git me some of that there aller vera right quick."

The old man's voice floated through the open kitchen window. "Son, why don't we sit for a spell while my woman fixes yours up? I do believe I could use me some liquid refreshment."

"Jasmine," the old man hollered. A young teen-age girl rushed through the kitchen to the front porch.

"Yes, Grandpa?"

"Be a good girl and git us glasses of my special lemonade. Make sure ya puts some ice in it. Pour a glass for the lady inside, too. They both look right thirsty."

Granny tried to wash the dirt off my face with a dish towel. The teen girl poured lemonade from a glass pitcher liberated out of the refrigerator. After removing most of the mud from my skin, the old lady rubbed on pale jelly. It oozed out of the green leaves the young girl brought in.

The old woman explained the remedy. "Aller Vera. It'll take the sting out. There. Much better. Let's go on the porch and relax. It's much cooler out there." We joined the men on the rocking chairs. A cooling breeze from building rain clouds blew across the veranda. The old man handed me a lemonade. The color was darker than normal. After the first sip, I knew why.

"Cooter, you old bugger. Were ya mixin' the Jack Daniel's in my pitcha agin'? What iffin' the younguns git into it?" Granny wagged her bony finger at the old man. A big toothless grin lit up his face.

"Now, now Granny, there's company here. We have to take right good care of them."

He winked at my husband. The three girls gathered at our feet. I guessed they didn't get many strangers around here.

"Now, young feller, you need to fess up to me. Are you runnin' from the law? Not that I care much one way or 'nuther."

"No, we're not. It's a long story, but we are actually running from our friends," Eric said while looking at me tentatively.

"Iffin' yer runnin' from yer friends, I don't reckon they be good friends."

"It's complicated."

"Where are you from boy?" Travis asked.

"Alaska. My brother and I have a crab fishing business up there. Linda lived in Naples until we married a year ago."

The teenage girl named Jasmine jumped to her feet. "I knew it. Yer the captain from the fishing show."

"What are talking about girl? What fishing show?" Cooter asked his granddaughter.

"The one on TV."

"Where did you go watchin' TV? We ain't got no such fancy gadget here at the homestead."

"At my friend's house. He's the captain." The girl blushed several shades of red. She leapt over to her granny, whispering in her ear.

"Now Jasmine. You know we don't tell no secrets 'round hear. It's rude. You go on and tell Mr. Eric what you just told me."

"I can't." The young lady turned beet red. Her shyness made it difficult for her to even look at Eric. With a twirl of her simple, threadbare dress, she turned away.

"Jasmine," Cooter said in a raised voice. "You tell Mr. Eric right now, or I'll tell yer daddy. He'll give ya' a right spanking for not listenin' to Granny."

"Gran Pa!"

Eric tried to diffuse the situation. "It's OK."

"Jasmine." Cooter folded his arms. The little girl looked up at the fisherman with a strange look of awe on her face.

"I said," she whispered so quietly we barely heard her. "That you is the handsome one. The cutest captain on the show. All the girls know that." Poor Jasmine fled into the house. Eric did a great job of keeping a straight face, though a touch of red stained his cheeks. This rosy glow could not be contributed to sunburn.

"Of course all the girls know that," I repeated, getting a laugh out of the adults.

"Well, doggone it. I didn't know we had a celebrity here with us."

"My gosh," Granny said jumping up. "I'd best be settin' a couple of mo' plates for supper. You will be stayin' the night with us tonight?"

"We don't want to impose."

"Nonsense. There's plenty of my home-made fried chicken. We also got us a nice clean showwa iffin' you want to wash up. I kin' find clothes in my daughter's closet that will fit the missus. Cooter, why don't you see iffin' you can fix up the captain?"

"Yes, dear." The old man winked at Eric. "After yer bath, we'll set out here and talk mo', maybe have 'nother drink."

Granny threw her hands up in the air. "Cooter!" She grabbed my wrist, pulling me inside the house.

"Don't you worry none, Miss Linda, we'll find you clean clothes. I'll wash up yours. After supper, you and the captain can sleep in the girl's room. They can bunk with their momma and poppa for tonight. They's only small beds, but their comfortable."

"Granny, thank you so much." The hospitality of these simple, country folk was overwhelming. After a good scrub in the cool shower, I found Eric still drinking with the men on the front porch. The three young girls were busy setting the table for dinner. Through the window, I watched a man and woman drive up in another beat-up truck.

"The youngun's momma and poppa are home. Why don't you head out on the porch and meet them?"

"I thought you could use my help."

"Nonsense, Miss Linda. You look right tired. Go out and rest a spell."

After introductions, we found out the girls' father was a local auto mechanic. Their mother was a cashier at Walmart. We spent the next hour chatting with them as Jasmine made a production of refilling our lemonades. She especially doted on Eric. He thanked her for every refill with his charming smile.

Capt. Marlena Brackebusch

My head spun from the Jack Daniel's, lack of sleep, and hunger by the time we sat down for dinner. Eric and I tried not to wolf down the delicious fried chicken, collared greens, and black eyed peas. After Granny stuffed us full of supper, a homemade apple pie was brought to the table.

"We even gonna top off this warm pie with Jasmine's vaniller ice cream. She made it with her own two hands." The young lady proudly scooped up the yummy looking ice cream, giving Eric the biggest plop. The dessert was even better than dinner.

"This is the best ice cream I've ever had." The teenage girl blushed when my husband winked at her.

After supper, we relaxed on the porch. The heat of the day surrendered to the cool twilight.

"We need to figure how to git the two of ya' to Ft. Myers, tomorrow," Cooter said while rocking on his chair. "Can't say I've drivin' there too much myself."

"Don't worry about it. We'll find a way. Could you tell me if there is a bank in town or a place we can get some cash?"

Travis slapped his knee. "Yeehaw. We're gonna rob a bank."

"I don't think he means to rob it, you old fool," Granny said. "He's probably got one of them little plastic cards. When you stick it in the machine, the money pops out."

"Exactly." Eric looked at me with raised eyebrows.

"The Injun casino is right down the street. They have lots of cash there. Maybe they got one of them machines, I don't rightly know."

"Sure, a casino will have a cash machine," I said.

"That settles it. I'll drive y'all over there first thing tomorrow."

The following morning we enjoyed excellent strong coffee while thanking our hosts for their help.

"Cooter." Eric sat next to the old man on the porch after breakfast. "Can I do anything to repay you for all your help? I'm not sure what we would have done...."

"Nonsense boy, we've loved havin' y'all here. I tell you what. Iffin' I ever get lost up in Alaska, I be lookin' you up." Grandpa laughed with a slap of his knee. Jasmine stood off to the side, staring at the fishing captain with wonder. This gave me an idea.

"Eric, why don't I take a picture of you with Jasmine. She can show all her friends at school the famous fishing captain who stayed at her house."

"Linda, that's a right great idear. Granny go find the Polaroid."

The old lady returned a few minutes later with an old beat-up instant camera. My husband put his arm around shy Jasmine. She beamed into the lens. Once the old machine spit out the picture, Eric autographed it for her.

As we were getting into the truck, I noticed the young lady sitting under the shade tree, staring at the picture with a dreamy smile on her face.

The Seminole Casino was busy for a weekday morning. The slot machines rang. We wandered around for a few minutes, taking stock of our surroundings. After a short search, we found the money machine over by the cashier's desk.

"Eric, I'm going to use the ladies room." While I washed my hands, someone grabbed my arm.

Next to me was our neighbor from the Cove Inn. "Linda, is that you? Oh, my God, what happened? Everyone in Naples is looking for you."

"Marlena, you can't tell anyone you saw me. Who are you here with?"

"Toby is over at the blackjack table. Where's Eric?"

"He's outside trying to get money out of the cash machine. Is Gage here?"

"No, don't worry. Let's go find the guys." Out in the main part of the casino, we came upon the crab boat captain. He did a double take on our friend.

"What the heck?" My husband looked like he was ready to bolt out the door, when Toby walked up.

The Naples charter captain reached out to shake my husband's hand. "Eric and Linda. What are you two doing here?"

"You guys didn't see us. Come on, Linda, we've got to get out of here." He grabbed my arm to lead me away when Toby stopped us.

"Do you two need help?"

"We could really use a ride. Please don't let anyone know where we are."

"You can count on us, Eric. Did you know Gage is turning southwest Florida upside down looking for you?"

"Did he call the police?"

"I don't know. Where are you two headed?" Marlena asked.

"To Key West. After leaving Linda with her sister, I have unfinished business to attend to."

"Are you going after that Carlos guy we've been hearing about?"

My eyes narrowed at my husband. "Yes, WE are going after him."

"I'm not arguing with you woman." Eric raised his voice, then lowered it again. "Let's not discuss this here. There may be ears."

"Why don't we go to my daughter's house? It would be a great place to figure out a plan."

"Where's your daughter's house?"

"It's right down the street. Come on." Toby led us to the casino exit. We barely squeezed the four of us into their Tacoma pickup for the twenty minute ride to a nice Mediterranean-style vacation home down a small side road.

The house sat on a very private lot surrounded by a chain link fence. The front of the house was obscured by Australian pines. Toby locked the gate behind us.

We entered the cool air-conditioned living room, plopping down on a comfy couch.

"Are you taking the ferry to Key West?" Toby asked Eric.

"Yes, that's why we went to the casino. I didn't want to use my credit card to pay for the ferry. Gage has friends in many places, who may be looking at our recent transactions. The casino should throw them off the track. We'll have to try to get on the ferry using false names."

"The only problem with this plan is the ferry company requires picture identification."

"We didn't think of that. I can't use my license, because Gage may have someone checking the ferry terminal. We'll have to deal with this issue when we get there. The ferry agents may believe our fake names."

"Yeah, Bonnie and Clyde." Eric frowned at my attempted joke.

"We'll figure it out." Toby reassured my edgy husband, who kept looking out the window.

"Eric, none of the gang looking for you knows about this house."

"Tell us what's been happening in Naples."

"Gage and Jake were at the Chickee bar talking to Jan and Cindy. We overheard them asking the bartenders if they've heard from you."

"Did they say where they were looking for us?"

"Yes, they said you had a boating accident in the Everglades. Gage told us Linda was injured. We overheard him telling the bartenders about a massive search party. He instructed the two ladies to tell him if either of them hear from you," Toby said.

"How about this for a plan." Marlena leaned forward in her chair. "We'll stay here tonight. Tomorrow morning, we can drive you to the ferry terminal. Toby will figure a way to get you on the boat."

My husband and I spent the remainder of the day trying to relax. Eric's nerves were very raw. While supper cooked, Toby pulled him aside.

"How about a Jack Daniel's? You need to relax, Eric."

"Great, Toby. Thanks." The two guys went into the man cave to shoot pool, leaving Marlena and I alone to chat.

"Are you doing OK, Linda?"

"About as good as can be expected. Our little jaunt through the swamps of the Everglades was terrifying. A snake swam right by my head."

"How awful."

"I'll be a much happier when this nightmare is finally over."

After dinner, we had a couple more cocktails in the living room.

Just before bedtime, my husband asked one more favor. "Toby, can I use your cell phone?"

"Of course."

The number was dialed from memory. The phone was set on speaker.

"Hello."

"Tom."

"Hi, Mom, how are you?"

"Are you alone, brother?"

"I'm at the Chickee Bar. No mom I haven't heard from Eric. He's still missing in the Everglades."

"I'll call you back in five minutes." After hanging up the phone, my husband looked at us. "Gage must be the bar. We'll wait a few minutes to call Tom back."

"Hey, where the hell are you?" The elder brother whispered through the phone a short time later.

"I can't tell you brother. Is Gage there?"

"Yes. He's hopping mad about your escape."

"Does he have any leads?"

"None he's shared with me. Are you and Linda OK?"

"We're fine. I'll call you soon."

"Eric, what the heck are you going to do?"

"Brother, we're going to meet up with Linda's sister in Key West. Don't tell anyone. I gotta go."

The rest of the night was spent tossing and turning in bed.

The next morning, our friends drove us to Ft. Myers Beach. Our assumed names and lack of ID caused a stir among the office people at the ferry terminal. Thankfully, Toby's driver's license, along with his assurances, allowed us passage up the gangplank. We walked to a quiet seating area near the front of the large ship.

"Thanks, man."

"I'm going to get off the boat. There shouldn't be any more difficulties, at least with this trip. You guys be safe." Our friend left the ship. He was stopped, on the gangplank, by one of the crew members, pointing at his watch. The Naples captain shrugged his shoulders before disappearing into the crowd.

"We made it." Eric tried to force a smile. "I'm going to look around."

"Honey, we're fine. There is no way Gage could know where we are."

"You're right, but if I know the Navy SEAL as well as I think I do, he'll be checking all forms of transportation. With any luck, he hasn't thought of this one, yet." My husband stepped over to the stairs, leading to the deck. He returned a few minutes later, right after the boat cast off.

"It's all clear. I didn't see anyone suspicious."

We relaxed as the big ferry steamed down the channel. In the Gulf, she picked up speed, flying along the surface of the water at a steady thirty-four knots. Only three and a half hours went by before tiny, round mangrove islands dotted the horizon.

The ship zipped by the entrance marker to the Northwest Channel. We docked a few minutes later at the ferry terminal near the Key West Bight. Eric and I hurried past the tourists, gawking at their first sight of the fabled land of Margaritaville.

We hustled along the board walk, past Conch Harbor marina. With a final jog, we skirted the walkway by the Turtle Kraals, finally arriving at the Bight. There before us was our destination—Merlin and Eva's trawler.

Eric stopped me near the turtle museum. We peeked around the side, scoping out the mass of humanity, flowing along the boardwalk. One sunburned tourist after another floated into and out of the local hangouts.

We didn't see anyone we recognized. There was no sign of activity aboard my sister's boat.

"The coast looks clear. We should hurry over to the trawler."

"Eric, what if they're not home?"

"Do they lock their boat?"

"No, I don't think so."

"If there is no answer, we'll let ourselves in. When we get inside the boat, I want to take a look around to make sure Gage doesn't have anyone staking it out."

"Eric, where are we going to go?"

"We'll see if Merlin will take us somewhere quiet and remote for a few days. As long as the few people who know we are alive don't give us up, Gage will think we perished in the Everglades."

We crept over to the pretty trawler. A gentle rap, on the teak door, brought no response. A couple of agonizing minutes went by. The door slid open, revealing my brother-in-law. We sighed with relief.

"Eric and Linda, what are you doing here?" Surprise was etched upon the boat owner's face.

"Can we come in?" my husband asked in a husky voice. Merlin stepped back allowing us entry into the main salon of the boat.

"What's going on. Are you two in trouble?"

"Have you spoken with Gage?"

"Yes. He said something about the two of you getting lost in the Everglades. Are you feeling all right, Linda?"

"I'm fine. Where's Eva?"

"She went shopping at Publix."

"Have you seen any of Gage's people around here?"

"No. As a matter of fact, Eva spoke with Tom last night. He said something cryptic about the two of you being OK, but as far as we're concerned, you are still lost in the swamp. Your brother told her the military guys were getting the park rangers and the Miccosukee Indians to help search for you."

"Excellent. They have no idea we made it out."

Chapter 22. The Marquesas Keys

Merlin called his wife, asking her to do a big shop at the supermarket. She sounded surprised from what we could overhear on the phone. When Eva returned to the boat twenty minutes later, she found out why.

My sister embraced Eric and I for a good long time before letting go. "I knew you were all right, the tarot cards don't lie."

"What are you talking about?"

"I read the tarot cards last night. They showed my near future would be very bright. Now you two are here safe."

Eric looked impatient as he listened to my crazy sister's explanation. Usually, he was much more tolerant of her eccentric behavior. "Eva, I don't mean to be rude, but we need to get out of here."

Merlin handed a couple of bags of groceries through the trawler door. "Where do you want to go?"

"I don't know. Is there a place we can go, to hole up for a few days until Gage gives up on the search?"

"The most remote place around here is the Marquesas Keys, to the west. It's a day's run to the atoll."

"Can we leave now?"

"Eric, I'm not comfortable navigating through the area at night with the abundance of coral reefs strewn about. If you want to leave now, we can head out to Boca Grande Key for tonight. It's only three hours away. At first light tomorrow, we'll cruise over to the Marquesas."

"What can I do to help?"

"Let me check the engine oil. Eric, why don't you remove the shore power cords?"

The trawler was a buzz of activity for the few minutes it took to pull away from the pier. We motored in a southerly direction toward Sand Key Light. After engaging the autopilot, Merlin stepped back from the console. His eyes scanned the horizon ahead of us. Eric paced like a caged lion. I pulled him over next to me.

"Remember our trip to Sand Key two years ago? That was the first time I went into the ocean after *Wind Rose* sank."

Eric managed a slight smile at the memory, though his attention was on the trawler's owner. "Merlin, do you have any weapons aboard?"

My brother-in-law looked through the passageway to the galley. "Good. Eva is busy with the groceries. I didn't want her to hear my reply." Merlin leaned toward us. "I may be married to a sixties tree-hugging hippy, but I'm not stupid. Sorry, Linda."

Our host grinned through his neatly trimmed goatee. "I have a Colt-45 and a Mossberg 500 shotgun."

"Where are they?"

"Linda, would you keep watch for a few minutes?" The two men went down into the main cabin, leaving me alone in the pilothouse.

When they returned, Eric slipped his arm around me. "The forty-five is in the top drawer of the forward cabin. It's fully loaded with a seven round magazine. The safety is on. The manual safety is located at the left rear of the frame. Make sure you take a look at it. The Mossberg is loaded with the safety on, underneath the port settee in the main salon. There are spare rounds in a box next to it."

"OK, Eric." My hand ran down the back of my husband's shirt. His muscles were tense knots. "Honey, you need to relax." A grunt was his reply.

We cruised down the channel inside Western Dry rocks, soon arriving at the pretty sand island of Boca Grande Key.

There were a couple of small powerboats dotting the white sand beach. The current ripped through the anchorage, giving Merlin a challenge while anchoring. Eva stepped to the bow with the remote for the electric windlass. The chain rattled out of the anchor well. After shutting down the engines, the only sound aboard the boat was the low hum of the generator.

"Eric, I'm going to take the dogs ashore for a walk. When I get back, I'll fire up the grill for steaks." Our host called the pups to the back deck. After launching the rigid dinghy, the two poodles jumped in for their ride ashore. Eva busied herself in the galley, mixing up a pitcher of cocktails.

I stepped to the aft deck for a look around. The pretty little island had a scattering of palm trees around the fringe. A couple of snowy egrets waded in the shallow water, on the hunt for dinner. The peace and quiet was idyllic.

Eric leaned out the back door. "Linda, get in here."

"What's the matter?"

"We need to stay out of sight. I can't afford to fall back into Gage's clutches. He won't give us another chance to escape. That would make it impossible to deal with my unfinished business."

"Our unfinished business."

"Linda, I'm not arguing with you on this one. When I meet up with Carlos it will be very serious, not to mention, extremely dangerous. You will not be involved."

Off to the left side of the trawler, an orange Coast Guard RIB pulled over beside Merlin. Our host was returning from the beach with the dogs.

They had a brief conversation as the Coasties looked over to the trawler several times. Merlin's answers must have satisfy the officials, because the orange boat sped off in the direction of Key West harbor.

"What did they want?" Eric asked our brother-in-law when he returned with the pooches.

"They were checking my gear. The officer wanted to know where we were from and how many people were on board. I told them two. Luckily, they didn't search this boat."

After a lovely dinner and a grand sunset, we climbed to the flybridge under the cover of darkness. The stars burst from the sky, allowing us a few minutes of peace.

Early the next morning, we were underway bound for our hideaway destination.

Eric studied the nautical chart. "Where do you anchor around the Marquesas Keys?" The semi-circular islands were surrounded by shallow sand banks.

"Most boats anchor on the west side. There's a better spot inside the atoll where we will be as invisible as possible. If we play the tide right, this boat should be able to sneak into Mooney Harbor. The entrance is shallow, but the tide should be near high when we get there. There is a small outcropping of mangroves with deep water nearby. We'll take refuge there. It's not on the chart, so not too many people know about it."

"Sounds like the perfect hideaway." Eric's nervous energy would not quit. He paced around the gently swaying pilothouse. The water around us was calm with a low swell coming on the bank from the deep Straights of Florida.

The water color alternated every few miles, between the emerald green of the murky Gulf water to the brilliant electric blue of the crystal clear Gulf Stream. All the mixing of currents created swirling whirlpools which tossed even a heavy trawler like this one off course. Merlin tweaked the autopilot to keep the boat headed in a westerly direction.

The mangrove atoll of the Marquesas Keys smudged the horizon at noon. The islands formed a nearly impenetrable circle forty miles west of Key West. I wondered how this shallow patch formed right next to the deep trench of the Florida Straights.

Unfortunately, history must wait as we all paid attention to the shallow spots near the shifting sandbars.

"See the small cut there." Merlin pointed to a narrow opening in the green, dead ahead. "That's the entrance to Mooney Harbor."

My husband squinted at the chart. "It's tough to see. You really need local knowledge to get in."

"Yes, the sandbars shift whenever a storm comes through. It makes a great hiding spot, if we can get in." Merlin slowed the trawler to a crawl. The depth sounder crept lower--ten, eight, six. We held our collective breaths as the keel skimmed over the bottom.

Suddenly, something shot out from under our bow, launching itself into the air.

"Wow, what a huge stingray. I wonder what he was trying to get away from." The gray monster belly flopped back into the sea.

"Linda, they often jump out of the water to get away from hammerheads," Merlin said.

The mangroves on either side of the tight passage were so close, you could almost touch them. After traversing the entrance into the harbor, the water depth returned to ten feet deep.

Our host felt his way around the large harbor, steering for a clump of mangroves to the northwest. The anchor was dropped in eleven feet of clear water. Despite Eric's warning, I had to sneak outside for a look over the side.

Directly below us was a sandy patch, surrounded by a large bed of sea grass, lining the bottom of the lagoon. A small ray glided beneath us, causing a tiny crab to scurry away in fear. Though I knew my husband would not go for it, I would love to strap on a mask and fins to check out this remote habitat.

"Linda, please come back inside." Sighing, I returned to my husband's side. With any luck, we would spend a few quiet days here, until Gage gave up on us. We would leave this nightmare behind. I was to the point where I didn't even care about revenge anymore. It would be nice to get my rings back, but with all the agony we'd been though, they were a small price to pay to get out lives back.

"Linda, are you OK? You have a strange look on your face." Eva grasped my hand, bringing me back to the present.

"I was just thinking about the ranch." Out of the corner of my eye, I saw the wistful smile on Eric's face. "It would be so nice to go back there to relax. Maybe take a quiet trail ride."

We spent the rest of the afternoon and evening cooped up inside the trawler. Merlin and Eva took the pups ashore for a bathroom break and exercise. Eric read a cruising guide to the area. I tried to tidy up the already neat cruising boat.

After dinner, we lounged on the raised settee in the back of the pilothouse, watching the sun go down.

"This is a beautiful place. Look at all the birds." The sun set over the dark-green palisade of mangroves.

"When things get back to normal, we'll come back out here, Eric," Merlin said. "All the keys around here are great to explore, not to mention the sea beds."

"I bet the spearfishing is great."

"Yes, it is. There are lots of mangrove snapper."

When darkness descended, we climbed to the flybridge. The night was pitch black. In response to Eric's request, our captain opted not to illuminate our anchor light. No one would enter this lagoon at night anyway, due to the shallow water. There was no point in advertising our location with a bright white light.

"It's always a little spooky out here at night." Eva gazed at the blanket of stars overhead.

"I was reading about this place in the cruising guide today. A Spanish galleon sank here in the 1600's after departing Cuba with a cargo of gold. Some sailors who have anchored here since reported seeing a ghost ship sail by at night."

"Eric," I admonished my husband. "You are starting to sound like Tom. What's next, the keys are haunted by killer coconuts crabs?" The full moon rose to the east, casting an orange-white glow on our faces. The absolute silence was broken by a seagull screeching in the distance.

"No, Linda, Eric is right," Merlin said. "I've heard the shrimpers talk about the same thing. They see a ghost ship, like an old sailing ship with torn sails, cruise slowly by."

"Can we stop talking about this please?" Eva asked. She looked extremely nervous.

"It's a good thing we haven't seen any boats, either ghost or real. Don't worry, sis."

After a few more minutes enjoying the moonrise, we decided to call it a night. The only sounds heard in the forward berth was the low hum of the generator and the occasional splash of a mullet jumping. In our heightened state of awareness, every creak of the old trawler was magnified, making sleep difficult.

Dawn arrived with an awesome sunrise. We spent the next day killing time with card games and playing with the dogs.

The full moon rise was spectacular the following evening. There was no discussion of ghost ships or other spooky spirits. Instead, Eric and I relaxed, knowing every minute which passed was in our favor.

Our Navy SEAL friend should stop looking for us. This would allow us to get on with the business of catching Carlos. It was obvious Eric still hoped for a shot at revenge. We would have to wait and see. Before heading to bed, my eyes enjoyed the pretty scenery out the windscreen. Some movement to the south attracted my attention.

"Eric, look." He followed my gaze to the outline of a shrimp boat offshore.

"It looks like a shrimper. There's nothing to worry about. He's probably going to anchor on the western side for some rest," Merlin said.

"You don't think...."

"No, Linda. I don't think it's Carlos. Relax. If the drug lord were around, we would have heard about it."

My mind was finally able to rest, allowing me fitful sleep. Eric tossed and turned, though he seemed more calm. A couple of jumbled nightmares caused me to stir during the night, but I pushed them aside while luxuriating in the quiet anchorage.

As the first rays of dawn crept in the small porthole, Eric bolted to a sitting position.

"What's wrong?"

"*Shh*. I heard something, Linda. The anchor chain moved."

"We probably swung around."

"Stay here." Eric grabbed the forty-five. The big pistol was tucked into the back of his shorts. Without a word, he disappeared from the room. The anchor chain snapped again.

After yanking on a pair of shorts and a T-shirt, I made my way through the dark passageway to the main salon. A shout was heard on deck. Not my husband's voice, but a familiar one.

"Cowboy, we meet again. I've brought your wife's rings. Come here and get them." My eyes peeked over the console of the pilothouse. Carlos stood on the bow. Eric was two-thirds of the way there, when the drug dealer raised his left hand over his head. With a flick of his wrist, he tossed two shiny objects into the sea.

"You son of a bitch, you're a dead man." Eric cocked his gun, taking aim at the drug dealer.

"Oh my, God." My sister shrieked from outside the door to the main salon. I rushed over to drag her back inside.

"Stay down. Go back into the aft cabin," I ordered her while peeking out the hatch. My hand blindly reached under the settee for the shotgun. The distraction of my sister's shout caused Eric to turn around. As he swung back, Carlos had a gun locked on him.

"Eric, I've waited so long for this moment. My moment to murder you has come. Won't dear sweet Linda be thrilled to go away with me. Trust me, I'll take very good care of her." His horrible cackle almost drowned out the sound of gunfire.

The drug dealer's bullet sent Eric plummeting to the deck. Carlos fell back a few feet, striking his head on the bow pulpit. My husband's gun flew through the air, as if in slow motion. It landing on the cabin top a few feet away.

I was at his side in seconds. He was unconscious. A steady trickle of red ran down the deck to the midship scuppers.

A sound to my right made me turn toward the bow. Carlos crawled for his gun. The firearm was halfway between us.

Eric's gun was closer. My knee banged on the cabin top. I leapt for the forty-five. Raising up on my knees, both hands clutched the heavy gun. My arms shook. I aimed at the dirty drug dealer. One finger slid to the trigger. A calming breath was forced from my lungs.

Carlos reached his gun. A nasty grin splayed on his filthy face.

"You would never shoot me, Linda. You are too much of a coward. Don't worry, I will teach you to love me. Throw down the gun."

Repulsion seared through me. I struggled to exhale. My finger squeezed the trigger. Carlos aimed his gun.

A seagull's screech eclipsed the thunderous blasts of gunfire.

Epilogue

My left hip stung. I collapsed forward, breaking my fall with my left hand. The blasts from the weapons rang in my ears. Using every remaining ounce strength, I pushed myself back to my knees. Was Carlos still after me?

Two arms enveloped me from behind. The gun was in my right hand. My right wrist was grabbed in a vise-like grip. My left arm was pinned against my body.

"No!" I had to wrench myself out of the grip of this new assailant. One of Carlos' henchmen crossed my mind. If I could only turn around enough to get off a shot.... The tight grip made this impossible. I snapped my head back to butt the attacker.

"Linda, drop the gun. It's OK." Gage's shout penetrated my terrified brain. "Let go. It's over. You're safe now."

The would be assailant was none other than our ex-Navy SEAL friend. When he painfully twisted my wrist, the gun clattered to the deck.

The tall Navy SEAL released me, to rub his sore forehead. "Geez, Linda. You almost broke my nose."

"Eric." My head swiveled to the left. I tried to crawl over to my husband. He was lying prone on the other side of the deck. Two men hovered over him. It was impossible to see whether or not he was breathing. Oh my God, he needed my help.

"Linda, stop. You've been shot. Let me get you to the pilothouse to have a look at the wound." The tall Navy man grabbed my left hand, while wrapping his other arm around me.

"Let me go, Gage. I have to help Eric."

"Tom and Jake are taking care of him. There are two Coast Guard helicopters en route to our location. They should be here any minute. Let me take a look at your wound."

The big Navy SEAL dragged me to the pilothouse, gently lifting me through the doorway. "Lie down on the settee."

"Is Eric OK?"

"*Shh*. Let Tom and Jake worry about him. You take it easy. Eva would you get me a couple of towels so I can stop this bleeding?"

Looking down at my left hip, I noticed my shorts had a hole in them. Blood splattered the cloth. A trickle of red ran down my thigh. My sister returned with two towels and a first aide kit. She had a horrified look on her face.

"I'm all right, Gage. Let me go to Eric."

My pleading fell on deaf ears. He kept a tight grip on me as the sound of a helicopter's blades, beating through the air, stopped directly overhead.

"They are going to take your husband to the hospital first. The second chopper will pick you up. This wound doesn't look to bad." The SEAL's eyes locked on mine. He stuffed a couple of gauze pads under my short's leg. The compress was secured with a tight wrap around my thigh.

"Linda, what were you two thinking?" He shook his head. A few strands of hair fell across his forehead. The question was interrupted by Tom striding into the cabin. My brother-in-law's hands were smeared with blood.

"Eva, where can I wash my hands?" The big fishing captain's eyes looked devastated. My sister led him into the cabin.

"Tom."

"Linda, stay still. I'm trying to stop the bleeding," Gage said.

It seemed like eternity before my husband's brother came back into the cabin, his hands discolored by my guy's vital fluid. Tom wrapped his arms around me, hugging me tightly. "Li'l Sis, are you OK?"

"Tom, how's Eric?"

"Not so good. He's lost a ton of blood."

"I need to go, now. He needs me."

"Li'l Sis, there's nothing you can do for him. Why don't we get you fixed up? There is a doctor on the chopper who will be taking good care of Eric."

A second helicopter approached. Gage sat on the settee with his hand on my shoulder. "The Coast Guard is going to airlift you to the same trauma center in Tampa. Let the paramedics do their work. Take it easy."

"I'm going with her," Tom said in a low voice.

"I'll make it happen."

The Coast Guard rescue swimmer poked his head into the cabin. After assessing the wound, he made a call over the radio strapped to his chest. "Send down the litter."

"Linda, we need get you outside." Gage and Tom helped me limp out of the cabin. They strapped me into the rescue basket. The helicopter swayed far above me. Fear flooded my brain.

"Tom."

He saw the look on my face. "You're not talking me out of sending you on a helicopter this time. Don't be afraid, I'll be there."

Once clear of the deck, the basket spun and swung. The wind buffeted me. The white chopper above drew closer and closer. Hands reached out, yanking me inside the fuselage. "Pull her in head first," one of the Coasties shouted over the wind. Petrified would be a huge understatement to describe my state of mind.

After securing me inside the cabin, they lifted Tom and the rescue swimmer aboard. The chopper buzzed to the northeast. My brother-in-law gripped my hand. I worried and worried about my husband's condition. Please, God, don't let him die.

The chopper bumped to a stop on the roof of the hospital. They whisked me away to the trauma bay.

The doctors and nurses tended to what turned out to be a superficial wound on my thigh.

"Please tell me if my husband is all right." Why would no one answer me?

Finally, the emergency doctor in charge leaned over to talk to me. "You husband is in surgery. He's sustained a very serious gunshot wound to his chest.

There are bullet fragments in his left lung, very close to his heart. We'll know more after the thoracic surgeon looks around. You can get dressed if you feel up to it. Your brother-in-law is waiting outside."

When I stepped outside the trauma room, Tom wiped his red eyes. He surrounded me with his arms. "You heard?"

"Yes, Tom. I want to go near the operating room until we get more information."

"Sir, you should take her home. She needs lots of rest to recover from the blood loss," said the nurse behind me. "Your husband will be in surgery for many hours. We'll have the O.R. staff call you as soon as they know something."

"Come on, Li'l Sis. There's nothing we can do here. Let's get you home."

"No!" My protest was not effective in my weakened state. There was no way to squirm out of the Tom's hold. Jake was waiting with a car outside the door. Soon we were on I-75, headed back to Naples.

Later in the evening, we gathered in the main salon of the *Diana*. Tom's cell phone rang. He spoke for a few moments before hanging up.

"Eric made it through surgery. He's in intensive care, but in critical condition. The nurse said we can come up in the morning. They are going to keep him in a drug induced coma until tomorrow. It may be longer if the swelling in his lung doesn't go down." There was a collective sigh among our group.

The next morning, we made the long three-hour drive back to Tampa General. It hurt like heck to limp through the long sterile hallway to the intensive care unit. The nurse led Tom and I to my husband's bedside.

The big strong cowboy who loved me so much was almost unrecognizable. Multiple tubes stuck out of him. His sexy hair was matted against a deathly white face. The tears would not stay inside of me. I tried hard to choke back the emotions for Eric's sake.

The doctor rifled through the chart. "He's doing better this morning. It's still touch and go. We will keep him in a drug-induced coma for another day or two. The ventilator will allow his lung time to heal. Your husband's a lucky man. One of the bullet fragments was only a centimeter from his aorta. If this main artery was severed, he would have died on the spot."

Tom's big hand squeezed my shoulder. My lips placed a gentle kiss on my soul mate's forehead. After an hour of quietly encouraging my unconscious husband to get well, my brother-in-law pulled me away. He ignored my protests.

"Linda, the doctor said you need to rest and that's exactly what I intend to see you do. We'll come back tomorrow."

"No, Tom. I need to stay with Eric. He needs me."

"Linda, dammit. I know you are stubborn, but listen very closely to me. There is nothing we can do to help my brother. If you don't rest, your leg wound won't heal. When Eric is released from the hospital, he'll need you to be at one hundred percent, to take care of him. I'm being completely selfish, dragging you out of this hospital."

"But, Tom. What if...."

"Dammit, Linda, I don't want to hear you say that. Eric will be fine."

The elder brother clamped his arm around me as we retreated from the building.

A couple of days went by, as Eric's wounds slowly healed. Tom and I drove repeatedly back and forth to the hospital to the north, spending a couple of nights in a local hotel. The day my husband regained consciousness and was transferred to a non-critical ward to recover, Gage called for a celebration in the dining room of the *Lady Diana*.

The usual cast of characters was there to help us rejoice, including Joey and Jan, along with Martin and Diana. Sloan sat by Tom's side. Jake perched next to me.

"A toast to our good friend's recovery." The tall Navy SEAL raised his glass of beer as the rest of us cheered. My relationship to the military man was strained since the whole escape from the Everglades thing, but we were regaining our mutual respect.

"Gage, I never did ask you if Carlos was...dead. My shot was at point blank range."

"Yes it was, Linda. Though the kill shot went right between his eyes. You're a pretty good shot, lady, but not that good." The former Navy SEAL grinned. "Did you know a nine millimeter bullet ended his miserable life, not a forty-five? It must have been the better angle I had over your right shoulder. Don't even think twice about it. You didn't kill him, I did."

It was unclear whether the Navy SEAL was trying to make me feel better or trying to remove any guilt from me. There would never be any guilt over shooting the bastard. The only feeling right now was relief because the whole nightmare was finally over.

The tall man reached into his pocket, retrieving a couple of items. "Oh, by the way, I have something for you." He placed them into my hand. After opening my fist, the gleam of my engagement ring and wedding band was unmistakable. These were the same rings Carlos stole from me last year.

"After the Coasties took you to the hospital, Merlin and I put on swim masks. It only took us a few minutes to find them."

"Thank you so much, Gage. How did you know we were in the Marquesas Keys?"

"We were real lucky. Hell, we chased you halfway around southern Florida. You'll have to tell me about your escape someday. Elton is still scratching his head.

"How we tracked you down in the Marquesas is another story. Our team followed Carlos' boat. He anchored near Rebecca Shoal ten miles to the west of your location. The drug lord hopped into his mini-sub, then headed your way. Flo and Jet were on a recon mission when they came back to the boat all excited." The Navy man stared hard at me.

"They led us right into the lagoon. Of course, if we had know you were there, we could have provided protection. Neither of you would have been injured." My sheepish smile didn't soften his serious glare.

Several long days later, my husband was released from the hospital. Back aboard the *Diana,* Martin called a meeting of our entire group.

"I am so happy to have Eric back with us. After discussing the situation with Gage, I have decided to offer the sailing foursome their jobs back. Once you are better, of course."

My husband's face contorted with pain as he spoke. "Martin, thank you. For now, I want to get back to the ranch to relax and heal up. I've had enough of drug dealers."

"When you are feeling better Eric, I would like to give you *Island Time*, to...compensate you for your injuries."

"You're very generous, Martin. There's no doubt your gesture will make Linda very happy." My husband winced. He reached his hand out to me. A tear slid down my face. "Gage, I have a question for you. Did you ever figure out how Carlos knew we were in the Marquesas Keys?"

"Yes, he picked up your trail in Key West."

"How the heck did he know we were in the Keys?"

"I'll answer that question in a moment."

The tall, lanky Navy SEAL rose from the table. "First, I have more unfinished business." He stared at each of us in turn with his deadly serious assassin's glare.

"We need to discuss phone calls made to Carlos, tipping him off about our every move." Gage did his big cheetah stalk around the room, sizing up his prey. He stopped at the head of the table, gazing solemnly at each of us.

"One of you thought you were pretty clever. You tried to deceive our team's efforts by giving away vital information. There's nothing I hate more than a traitor." The big man slammed his fist on the table. Everyone flinched.

"Luckily, you missed one very important fact. What I really want to know is why did you do it?"

Those anthracite black eyes of the special ops man seared through each of his quarry. "Why would you hurt your friends and allies to help a dirty scumbag like Carlos? These actions nearly killed Eric and injured Linda."

Gage placed both of his palms flat on the table. "I expect an answer to this question.

"The small piece of the puzzle you don't know, is every phone call placed through the satellite system aboard this yacht, is electronically logged. So how, you ask, did I figure out who was making these calls? It was easy. Simply cross check the outgoing calls to see which ones closely coincided with the calls to Eric's cell phone. Later on, I checked the calls on *Island Time's* satellite phone."

"Early on," Gage continued. "I wasn't even sure the traitor was one of us. After the call was made to the satellite phone on the sailboat, there was no doubt one of you was the snitch. At first this fact really pissed me off. Now, I'm saddened to find my trust was violated."

The Navy SEAL stalked around the table, again. Everyone looked at one another.

"Well, I may have told Carlos a thing or two early on, but it was only to get back at my husband."

"Diana, what are you talking about?"

"Martin, some days it feels as though you don't even know I exist. All you care about is this stupid boat and going after drug dealers." Her voice rose to a very high pitch, as if she were about to scream. "Will you finally stop obsessing about your brother's death, for goodness sakes? Try paying attention to those of us who are still living."

"Diana, I can't believe you tried to sabotage my project. How dare you!" Martin leapt up from the table. The irate man towered over his wife with his hand raised, about to strike her. She cringed. Gage intercepted the enraged husband's palm a mere foot from his wife's face.

"Easy, Martin. My belief is Diana was simply play-ing games. I even overheard one of her calls. She was taunting Carlos as a way to get back at you. To my knowl-edge, she never revealed any important information."

"I most certainly did not," Diana said with a huff.

"So who did? Who was feeding all the critical information about our every move to Carlos. Who told him about the birth of Eric's horse? The foal nearly died because of it."

"It most certainly wasn't me," Diana said. "I would never hurt an innocent animal. So who did it?"

"I asked myself the same question. If it wasn't Diana, who was it?" Gage stood at the head of the table. "Who is so heartless as to hurt a defenseless baby animal?" All eyes followed the Navy SEAL's to Tom and Sloan. His eyes rested on the pair for only a second.

"I could eliminate some of the phone numbers right away. Of course, neither Eric nor Linda would hurt their own horse. Jake and Rick I trust implicitly. They were crossed off the list.

"Martin? No he wouldn't endanger his own project."

"What about Joey?" Sloan asked. "We all know he was really angry with Linda for running off with another man."

"Oh for Christ's sakes, I'm already long over her. She was such a waste of time."

"Thanks, Joey."

"No, I knew from the beginning it wasn't Joey. He had too big a score to settle with Carlos." Gage sat down in his chair. He entwined his fingers together, with his elbows on the table. His chin rested on his fingers.

"This only leaves two people. Tom and Sloan."

"I would never hurt my brother."

"That's pretty obvious, Tom. Why did you do it, Sloan?"

"What? You have to be crazy. I didn't make those calls."

"The phone records don't lie."

"Jesus, Sloan. It was you?" Tom yelled at the dolphin researcher. "You almost killed my brother." The elder crab fisherman jumped out of his chair. He was about to grab his now former girlfriend when Gage stopped him.

"Hold it, Tom. Let's find out why she did it, before you beat the heck out of her."

"You guys are crazy. I didn't do anything wrong."

"The phone records don't lie. Why did you do it?" The two big men towered over the scientist. The former Navy SEAL grabbed her when she attempted to make a dash for the door.

"Not so fast, lady."

"Martin, you son of a bitch. You never cared about my dolphins." Sloan's voice rose to a screech. "It didn't matter how much danger you put them in. You would never listen to me. I couldn't stand by and watch you endanger their lives. I'm leaving right now with Flo and Jet."

"Oh, no you are not. The police are on their way here."

"What? I've done nothing wrong other than make a few phone calls. The last time I checked there was nothing illegal about that."

"You gave away critical, confidential information about a United States Coast Guard cutter, endangering her crew. That's a federal offense," Gage explained. "We are going to attach conspiracy to commit murder."

"Murder? You are insane." The lady scientist unsuccessfully tried to wiggle out of Gage's clenched grip.

"You are the one who told Carlos about Eric and Linda's whereabouts in Key West. With all the low-life's down there, finding them was no problem for the drug lord."

"Gage." Eric looked to the Navy SEAL. "How did you find us?"

"While you two were playing in the Everglades, we picked up Carlos' trail. Flo and Jet were tracking the mini-sub, when he snuck into Mooney Harbor to attack you two. The dolphins came back to the *Diana* all worked up. Tom, Jake, and I jumped into the inflatable. Unfortunately, we arrived at the trawler a little late."

"Shit," Tom said with disgust. "Eric. I'm the one who told Sloan you were heading to Key West. You bitch." The crab fisherman gaped at her with pure hatred.

"It's OK, brother."

"Sloan, the dolphins will be old and gray by the time you get out of prison." The Navy SEAL hauled her away from the dining room table to the waiting police officers.

"Tom, I'm so sorry."

"You know, Linda, there was always something not right about her from the beginning. I couldn't put my finger on it. When we pulled you from the ocean, I shouldn't have let my brother be the only one to pursue you. You are definitely the best catch of them all."

"Thanks, Tom, I love you too."

"It's a damn good thing I'm so weak or there would be hell to pay for that comment, big brother." It was great to see the grin on my husband's face.

When the former Navy SEAL returned to the room, Martin asked him one last question. "Gage, why have I never seen this record of the phone calls? I didn't even know it existed."

The ex-military man sat down with a grin.

"It doesn't exist. Sometimes you need to know when to bluff."

Capt. Marlena Brackebusch author of *Nightmare Voyage, Treacherous Voyage and The Ultimate Voyage.*

Capt. Marlena Brackebusch grew up in New Jersey and started sailing small dinghy sailboats at the age of seven. After being away from the sea for several years, she resumed sailing in Boston during college. She taught sailing for U-Mass-Boston, as well as several renowned sailing schools around the East Coast of the US and the Caribbean. During the late 1980s and early 1990s, she and a friend completed a four-year World Circumnavigation aboard their thirty-one-foot sailing yacht. Since then, she has been teaching sailing for the American Sailing Association, delivering yachts all over the world, and chartering boats in Naples, Florida. The sailor/author now resides in Naples, where she is owner of Island Sailing, a Naples company dedicated to providing fun sailing adventures. Capt. Marlena is a U.S. Coast Guard Licensed Master Mariner, an American Sailing Association Sailing Instructor, and a PADI Certified Scuba Diver.

She is a certified EMT.

Capt. Marlena Brackebusch

In July of 2013, Capt. Marlena completed a tactical firearms course taught by an ex-Delta force instructor.

Two months ago, she hosted a training event for the Naples SWAT team aboard Island Dreams.

"I hope you enjoyed reading The Ultimate Voyage. Be on the lookout for my next adventure. Just over the horizon," Capt. Marlena.